I0818149

A Crime for all SEASONS

Copyright

Front and back cover illustrations by
Stephen McCormack

A Crime For All Seasons Hardback
ISBN - 978-1-7396006-5-5

A Crime For All Seasons eBook
ISBN - 978-1-7396006-0-0

Also by the same author -

A Crime for all Seasons (Paperback)
978-1-7396006-3-1

A Crime For All Seasons (Graphical Novel)
978-1-7396006-1-7

A Crime For All Seasons (Audio book)
978-1-7396006-4-8

Some Kind of Record
978-1-7396006-2-4

Dedication

For my sister Paula Quinn.
A lifelong reference for all that is good in the world.

It is impossible to know the full and final consequence of one's actions.
- Anonymous

Be daring, be different, be impractical, be anything that will assert integrity of purpose and imaginative vision against the play-it-safers, the creatures of the commonplace, the slaves of the ordinary.
- Cecil Beaton

To Kenny for keeping his head while so many around him failed. Themselves and humanity.

To Boeing Aircraft Corporation for their intricate unfolding mechanisms.

To Richard Russell.
Your aching for meaning made you pay the ultimate price. The most precious of passengers. This flight does not leave without you.

Most of what follows is true

Table of Contents

Foreword........8
Act 1 Before The Deed........10
Chapter 1 A walk in the wilderness........11
Chapter 2 Turning a corner........16
Chapter 3 Home for Christmas........23
Chapter 4 Change........33
Chapter 5 The plan........40
Chapter 6 Communications........45
Chapter 7 Device........51
Chapter 8 Disguise........58
Chapter 9 Briefcase........64
Chapter 10 Air-Stream........69
Chapter 11 Reconnaissance........79
Chapter 12 Private hire........84
Chapter 13 Look before you leap!........91
Act 2 The Deed Indeed........98
Chapter 14 Early morning........99
Chapter 15 Getting on board........103
Chapter 16 Excuse me, Miss........108
Chapter 17 Enter Tina........114
Chapter 18 A rattle in Seattle........120
Chapter 19 Landing prepared........128
Chapter 20 Tension on the tarmac........133
Chapter 21 Troubled Flight 305 for takeoff........145
Chapter 22 Into the Sacred Black........152
Chapter 23 Home and not so dry........167
Act 3 After The Deed........178
Chapter 24 Vanished!........179
Chapter 25 Watching the dust settle........191
Chapter 26 Bitchin in the kitchen........197

Chapter 27 Meanwhile back at the FBI........................205
Chapter 28 When crime meets grime...........................212
Chapter 29 Kenny loves Bonny...................................219
Chapter 30 The real McCoy..224
Chapter 31 The spirit of Richard.................................231
Chapter 32 The crime of all seasons............................242
Chapter 33 Enter Tena Barr...249
Chapter 34 The sands of time......................................260
Chapter 35 Kenny dead...269
Chapter 36 Life After death...276
Acknowledgement..282
About the Author..284

Foreword

When I was just a boy of five my family had recently moved to a distant suburb of Dublin, Ireland having departed Cork city for the capital. My memories of the new, sleepy location were of boredom and blandness for the first year. Nothing ever seemed to happen except the weather and that was always bad. The only thing that gave me cheer was my first musical experience of hearing "Snowbird" sang by Anne Murray on the radio which filled me with wonder

Spread your tiny wings and fly away

And, for a brief moment I saw Daniel Boone and found it uplifting despite the intermittent reliability of the Black and White TV which had the dubious brand name of Murphy. This was later replaced by a Bush model which seemed to be more promising.

One Sunday evening at the kitchen table I was attracted to a colorful Comic Book left lying around by some of my older siblings. When I opened it the color and illustrations drew me into it and seemed in such stark contrast to the blue-gray surroundings of our kitchen. I could not read much. In fact the biggest word I knew was Marmalade but still I swept through the exciting pictures soaking them up by the second. I do recall that the first page of the story depicted a bus with a passenger getting on board at a stop in the dead of night while the rain hammered down on the driver's windscreen, just like it was hammering on my kitchen window outside.

Looking through the book's adverts in between the graphical stories, I came across a dollar sign for the first time and I understood it to be an American publication. From America. Just like my aunties with their strange accents.

It is notable enough that while I was looking through this book in Autumn of 1971, people were plotting and planning a weird and mischievous event far far away in that very same America. Bad things. Big boys. Men. Bad men.

Of course I would not get wind of such a thing for many a year. Indeed a whole generation, lifetime and country would come to pass before I would discover this tale. There I was battling the Mediterranean heat of sunny Spain in 2009 while listening to Internet radio from USA. You know I loved to listen to radio from America. The Diane Rehm Show came on NPR in the hot afternoon and a report on this unassuming story caught my attention. I think it was one of those moments where I knew I had to process the topic to the full as soon as I heard the report, whatever that would mean in reality. Perhaps simply researching into it more or exploring the story but I somehow felt I might be able to contribute to this, enthralling little distraction, as I saw it.

And so we have arrived. And as someone said to me recently, you're never too old to have a happy childhood.

Act 1 Before The Deed

Chapter 1 A walk in the wilderness

Admittedly, I teared up a little while running through these pages. This is the tale of someone honest who did a dishonest thing. Someone who was down-trodden as a result of always trying to play it fair. The response was not a correct action but a criminal one. Yet it was done with justice in mind.

* * * * *

Back in December of 1970, a certain guy by the name of Kenny Christiansen kicked his way down the snowy runway on Shemya island. Located closer to Japan than to America and roughly four-by-two miles in area, a grim and cheerless platform for sure. In the middle of the North Pacific Ocean. For Kenny, this was hardly a starting point for anything but an abundant reminder of his misery and that he was in every sense at the bottom of the barrel. In his life and in his career.

"Damn, it's so cold here" he thought. "I can never get used to it."

As he headed over to the creaky looking aircraft hangars, he wondered if any food was going down this time of day in the main building. That was the place beyond the hangars that looked like something out of the cold war.

Shemya island was one of many used by the United States Air Force as a refueling and service base during World War 2. Just as it was still being used now, except by commercial airlines like North West Orient Airlines (NWO).

NWO like the name suggested, operated out of the central and mid USA and covered most of the pacific ocean with flights. A happy-holiday public image was given by all the adverts and staff uniforms along with the blue and white stripes on their aircraft with that cute red tail. "We give you half the world" ran the advert slogans in 1970. And they kinda did. The Americas were well covered with their flights as well as a reach into the vast Pacific region.

While the word "Orient" in the company title has a tendency to charm and disarm the customer, Kenny had really bought into that too for so long. He still loved aviation as much as ever but a piss-poor income did not bode well for a guy in his late 40s and he frankly saw little future for himself. He was living on the breadline mostly, hardly able to put food on the table and often in arrears with rent or bills. The grinding financial state had cast a pretty gray cloud over his life and Kenny wondered if he might at some point be battling to avert some kind of clinical depression. Fingers crossed . . . he had enough to deal with besides something of that nature.

He may have long romanticized the world of aviation but bad treatment by NWO company officials and all the pressures had meant he had to shelve his enthusiasm to the point that it was collecting dust in his mind.

He made his way into the hangar and strolled across the floor. Two mechanics were stuck in a radial engine mounted under a large wing. He could feel the heat in his face as he slipped back his hood. "Man how long now have I been coming up here? . . . " he thought to himself. "Working long hours and still not able to earn enough to survive . . . "

He was normally based out of Seattle but was no stranger to this place having been sent here for long spells on and off for years. He had joined NWO in the fifties after enrolling in a trainee program for Aircraft Mechanic and Fitter. Airplanes took lots of work and maintenance. Specialized stuff. So Kenny felt good at the time about his move into a pretty solid career. One that could give him a good level of living, that could pay the bills.
So, how did he get to this stage then of not being able to make ends meet? After nearly twenty years on the ramp, working every end of aircraft service, maintenance, fitting, repair, refuel systems, you name it. Like many a young recruit he was quick, enthusiastic and the size and infrastructure of the company was reassuring to him. He had really loved being there. But now here he was at his age.
Accomplished and experienced yet impoverished.
Well, the answer it seemed to him was two fold. Kenny's personality and the company's personality.

Although Kenny was sharp and thoughtful he was always a bit shy, quiet and in truth, a gentleman at heart. He was never a grabber or someone who was rude and pushy. He could not stand such folk and by and large he had only encountered one or two like that at his level. Most staff were regular sorts and at ease. And any unsavory person he had met on the way suffered some consequence or other. Like being fired or having a bad reputation. And rightly.
At any rate Kenny sometimes regretted being so outwardly

soft. Not that he had missed too many tricks but somehow he felt it was a trait that was unhelpful to his cause. It bugged him a bit.

The other part of the explanation was more tangible – and bitter. The upper hierarchy of NWO was a different ballgame from the blue-collared people of Kenny's circle.
The decision making executives at the Airline really beat to a different drum. They were forever eroding the unions, or trying their utmost to push back on any progress for better pay to Airline staff. Worse, they had messed a lot of people over with diminished pensions and benefits, including Kenny. And he knew that his situation in the company was far from being an exception.
They had also killed off career paths within the company in order to save money, resulting no doubt in a fat bonus for themselves. And the pompous arrogance of these overpaid pricks who never had a tough day in their lives made his blood boil. How he managed to keep calm on the outside he could never quite figure out. Then again that was definitely a thing he was very good at.
If only he could get paid for it.

He made his way over to the main building and turned into the entrance which was snow-blown. About a foot and a half had fallen the day before and the building was frankly, not the homeliest you could imagine. Still it was warm inside. He started thinking about food again and worked his way through the corridors. He was tired. Of everything.

Turning a corner he saw two managers and a female companion chatting with the office door ajar. Two guys in their slick, shiny suits and a cute woman who might have

been an Air Hostess but he didn't know. Wearing short turned-in hair and a pouted look on her face. She thought she had entitlement for sure. There were not too many lady workers based on the island.
He overheard one of the guys speak in such a posh tone. He was the guy with the amazing brown briefcase and every part of his apparel had so much attention to detail. So measured and aware. "Sally and myself are heading to Florida at the weekend for a game of golf. Why don't you ask Julie if she wants to come along."
They perked a little when they noticed Kenny approaching. He knew his face was red as ever from being out in the cold. And his workshop steel-capped boots were no doubt unsightly. The girl slung him a glance over her shoulder designed to make him feel like pond scum. A look he was well used to and one that meant nothing to him. That was the normal look you got if you were a creature from the hangar. Kenny passed them saying to himself privately "Well I do declare. You're going for a round of golf with Sally on company dime after screwing me and the rest of us down on the ramp. Yeah – us. The people who make your very flight possible. Well, ha-bloody-ha!"
Specifically, he didn't know of the detrimental involvement of these exact people, at least in terms of evidence. But still . . . he knew it. He had been through the mill. He had seen this movie before. He had no regard at all for that gravy train and would be happy to burn it to the ground sometime.

He ate a solid hot meal in the canteen because he knew he needed it but in fact he had strangely lost his appetite. It was a filling episode, not an enjoyable one.

Later he made his way to the sleeping quarters. In his case to one of the semi-circular galvanized huts which were a hangover on the island from the days of the war. They were still in good nick and very warm being aerodynamically designed to cheat the wind. Quite appealing actually. Rugged and very much his cup of tea. Still he could not imagine white collared NWO management being assigned one of these.

Before bed, Kenny was going over some paychecks and doing his mental sums on finances. Something he hated. For a recent monthly paycheck the take home pay was 512 dollars. And that was for a full month. He did not always get a full month – if only . . .
And now with these airline strikes that were in place he had found himself writing home to his brother Lyle in Minnesota looking for help. He wrote "They have multi-million dollar jets sitting on the tarmac while I am down to peanut butter and bread."

Chapter 2 Turning a corner

Next day there was a meeting in the main building for unions who presented the workers striking position.

Kenny had always been a bit suspicious of these meetings which management agreed to hold at outposts like Shemya island. It was a way he felt, of foot-dragging and avoiding confrontation with union and workers. Not to mention a way of even completely avoiding dialogue, where possible,

with operational staff while they actively melted and morphed company employment policy.
Anyway, he decided to go through the motions and put on his NWO uniform which he had to admit looked pretty smart. Shirt and tie and all. That he expected was going to be the only positive aspect of this get-together.

So Kenny went along to the meeting room where the usual set of chairs and tables were set in a circular layout round the place. Just like the United Nations but, well, a whole lot more humble. In walked the usual few heads representing the unions and one or two from management who he knew to see from previous meetings. Nice people overall - just at the wrong side of the fence.
The assembly got underway in the usual courteous manner and after about 20 minutes Kenny found himself drifting a little bit as he detected no change or nothing newsworthy. He felt like yawning but fought back a bit. He lit a cigarette. He did not want to look bored as it was something he was not comfortable with. He being a nice guy. He never wore that skin well.

Suddenly, the door opened and in stormed – who above all people, Mr. Florida Golfer himself.
Never mind that fact that he was so late but from the word go he assumed that he was the boss - and boy was he here to boss. Even before he took a seat the tone of verbal junk from him was unbearable. His swagger was comical. As if the whole meeting was arranged for him and nobody else was worthy of anything.
"Lance Shaw is the name. Been sent over from mainland to enlighten you on a few essentials."
"I am here to convey management's concern about NWO

moving forward. I'll get to the point: The central preoccupation in our analysis is company performance. We have been leaky on profits, more and more and shareholders are not happy. The pressure on us now has been greater than ever from competitors . . . "

And so on and on he went with this garbage.
At first people were taken aback, Kenny too. But after a few minutes of this insufferable riddler he twigged it. He had been sent by management as a tactic. A distraction from taking anything on board to bring back to top company management but instead put a scare down the ranks about mass lay-offs. The best form of defense being the attack. Right.
He continued on with listing various points he wanted to implement improvement on. Cutbacks on pay, winding down company expenses and expenditure. Shorter hangar time for Jet servicing and so on.
Kenny found all this depressing. In part because it might have some truth in it, signaling a harsh road ahead. But also because it showed just how rotten NWO had become.

Now at this point it should be mentioned that Kenny was a gay man. A Homosexual as it was more often referred to in those days. But it was not a good term back then. Gays were hounded and despised across America. This was still a few years before Oliver Sipple and Harvey Milk. Unless you lived in Greenwich Village or San Francisco you would not dare be openly gay. And Kenny was certainly not that. He was very private.
To Kenny, this guy Shaw was actually quite good-looking eye candy. But he knew that anger transcended such matters of desire, at least for him it did. The mechanisms of

aggression scared him sometimes and so he generally steered clear of it. It was like ecstasy, like a drug. His instinct was always to pipe down. No talk was better than the wrong talk. A motto that had served him well.
Still, he was in no mood to cozy up to this raving peacock across the table.
He decided there and then to take a measured step into the conversation.
"Well" he cleared his throat. His soft voice was in contrast to the loud crispiness of Shaw's output.
"I think I can speak for a size-able contingent of ground staff in NWO. Many of us, like myself, are struggling to put food on the table. Bills are unpaid etc. Therefore what you are saying does not mean much to us, frankly."

Kenny was careful with the phrasing of this but judging from the frozen faces round the table he felt that his distain must have seeped through, somehow.
He continued "We have been working hard for years and with deterioration in benefits. Where do you propose to get increased performance if you are not going to hire more people? You are asking us to do even more for compensation that is already inadequate."

This seemed to frighten Shaw's horses a bit. His response was staggered. Back-peddle, back-peddle . . .

Of course Kenny had heard him in the corridor the previous evening being a good old high-lifer. And he knew that Kenny knew he was a high-lifer.

At this point Kenny was not really interested in what he had to say. He knew it would be nothing good. Shaw recovered his composure somewhat and it all looked even more awkward and pathetic now.

Leaving the meeting, Kenny was thinking "What a loada crap!. I have to stay here and be responsible as well as responsive to any work that comes in. But I don't get paid anything like enough for my time. How did I end up in this dead-end joint of an Airline?"

There were other Airlines to apply to of course but all the evidence was to say they were just as bad. Same shit different bucket. They were all watching each other. If one introduced new practices everyone else was sure to copy and follow. You could always rely on corporations for herd mentality. It probably was a good idea sometime to send in a few applications but he had just been too busy as well as being stressed out.

He wondered if there would be any backlash in the company for his straight talking at the meeting. He did not put it past management and he might have made a mistake by speaking out. But in all honesty he was too tired to process the thought. He felt that life, whatever it had to offer, was too short for that.

Living for the day was an approach he had to take quite often. So, he decided to take the most cheerful option available on this barren gray slab in the middle of the ocean. To pay a visit to the hangar. To him the whole world of aviation always seemed so right - if only he could leave out the bad players in companies like NWO.

There were always so many things to see in an aircraft hangar. The different planes, the tools, the designs, the performance. Even the documentation.

There was a Boeing 727 parked up slightly diagonally when he got indoors. The 727 had been a very successful workhorse of the Airlines. It was able to carry close to 200 passengers and felt very much like its full-blown 747 sibling, except not as monstrous. But everything about it was decent. It was never going to be a vomit comet.

But this one on the ramp had a surprise today. It had a rear staircase opened down from its under-body at the tail end.

"Wow" Kenny looked on in amazement. "That looks so slick."

Actually all 727s were fitted with these rear stairs trailing out of the back when in use but he had never seen one opened and had really forgotten about them. NWO just used the normal side entrance for passengers and crew. He imagined how it would look so party-like if you owned a 727 as a private jet . . . arriving in the tropics with Palm trees swaying in the breeze and stepping out of the back like this. If only you could own a 727 . . .

To make way for this strange configuration the craft had two jet engines either side of the tail and then a third on top of the tail in piggyback arrangement. It was actually a neat aircraft with all the engines down the back.

He made his way up to the top of the stairs and into the interior of the craft. There were two of his colleagues engaged in the removal of some seats. This vehicle was evidently being converted for cargo.

"Hi guys" greeted Kenny. "Wow, isn't that back stairs a work of art! Man, it's so neat. Never saw one opened up before."

The reply he got from one of the guys was a bit sharp - "Yeah, that's for folks like you so you can take a jump!"

This brought a little silence all round. Kenny glossed over it as best he could by buzzing casually back down the stairs and out of the plane. He was the type of person who would internalize such comments when he heard them, wondering what he had said or done that was wrong. He decided not to take this too personally. But he had always been like that – over enthusiastic about seemingly trivial stuff that he thought was really interesting. It was in his nature. It wasn't going to change now. He also knew that with just a little security or prosperity he could probably be the happiest man in the world, despite all the difficulties he was having. Maybe not everybody in his company could make that claim.

Kenny had grown up on a farm with his brother Lyle back in Minnesota. Life was tough, rigorous and they were used to humble ways and means just like in a lot of rural settings. The boys grew up steady with their mum and were fit and resourceful. They had to be. When opportunity arose to go farther afield Kenny had always appreciated every moment of it. For him, appreciation was a big factor in acquisition.

Anyway, he was heading home tomorrow for Christmas. Back to Seattle where he was normally stationed these days and to spend the usual holiday with his friend Bernie and his wife. Between their hospitality and his own crummy apartment that he rented across town, he hoped to be able to relax about things a little.

Chapter 3 Home for Christmas

Within a few days Kenny departed the isolated rock known as Shemya island on board a jump seat of an NWO aircraft. This particular craft was headed to Vancouver, the guts of 3000 miles distance, where he would get a connecting flight for the final short hop to Seattle.

He slept a good deal of the way and did not find it a very long haul. It was nice to look down at the mainland once again even if it was snowy.

Strolling through the airport terminal building at Vancouver he decided to take a look at the newsagent stand. He fancied something to read through the holiday period.
Kenny had always loved international airports. These were the holiday hubs of a city in his view. The collection point for jet-setters and travelers. Whether you were a worker at the airport or a passenger it was a positive and uplifting place to be. And the aircraft all seemed to dance in harmony with their large wing spans. A different world indeed.

He had been browsing through the newsstand and the magazines when he spotted something unexpected. Something that would accost his day completely.
In the Comic Book section, Dan Cooper – French speaking paratrooper and adventurer. A comic book hero who jumped out of airplanes for a living . . .

He stood rooted to the spot, stung. The hemorrhaging past poured into his mind. He remembered as a young man of just 18 being recruited as a trainee paratrooper for the United States Air Force, months before World War 2 had ended. Stationed in Japan, he loved every moment of it but did not see much action there.

Out of a large contingent of trainees recruited he was one of only a handful to succeed and qualify in what was a savagely hard test with parachutes, training, physical fitness and jumping. As one commentator would later say of him, Kenny was indeed a tough guy.

He got deployed only about a month before the war ended. So the timing had been bad. Still, who knows, he might have been killed if he was too heavily involved in it. Maybe it was all for luck. If only there had been a way to continue Skydiving for a living.

After the war this beloved activity tapered off as there was no demand for it and of course it was expensive to do as a hobby. It had always been paid for in the military when he had done it.

Kenny scraped through his early twenties looking for work and trying to shape out a meaningful career of some sort. Doing odd jobs and whatever he could. He even tried door-to-door selling encyclopedias at one point. But if there was one thing he could not do, it was to lie to people. He could not, as he felt, insult people's intelligence. And so no, he was not a salesman. Gradually, he steered himself toward some kind of career in Aviation. A move that definitely made sense. At least in the early fifties.

He just couldn't help but buy the comic book. He was a sucker for anything engaging like that. Even if it was in French. He could look at the pictures and reminisce.

* * * * *

Kenny always spent Thanksgiving and Christmas over at Bernie Geestman's place. He and his wife had their home in Bonny Lake, Washington. Kenny and Bernie went way back to the early fifties together where they first met as he came to the hangars in NWO.
Bernie had already been there and was supervisor to him.
The two were always good old friends who looked out for each other's interests.
They pulled well together as a team but it's fair to say they were quite different in terms of personalities. Bernie was always proactive and assertive whereas Kenny was more easy going, a better listener and quieter. Somehow the two molded together well.
Bernie was more shallow, more transparent and direct in his approach. He did not hide things that well, especially to somebody who knew him. Kenny by contrast would always think things through a little deeper. That is not to say that Bernie was not an able guy and very streetwise. Having a more striking, sculpted face than the plainer looking Kenny, he also had accumulated more stuff and property. Pretty good at networking and communication he had been promoted as a shop floor coordinator at NWO, having punched his cards in the world of aviation mechanics and all things related.

After the war, Kenny found himself posted in American occupied Japan. He then went back to Minnesota for a period looking for suitable work. He had certainly got travel in his veins by that stage.
When Kenny started out life with NWO he was hired as a

general laborer. An all-round guy. He was posted to Shemya island for an initial eighteen month period but did a second term there, staying on over four years in all. After that he spent six months in Bikini Island in the south pacific. Bernie had left NWO at this point and went working for Boeing.
More recently Bernie had left the airline and went working for a Tug Boat hauling and salvage company in the Washington area. His background and experience no doubt weighed for that job.

Bernie's wife was Margaret, whom Kenny really got on well with. They would sit for hours talking and chatting. He had in fact been to their wedding in the late 60s. She had a ranch out in the country and had given Kenny some work from time to time, digging trenches and other things for which he was so grateful during such lean times.

This year, the Geestman household had another addition, his sister Dawn had moved in with her kids following a recent divorce from her husband across the country in Minnesota. So the home was becoming a lively place of late. Kenny very much enjoyed the atmosphere there. He had never thought too much about having a home of his own but the idea was becoming appealing.

So Christmas came and went, going down pretty well for all concerned. Kenny was glad of the break, even if it was quite short. He needed to monitor things in NWO and try to stay in the picture so as to get some half decent hours. Seattle was the home of Boeing so it was a fairly busy place with regard to aviation overall. He was always going in and out of the hangars as he needed to get his name down for hours whenever possible.

Over time the company had seen sense in re-directing workers like himself to do more diverse jobs, such as flight attendants on some routes round the pacific. This got him out and about and to work with the air hostesses, who sometimes had an opinion of themselves

He remembered the very first day on board such a flight working with them. He was receiving a bit of ice all-round for the first couple of hours. They were a bit unapproachable.

One of them finally referred to him directly, "Let's see if the new boy can hurry up a little bit."

Kenny did not think much of this kind of cold shoulder but he knew how to give as much as he got.

"Don't try that juvenile crap with me girly" was his response, looking directly at her. She turned away somewhat in shock trying to compose herself.

At times it seemed that he was either very nice or very sharp as a person. Maybe he needed to practice diplomacy. Yeah, that in-between stuff. But no doubt some people rubbed him up the wrong way and he was feeling too old for giving a damn about what they might think.

Then there were the pilots . . . the mile high part of the mile high club. As a rule, guys who came from the ramp could rarely stand them. But he didn't mind them so much having never had any reason to have a run in with them. He just reckoned he was being paid far too little to be bothered by them. If anything they amused him. Of course the Pilots attracted lots of attention from female Air Hostesses - it was a good hunting ground for both genders.

But not for everyone, occasionally there was an honest hard-working hostess who did not suffer any delusions. He could work with them pretty well.

Somehow he ended up doing the job of flight Purser. The person who handled all cash on-board commercial flights. He had a bit of responsibility at this task and maybe some pressure if things did not balance on the cash counting at the end of the day. Still he got to know some things about cash transactions and banking procedures.

Being assigned to flights was great as it meant you were likely to be working on the trot for a few days as you were away most of the time round the Pacific at various destinations. Although you were busy getting to sleeping accommodation and back for the returning flight next morning, not to mention the actual work on the flights, it was enjoyable for the most part. He loved jet setting. Who didn't?

Just before the Christmas break Kenny had called into the Seattle NWO office to check the schedule. He was penciled in for a trip the week before the New Year. "Great!" he thought. "Some work and a nice change in the middle of winter." Quite apart from the money, he loved work. Something so sweet about early mornings and keeping the mind filled with variety. And in flight he got to wear a nice uniform. He tried to look his best and be a good ambassador for the airline, in part because it might increase his chances of getting called up again for more work.

It was actually on that work shift that he was waiting with an NWO officer in the kitchen area of an airplane about 30 minutes before boarding. They were chatting away and this guy whom he had never met before was a real motor-mouth. He talked a bit much to be fair and was a trifle wearisome. Let's say that he was hard work.

They had been talking shop – about the pursing procedures and cash handling. As with all things this guy had a lot to

say. During one of his lengthy verbal excursions Kenny removed his flight attendant's cap and was trying to address the sweat building up on the inside rim when he heard him say - "they always gotta keep money in reserve at SeeFirst bank here in Seattle in case of crisis for the city."
Was that so?
"Really?" Kenny was a bit surprised.
"Oh yeah, sure." was the reply. "In fact every city has to plan for sudden outlays at all times so they keep a certain amount of cash on standby in vaults. Ya know for Secret Service stuff and all that. Apparently they have to keep a certain amount of marked dollars in store – probably goes into the millions."
Kenny interjected before heading down the aisle of the plane, "I guess it's a security headache for them in that case."
As Purser he had to make the odd run to these cash sorting offices but of course he never knew anything about the internal workings of these places, only the interface with his end and the cash handling. Anyway, the flight would be taking off soon so that should mean some measure of relief from getting his ear bent by this empty moron he had to work with.
But these rantings he had to listen to did put him thinking about things. It was not that he needed to rob a bank but it kinda would solve some problems. Of course, he would not dream of robbing the Seafirst bank or any other financial institution. He would feel bad about ever doing such a thing. He had no quarrel with them. He even had a bank account with Seafirst in Seattle. Not that he had too much money to put in these days.
But robbing from his employer for compensation for bad treatment might be a different matter. He would never tow

the same line of guilt in that case. If only you had some way not to be caught. As far as Kenny knew the vast majority of bank robberies were solved by the police and the thieves caught, it being impossible to pull off a big robbery without some clue being left behind. There was no such thing as a perfect crime. To even think about planning such a thing you needed inside knowledge at the very least. Ideally, you would need to create some kind of double or triple partition between you and the law. A kind of a proxy situation, maybe where someone else was unwittingly doing the stealing for you without knowing it. But how on earth does one do anything like that? . . .

Actually, he did have a fair amount of inside knowledge when it came to Northwest Airlines. But as far as he knew they did not have vaults with mountains of cash. The banks dished up that particular service.

Sure enough, the odd tool went missing from the machine shops and hangars down the years. Workers signed things out and conveniently never brought them back but that did not exactly constitute a sizable enterprise. You might get some supply of material for your home project here or there but it could not be turned into tangible profit needless to say.

There seemed to be no goose that laid a golden egg. Northwest did not handle really big cash amounts except at certain times of year and it was questionable how much they would be carrying. Certainly no gold bullion being transferred on a regular basis or anything like that. You would first have to generate that situation which would be highly exceptional. Then you would need to intercept such a transfer of cash. Then deal with security and escape. Then cover your tracks.

It was a dead end. The company had it all sewn up.

The following Friday was New Year's Day and after a long week at work Kenny was happy to be off work for a couple of days. Nice. He went into a local bar in Seattle about 7 pm for a shot of Bourbon which he loved with his Rayleigh cigarettes. It was a usual haunt for him and he would see the odd familiar face. Airport staff sometimes went in there. Sitting at the bar, there was a TV at the end blaring away with the typical news and politics stuff. He had been there for some time slurping whiskey when he noticed NWO came flashing up on the news item across the screen. He cocked an ear, expecting it might be about strikes or layoffs. Sure enough it was but with a different flavor this time.

"Reports continue to come in about North West Orient Airlines financial woes. The company has been flooded with strikes and industrial action in recent times and now it seems to have taken its toll on at least one member of staff there who was found dead after committing suicide due to pressure brought on by changing company policy resulting in layoffs."

Kenny stepped out of the bar feeling all too sober, frankly.

He did not recognize the name of the dead person mentioned on TV but that came as no surprise. NWO was a big company with lots of employees spread out in different locations.

As far as he could see there was nothing company officials and big business would not lie about. Greed had become such a driving force in America he sometimes wondered what it was all about. All that freedom spirit and the Founding Fathers stuff. Sure, there was a sense of freedom in America but only if you were rich enough to afford the freedom. That was where the buck stopped or rather, the intellect died.

To Kenny, there were so many amazing things about life, from nature to our technology and inventions. Why did these fat cats at the top not want to allow a working wage to be a living wage? A chance for everyone, so many of them being just like him, not wanting much really. They would still all be rich and have all their benefits. It probably would not impact them at all at the top of the hill. But with the way they scrambled hastily to maximize profits, anyone would think they were running out of Oxygen. Like wild animals that had not eaten in a month. Had the right things been implemented in this regard the whole of American life could be a celebration instead of a suffrage.

Kenny had a grown hatred and resentment of the super-rich ruling class. Those who were at the top and toyed with the rest of the world while conscientiously maintaining the very monetary system that enslaved everyone else. Like a hobby or a game for the elites. Meanwhile all the rest down the food chain galloped endlessly to survive or get a meal, life being a continuous stream of uncertainty and worry. And, as if that were not enough, they were expected to carry the burden of shame for poverty, failure or lack of affluence.

At this very point he had always felt a blind rage. Like so many he was the victim of a capitalist system he had not invented, yet he was supposed to feel apologetic about it. "No" he decided. Not a chance. Let the rich live with that burden. That was their responsibility for the rot they had created in America. Let *them* carry the shame of their design.

And what about the Government? Was it not their job to ensure that certain minimum requirements were in place to protect ordinary people, in this, the richest and most advanced country in the world? Was that not what good governing was supposed to be about?! Oh then he remembered that politicians were some of the greatest deceivers of all time. Yes, those slime-balls who went along with war in Vietnam. But of course they did not have to go to the front line. It was not their family members who came home in body bags. Had that being a real prospect not a single one of them would ever have voted for such a thing in Congress. No sir!

No, whatever he took to better himself, he alone would have to wrench from the grip of companies. This world did not give. It only took. No doubt it was easier for him to disconnect in this way. He was, at least potentially, mobile and free to roam and do what he wanted. For the many who had families to feed it must be a different story.

He needed change from the rut and mediocrity of his life. Yet he could see no way through really.

At that very moment he could not have predicted it but change was to come indeed. He did not foresee what was about to happen.

Chapter 4 Change

There comes a moment in everyone's life, surely, where we feel we know that some big fantastic idea can really hold up. That it could really be. That it could possibly happen. We feel this based on previous knowledge or wisdom, maybe intuition. Like we have the solution to hand – we just need to work out the details. Like the inventor perhaps. We have confidence, even clarity. We just need time.

This is how Kenny Christiansen must have felt about the plan he hatched over the coming weeks. He did not quite know what inspired him. Maybe it was his age, maybe it was his expertise in certain areas. Maybe it was the amount of Bourbon he drank. Maybe it was a personality change. Whatever it was he somehow knew he had the possibility to do this. And now he was energized. He just needed to get it done.

There was a touch of irony for sure because here he was planning theft just like those at the top he hated so much, except that in his case it was brazen, not protected by legislation. It was based on a sense of justice not plunder. But Kenny never stole a thing in his life and hated common thieves of any kind. It would be fair to classify this as uncommon theft.

He knew he would never have a streak of guilt about taking from the fat cats of upper management at the airline. They and politicians were white collar criminals that could legitimately steal large amounts of cash and never face justice.

So this was not white collar crime in his view – clearly it would be an undisputed act of criminality. Was it blue collar? Hardly. It was difficult to categorize. Time would tell.

Also, it was not in his nature to rob. He was making a decision to do something criminal as a means of righting a wrong. Not in a legal sense – there was no mechanism to defend him legally but in an everyday sense – in a moral sense. In a sense of fairness. Something society as a whole did not address much despite all the congressional and constitutional declarations to do so. Those were put in place by the people at the top to serve themselves. The ordinary people had long lost most of their access to the control levers of state. Not that they ever really had it in the first place.

He was unlike those for whom stealing was a way of life or indeed an addiction. Much wants more. He would know when and where to draw the line and stop. Or so he hoped.

While a big part of the motivation was righting a wrong, some of it was satisfaction at following his curiosity. He had gone in his own mind where, probably, nobody had ever gone in intellectual terms. It was uniquely his idea. It was his brainchild. He knew he had something and wanted to make good with it. For better or worse . . .

But committing a crime was one thing. Getting away with it would mean breaking the heart of the FBI. That would have to be addressed in due course. And he also had to take into account the possibility of danger to himself and to others. That was the most difficult aspect. He did not want to leave behind any victims of any kind: traumatized victims, physical victims. Even financial victims. He wanted no part in that. He was very clear on his ideology. But he would need to work hard on his practical methods.

He decided to run his big idea by Bernie. He knew him well enough to trust him. Though they were definitely different people, his buddy was used to bending the odd rule if he thought he could get away with something. He knew tricks for nearly every trade. He often had a deep understanding of the gulf between official stuff and practical stuff. He had a healthy appetite for that sort of thing and was definitely the type who would jump at some big cash prospect provided he was not at risk himself. And Kenny was confident he could persuade him that his plan was viable.

He felt that there was that spark of teamwork about them when they put their heads together. In some other circumstance they might have had a business together. They might have had different ways of thinking but that would introduce strengths into the fabric of the project. Two heads were certainly better than one.

He was tremendously excited and could not quite understand where the optimism had come from.
Besides, he thought, you only live once. And he had never lived yet. Never sang his song. Time to break the gray spell of mediocrity and do something fantastic. Time to express himself. Time to live!

So a meeting was arranged with Bernie one afternoon in late January. They were in a park in Seattle on a cold day, sitting on a bench like two birds on a fence looking into the west, toward a watery sunset. Chatting.

After the explanation was rolled out in detail to Bernie he put his two hands to his eyes, rubbing them. "So you are talking about robbing from an aircraft and then jumping out of the hatch with a parachute in order to escape with the money . . . are you out of your goddamn brains?!"
Kenny's response was "Maybe, but I don't think so." He had spent a lot of nights dwelling on this. He was well worded.
"I will need somebody on the ground to pick me up and clear out of the zone before anyone knows what happened. It's really important that it gets done quickly before daylight comes. And we can leave it all look seamless so that this appears to be your only involvement. Nobody ever has to know you were not simply responding to a call from your

old buddy who was looking to go for a drink."
He continued "And what makes this all work is that life goes on as completely normal for the both of us. We continue to work in our jobs. Humble folk. There is no visible change."
"So, lest I forget to say, let me emphasize that point. Life goes on as normal. You do NOT spend money on a new Cadillac – nothing of the sort. Never! This money is to be spent $20 here, $20 there. A fill of gas. A payment in a restaurant. Small stuff. Pay some household bills in cash maybe. Absolutely no bank movements or big credit transfers. None. This money is to take the pressure off everyday spending not to use to flash wealth - forget it! "
"Also," he added "If the law ever gets suspicious of either one of us, they will surely make a point of questioning the other. So, it will mean we are in this together, regardless of what other differences we may ever have. *Your* cover is *my* cover."
He lit up a cigarette "Most guys who wind up in jail are there because they have not thought things through. They plan the event all right but do not plan the aftermath. And most of them do not imagine using the loot to pay only for ordinary things. They make the mistake of going big and glamorous. Too visible and it attracts attention. As soon as questions are asked by the Law the answers need to be quick and solid. Tracks must be covered properly. And the best way is to never flag any attention in the first place, not to suddenly change behavior and make it visible to all."
He took another pull from the cigarette "That is not how this works. We have to be sharper than that. We can't just plan things at our end. We have to know how the law works. We have to view it as they do."
"Now," he stretched his legs "I am confident I have every

aspect of this gone over. If at any time you don't like the sound of it or you're not happy about something, you can pull out. I am not going to try it without you."

Bernie had his doubts "But - and it's a big but – I'm not convinced that this will go smoothly, just like that. You have so many things to go wrong . . . This is a protracted operation – landing at night in a parachute. Man you don't even know whose house you're going to hit or what rooftop you'll get stuck on. Or in a river – you could land in the drink at freezing temperatures in the dark. Jesus I mean . . . that's wild stuff."

But Kenny was reassuring. "The key here is preparation and rehearsal. So feel free to speak up at any time. Not only that. I will be looking to build in as much flexibility as possible. We should examine various scenarios for whichever way the flight pans out. And if at any time you don't like it you can pull the plug on it."

Gradually Bernie seemed to come round to the idea, at least provisionally. "So, even if I am happy with things from my end – I just have to pick you up and drive you home, there is definitely a big risk for you long before you touch ground."

He turned squarely to face Kenny. "You're like a guy who doesn't care what happens to him. It's like what someone would do to get their kicks."

Kenny looked around at him, saying "Well, there is that aspect to it a little . . . but look" . . . He stopped as the moment was getting a bit awkward.

He waited for a deep breath of air. "Well, it doesn't really matter I guess but . . . you know that I am Homosexual, right?"

Bernie looked at him calmly "Margaret did suggest it to me once, seeing that you are a single guy and all but I never gave it any thought."

Kenny's face was now red. "It's a private matter so it's not exactly relevant. But I guess it might go some way to explaining why I have a certain perspective."

He elaborated slightly."I mean, don't get me wrong, I value my freedom as much as anybody but the prospect of being locked up in prison with a few hundred other guys might not be quite so devastating for me as it would be for you."

Bernie's mouth opened up in amazement. He did not see this coming. His whole face morphed into a smile and he held his hands to his head, laughing aloud. "Man, you're off the hinges – you know that? Well, I gotta hand it to you. I mean you're good for comedy if nothing else."

Kenny was chuckling now also. "It's the way the cookie crumbles."

"Look," he said, wrapping it up "all I am asking is that you stay true to your word on this idea of mine, regardless of whether you are in or out in the end."

He extended his hand to Bernie. They shook on it.

Kenny added "Just make good with everything along the way, even if you change your mind at the last minute. I won't be able to do it without ya. And of course not a word of it to anyone. Ever!"

Chapter 5 The plan

What about this plan of Kenny's? To jump from an airliner, mid-flight with a large loot (he hoped) and to quickly disappear, never to be seen again.
Easier said than done. It had never been done before in any criminal, big-heist capacity. He had never even committed a crime before of any kind, let alone try something this bizarre. No doubt it would need to entail the element of surprise in every respect. And be well planned. No question, everyone who ever lived would call him crazy.
But there was something about our Kenny that had a way of inventing possibilities and making connections in order to achieve things. We may recognize it as a talent yet most would pass over it. To some uncharitable folk, far from being a champion, he was a loser. Perhaps the sheer spectrum of personalities in society would be a help just enough to allow him to succeed. Who knew?

But for now he would have a lot on his plate.

All along the Northwest coast, from the Canadian border down for hundreds of miles toward San Francisco, There lies a dense and lush strip of forest. Pretty and scenic. Heaven forbid that this should ever change. In the most Northern region around Seattle it was about 200 miles wide before giving way to the open, rocky terrain of Washington State toward the east. This, in Kenny's view, was a great ally. If you could parachute down there in darkness you stood a good chance of not being seen by anyone.

The problem of course was that you could have a mishap with where you landed in the dark. There were places to be avoided if you could. Getting stuck on tree-tops was not a thing he was afraid of provided he carried a knife to set himself free and a little flashlight for the dark. But for sure this would take time and there were a lot of trees.

He was most interested in a route directly south out of Seattle. Slightly off course and to the East were volcanic mountaintops – three of them. These looked majestic in the daytime jutting up high out of the surrounding forest. Natural monuments. But they represented large rocky barren structures and were to be avoided on his jump. If he came down in any of these, he would have crazy rock-climbing and would likely have to wait till daylight. That would be disastrous with helicopter police combing the whole place – a 2 or 3 mile diameter rock would make him easy to pick out in daylight from the air. He would be a sitting duck.

Still he was not overly worried about these as a threat. They were mostly to the east and he reckoned they would be easy to get around. Besides, aircraft generally avoided flying over them, as far as he knew. Another obvious potential disaster would be to land on cities or towns. Like trying to gather up his parachute in someone's back garden or under a lighted street. Or on some old granny's rooftop, trying to be discreet . . . Imagine living that one down in the state penitentiary.

Then there was the, hopefully slim, possibility of landing in water. The Columbia river swept across the region where Kenny most wanted to land, more or less bordering it on the West and South of the region. He wanted to avoid it.

Immediately South of the river was Portland city which would absolutely be a no-go jump. If it was in that area things would be a little more difficult. It would be farther from home and they might be less familiar with everything leaving it harder for Bernie and himself to hook up. Also, around the main highway south of Portland the forest area thinned out a lot and there were
fewer roads to get to. You could easily spend a long time off the beaten track. That would mean longer to haul around parachutes and he may have to abandon it which leaves a trail of evidence. The longer you were out there the more likely you were to be seen by someone who would surely pass on strange incidents to the police. And that was just in the dark. If daylight came it could be a real disaster. He really did not want to entertain that notion. The last thing he wanted was to be seen or even have to ask directions or interact with anybody. Better to be gone from the scene as fast as possible.
Seattle itself was situated about 90 miles inland from the west coast as thc crow flies. If he was looking to exit the plane south of that he would have to, literally, look before he leapt. Passenger Jets moved awfully fast – like five or six hundred miles per hour. If for any reason it was in the wrong direction or drifted it could be over the ocean in no time and a jump into the cold waters of the Pacific might not be so good for his health. Hell, there was so much to think of.

So he felt he had a workable plan. But he would look to improve it over time. Meeting with Bernie he rolled out a large map showing the area. Kenny had marked out in black the area where he thought was most desirable to land at night.

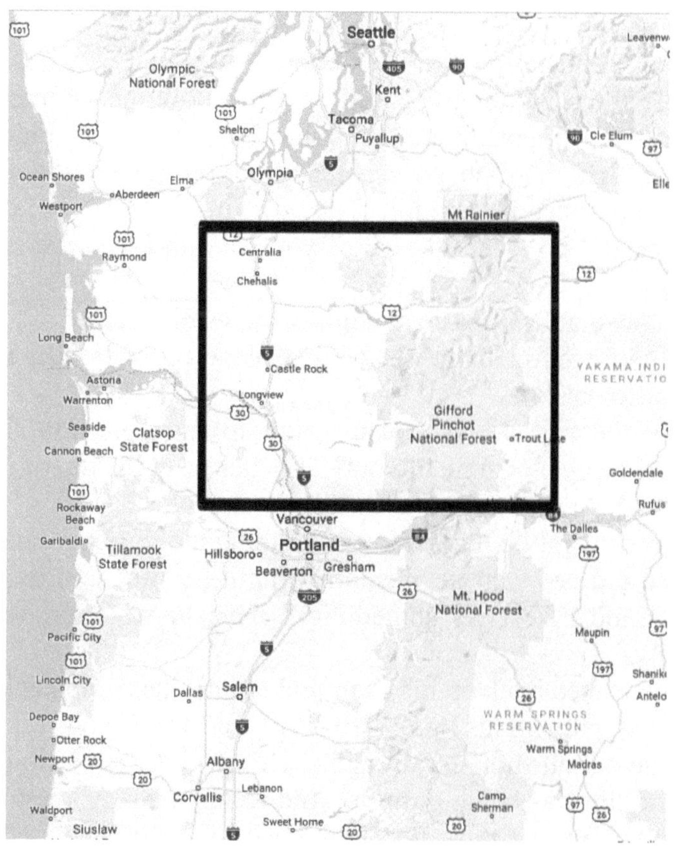

Bernie looked at it with his mind in a busy state "That means you have to jump fast, soon after leaving Seattle. These planes move real quick."

"Yeah." Kenny was looking serious, like he really felt it.

"So," continued Bernie "What height do ye parachute guys normally jump from?"

"Typically, 1500 feet. 2000 feet maybe. Doesn't matter too much but it's in that order."

"Oh Christ!! 2000 feet. Man, a 727 reaches 30,000 feet in

about 3 to 5 minutes."
Kenny was aware "Yes I will have to stretch it a bit – maybe to something like 10,000 feet."
Bernie looked dubious. "Well as you know the ceiling is about 15,000 feet from the point of view of breathing. Above that there is no oxygen. So you can't be going anywhere near that limit. The maximum that you can realistically go is 12,000 feet if you want to be on the safe side."
He knew that from basic aviation stuff, as did Kenny.
"So, you need to jump out of that plane pronto – like not long after takeoff."
"Also" he added, "If you're going to make it into that critical black box zone of yours, it better be at the top of it – only just. At the very north of it."
Kenny thought he might have something more up his sleeve but he did not want to mention it until he was sure in his own mind. "Yes, it's something I have to work on very closely."
Bernie leaned back on his chair and put his hands up behind his head, pursing his lips "Well Mr. Paratrooper, you reckon you have it all thought through?" He was part sarcastic but part of him was being positive. And Kenny already knew it.
"I am confident I can get it right." was his reply. They sat in thick silence.
Bernie was inclined to believe him. Kenny had the ability to deal with complicated things. His companion had always found him a very positive individual despite being a soft touch in everyday life. He could not quite understand why that was. He could not really explain that aspect of his personality. So for now, he would take it at face value. And assume that he could pull it off.
Kenny had to point out "We are going to have to be well

familiar with all the roads in the region. That means by numbers and for you, you will need to be good at driving wherever you need to so that I get picked up as soon as possible after I land. You will need to be agile and flexible. Remember, getting back to base quick. That's what will gut the FBI. If we delay in doing so, it will only play into their hands."

Chapter 6 Communications

Bernie had a shop unit he often rented out, south of Seattle and about a third of the way to Portland in a place called Oakville. Located farther to the east and just half an hour's drive from the coast. A simple commercial unit facing onto a street front. A typical shop or office for a small business. Modest in size, it had some room in the back and he was in the process of renovating it at this time. It needed some updating. The usual stuff, resurfacing and painting so that it could be presentable again for customers. But it already had one thing that might be vital for Kenny's plan: it had a telephone line installed.
Far from sitting at home waiting for Kenny's call from the side of the highway to be picked up, it was a much better idea to be waiting for the call at the shop. Alone. This would be no time for talking over his shoulder at family members – like his wife.

Having been full of concentration Bernie turned to his companion "Unless I'm mistaken, what we have to do is go over all these roads concerned on our map and mark all highway labels as well as the location of any obvious roadside phones."

Kenny looked up "Correct, and we particularly need to mark out all key locations on paper for me. I probably need to keep it with me so as to give me some clue as to where I am."

He went on "We already have the highway markings on common maps but the phone locations could be crucial or anything else we see along the way that is relevant. Therefore we need to get out on the road and drive through all these locations, marking everything as we go. It's called doing our homework."

Bernie considered what he was saying for a moment. He didn't relish the idea especially, driving all over the region. But he agreed. It needed to be done. And anyway, Kenny was the one who was putting his neck on the block.

Thankfully, payphones were plentiful being at every gas station and corner store. So if they got to know the main target zone it would be a great help.

Said Kenny "We can do them on the weekends, giving priority to that black box area on the map and working our way outward. We'd get them covered bit by bit."

He added "It means that if I am making my way onto a road in the dark, as soon as I see a significant signpost or a road marking, I can locate it on my own sheet that I have for reference and I can see from the same sheet where the nearest phone is. That way, I know where the hell I am and which direction to head to. So that when I call you from the phone box there would be a number we have marked on the map corresponding to that phone box. You would have the same information in front of you and can see exactly where

I am. I will try moving away from the phone box while waiting and out of sight, so as not to draw attention."
Bernie was looking a bit daunted at the scale of the task. "There's bound to be a lot of stuff to put down on one sheet of paper."
Kenny smiled "We won't run out of paper – use 10 sheets if we have to. Nothing that your car can't handle. Fill her up with gas and let's get crackin! But before we start mapping, let's talk radio equipment."
He now had Bernie's complete attention.
"First of all, it goes without saying, your standard Air-band radio is a good idea to keep track of airport activity with flight departures."
"Of course" said Bernie with a smirk "I think one of those made its way to my home when I worked at NWO, once upon a time. Not sure if it's working actually."
Kenny continued to lecture "They are easy to get from the likes of Radio Shack. It's no harm to listen in and get used to the Jargon used by Aircraft Control. So that you can identify when the plane takes off and take note of the time. Only remember, do that type of thing when you're on your own – like going along in your car or sitting here in this shop unit of yours. Any changes of habit like that must be seamless to the outside world and appear like a gradual hobby on your part."
Bernie agreed "Think I might hold off renting this place out for a bit longer."
Kenny looked thoughtful "There's my place too. The dingy apartment that it is. But this place is definitely handy being located south of the city and non-residential."
He lit a cigarette and saw the sun was coming out and illuminating the whole street, filling the empty store inside as well as himself with magnificent cheer as it had always

done, so reliably. All his life. Its immense ocean of warmth and light could never be matched.

It was Saturday morning in mid-February. He felt they needed to get the skates on with all this preparation.

All this brought out an energetic burst "In addition to Air-band stuff we need to get two-way radio communication."

Bernie started to look vaguely like he was in pain "Is this going to be more spending of my money?"

"Why exactly!" was Kenny's response. A beaming smile was breaking out on his face, spilling into laughter. "And you thought I would just rely on calling you from a highway phone in the dead of night at a moment like that. And we all live happy ever after. Geestman you red-neck. If it was left up to you, the cops would have us slammed in jail with ease – lights out. Thanks uncle Bernie!"

They both laughed. Bernie was always reaching for the bottom line. Cash was king. And Kenny understood how this habit stifled his thinking. Sometimes at least.

"Anyway" he said "You'll be well compensated. Right, let's go shopping for radio gear. As we go we can pick up a road atlas for the region and some paper."

And off they went.

In the 60s and 70s the pinnacle of the intellect was arguably Radio. For the rest of human tenure on Earth
there will probably always be beings who will hold it in the highest, irrespective of any other developing technology. The great Nikola Tesla has a lot to answer for.

But in Kenny's day the case was certainly very strong. Its use was rife in Aviation. Armstrong had walked on the Moon in 1969 with the role of Radio at center-stage as the world looked on. Radio hobbyists were all over the globe talking to each other and listening in with their large HAM rigs stationed in their bedrooms with powerful valve-amplifiers and mast mounted antennas. There was a variant for truckers and people on the move, often called CB (Citizen band) Radio. So it was natural enough that our two boys in Seattle would want to tap into it.

While there might be some scope for borrowing some gear from work both from Kenny's job and from Bernie's work on the boats, it was important not to raise any eyebrows with colleagues. Rather it could be implemented under the guise of a casual hobby with Bernie putting a unit in his car. One that he purchased from a typical outlet. Being the normal hard-working honest guy that he was.

That said, the SEATAC hangars and the Tugboat company were certainly a good resource with regard to information and manuals on all things related to their little operation. And they would use it wisely.

Normally a ship or large aircraft would nearly always be fitted with large radio transmitter and receiver decks. These were very powerful and quite wonderful but required a lot of expertise to operate. They could be totally confusing to the novice. Hence, the preoccupation for hobbyists and many was the specialist Radio Officer recruited by Marine and Aviation.

These decks were available as Transmitter/Receiver units combined for conversation or just Receivers for simply combing the various frequency bands and listening. But they both felt that they were too big, complicated and unnecessary for installing in a car. They favored the standard mobile unit but with a heavy amplifier installed. This meant being able to transmit longer distances with more power and also to better pickup transmissions for the smaller hand-held unit that Kenny would be carrying. This idea was what basically enabled, say, a guy on the west coast of Ireland with a modest 40 channel rig to talk to a trucker in Virginia, at least occasionally. The larger power of the unit in the truck could carry the conversation. So for the 100 mile radius of their little venture this would be comfortable. They managed to buy a second-hand rig to keep the cost down which was great. But Kenny would have another reason for over-engineering, he just didn't want to load Bernie with too much yet.

They also picked up two hand-held units that this would reach and were to have fun testing them out on the road. They actually worked quite well in daylight but had difficulty at night and were a bit unsteady. This was a general problem with terrestrial radio transmission after dark.

To test it out, Bernie dropped Kenny off in a forest picnic resort near Castle Rock then headed off up the road driving and talking on the radio with him. They found that once they went over 10 miles distance the reception was very patchy and not up to it.
They sat having a beer and wondering what to do. The hand-held units might carry a voice to 20 or 30 miles on a good moment but not likely. Most of the time you have to be just over the road – not more than a few miles. Having a large whip antenna with magnetic attachment on Bernie's car would no doubt be a help but it would also attract attention. Then Bernie mentioned the idea of carrying a 40 channel car unit.
"Would it be too heavy for you to carry?"

Kenny thought about it "Not really, I would just need a good 12 Volt battery to power it. They are definitely better for transmission than the Walkie Talkie."

And that was exactly what they would settle on. They found that it improved everything and they had no problems with reception no matter what terrain they were on. The only problem now was to source a suitable battery for mobility and how to carry it on the go. In addition to everything else that he would need to carry for the occasion.

Chapter 7 Device

What a difference a month would make! Kenny had gone from the dismal depths of winter in every sense to being energized totally and was having the time of his life.

With gradual improvement in developments he and Bernie were implementing, so too increased their confidence in the plan overall and in their ability to carry it out.

Bernie at times needed reassurance and his nerves needed to be settled. He was always the type of guy who was no stranger to breaking some rules but of course he had never done anything of this nature. Kenny felt that he would stay on board as he became more familiar with the whole territory and details of what they were rolling out.

But the guy who hides the truth can't remember where he put it. And Bernie had a habit of spinning off casual lies without covering his tracks properly. He seemed to sometimes underestimate the intelligence of those around him. He was not actually great at keeping calm when he was spinning a yarn. Still, it would have been very negative of Kenny to say this to his face. That was not his style. He would prefer to influence people by example and hope that all things would go well. With a bit of luck.

The more options the two had the better their chances of success. This was Kenny's conviction and he was also a great believer in rehearsal and preparation. How else were they going to pull it off if they did not keep the finger on the pulse?

So Kenny had a new member he wanted to introduce into his electronic family: a homing device. Having upgraded the radios he was encouraged and somewhat relieved to see that the system would have strength enough to go some distance at what was going to be a vital moment. This was a far better idea than simply relying on the public pay phones around the countryside. That might be a good last resort but really it could invite trouble when in fact what he needed to do was disappear from the zone quickly. In the dark. Be gone.

Then, if there were unforeseen complications on the night in question – like the plane moving too fast, getting delayed somehow before jumping . . . he might be hundreds of miles south, in trouble and god knows what territory. Given the potential the radios had for working so well he thought to himself why not include a transponder?! But he would de-emphasize these possibilities when talking to Bernie. No point in generating undue worry.

So a sense of fear and dread as well as some curiosity drove him to introduce another toy to the collection. For this little number, Radioshack and other discreet electronic suppliers were vital. This way you could copy some circuit from a project magazine (or draw up your own as the case may be) then build it yourself. This was a bit safer than making a dramatic purchase that would look suspicious. Not that he had been able to find such a thing as a commercial homing device or transponder when he shopped around. He had to come up with his own plan and solder together the components.

In the case of his device this consisted of some resistors, capacitors and half a dozen transistors on a so-called breadboard for building little circuits. The board gave it structure while he soldered wires to interconnect the various components together. It was en-housed in a plastic casing about the size of a cigarette box. It included a small 9 Volt battery power pack to power it and a single switch to turn it on or off. Two wires ran out of it that carried the signal into his radio transmitter and were connected in parallel across the hand-held microphone switch. That way, when he was not speaking on the radio to Bernie it was transmitting the signal. When he pressed the mic switch to speak, the transponder signal was immediately over-ridden. Therefore, Bernie could either hear him speak or he could hear the signal, provided they were both tuned into a nominated channel on the CB sets. And this would, hopefully, enable him to track Kenny and home in on his whereabouts even when the latter was doing things in a forest and too busy to talk to him. The signal would continue to send its beeps . . .

Still, a little bit of practice and training was needed to actually make use of it. Bernie called into the apartment in Sumner to have a look.

He quickly found himself gazing at the little gray plastic box that Kenny had assembled."So what's the story with this?"

Kenny explained the basics of it to him. He then lit up a cigarette. "Now I intend to turn it on when I land with the parachute – but not before."
Bernie protested "Why not? It would be great if it was on all the time from takeoff. I could try to track you all the time even before you jump. That would mean I could get on the move in the car as soon as possible."
Kenny had his answers ready "Yeah I hear ya. There are two reasons. First, I am not optimistic that the signal will be transmitted out of the plane properly. The metal in the fuselage serves as a mesh and blocks the signals. In principle you might have something magnetically slapped onto the undercarriage but that is tricky and it ultimately might be traced back to us. Bad idea. I don't want to leave any trails behind."
He continued "The second point is that, while it might be OK to switch it on just before I jump, I'll be too busy at that very moment and also I don't fancy having law enforcement all over the signal and being able to trace it while I am coming down in the chute. There are all kinds of clever HAM radio people out there and if any of them were very quick-thinking they might make it to the scene to greet me before you get there. It's inviting trouble. I don't fancy it. Better to turn it on when I reach the ground."
Bernie seemed to be less than convinced about this stuff. "So how is this going to work exactly?"
Kenny summarized "As soon as you hear the signal you know I have landed on the ground because I won't switch it on before that. Now I have adjusted the circuit here to be recognizable to us but not to the average Joe who happens to come by the channel, listening. So, by the way, if it should be that somebody happens to be using that channel, their transmissions will cancel out the signal and so we will

know to move away to another one. Again, you will know the signal when you hear it. It takes a few seconds to identify it because to the passerby it is nothing special."

Kenny went on to explain and demonstrate the sound of the transponder signal. It would have two quick beeps followed by seven seconds followed by another two beeps followed by eleven seconds followed by another two beeps followed by fifteen seconds. Then it repeated over again from the start, in a loop.

"So when you hear BEEP BEEP - 7 seconds of silence, BEEP BEEP – 11 seconds of silence, BEEP BEEP – 15 seconds of silence – that's us. 7, 11 and 15. That means you will have to listen for about twenty seconds to make sure it's our signal. I set it this way to be discreet and not attract attention, instead of some continuous squeaky annoying sine wave that would be really noticeable. So it's just a pulse followed by silence. With a bit more testing we can decide which of the 40 channels to use for it."

But he had more to add. "Now in order to test this out, it's tempting to just set it up here in the apartment and leave it running for a few days straight. That way you could just simply drive round the state at your leisure and check the reception, while you get to know it. However, the problem there is that if the signal is coming from the same place, day in day out, the HAM radio community might do things like record it, and who knows what techniques they might have for tracking it over time. And I don't even know what laws I would be breaking at that stage. But then, in the aftermath of our big job, the police would be running an investigation and who knows what smart-ass technical wiz-kid might step forward. That could be very incriminating against us. We don't want to entertain it. We should not underestimate

the enthusiasm of amateur radio folk."
"So we need to test it while on the move. From different places and maybe different quiet channels, spuriously."
At this point Bernie interjected "Why do we need it exactly? What's the advantage, since it is using the same radio transmitter as your talkie. It's not like you are using a separate transmitter in case the main one breaks down. If you were, it might have some merit . . . "
Kenny agreed in part "That's a fair point. The main benefit is that it can help to keep us off the air – we need to keep talking to a minimum. Also, if I am busy cutting my way out of some crazy ditch, parachute straps and whatnot the transponder can come into its own, working away. Quietly sending out its signal. Once I have it switched on."
"Not only that," he added. "for the duration of the signal, the intervals where it's not bleeping, the 7, 11 and 15 seconds between the bleeps – for those silent periods, the transmitter is switched off, though the circuit is running away and counting. This means we use far less power from the battery than if we were talking."
Bernie could now see the light "Oh right, right yeah I see what you mean . . . So that means that others could use that channel and the bleeps would not really interfere. So it's off the air most of the time. You really have been thinking all this through, haven't you?"
"Well" replied Kenny, "nothing all that special. Just a matter of being fairly thorough. So as we go out and about, testing, you should be able to get some indication of its distance from the signal strength in your car. That way you'll know what to expect. We can go out to the car and I'll show you what I mean exactly."
So they went outside into the car park where Bernie's big V8 station wagon was parked. It was fast, spacious and

reliable – just exactly what they would need on the night. Kenny pointed to the voice meter needle on Bernie's car receiver. Normally this needle deflected in real time to show the signal strength of someone's incoming voice when you were talking to them. Kenny's idea was to set both the car and portable radios to, say, five (midway in volume). Now, with a fixed setting like that on both radios, having been synchronized as such, the signal should roughly reflect the distance to the transponder. So Bernie would have some idea of how far away Kenny was. As he drove closer to the parachute landing site the signal beeps every few seconds would increase in deflection, getting louder and creeping up toward the distortion reading denoted by the red part of the gauge. So if it was reaching the red region then the transponder might be very near. If it was only reaching the 50% mark, it could be 80 or100 miles away. They would need to get to know it in order to give a good estimation. In this way they would have a crude calibration.

That was in theory at least. It remained to be seen just how useful it was. But they both agreed overall that the transponder was a good idea. Even though it seemed primitive, the concept was good. Now to put it into practice. Kenny stood some yards away from the car with both the mobile radio and transponder slung into a shoulder bag. He reached inside the bag to switch it on as well as the signal from the transponder. He turned the volume half way up. Seconds later his comrade flashed his headlights across the car park in acknowledgment. He drove over to pick up Kenny, saying "That was very clear with the volume setting only to five."

They now felt they had done enough shop talk and Kenny was anxious to try it out for real.

So Bernie dropped him off in a park near the city before

making his way, driving south toward Portland. With practice they found both the speech and signal quality pretty good. The signal was lower in level than speech so they learned to manually adjust the levels up when they were not talking.

The following week they got a chance to test the signal and voice transmission for long-distance. Bernie and Margaret were taking a trip down the coast to Newport where they were staying for a couple of nights. Kenny deliberately left the signal and transmitter on for a few hours throughout the Saturday night. Newport was about 100 miles farther south than Portland, so he decided to bring up the power a notch and wait to see what Bernie discovered when he tried it. To their delight he could still receive it quite well. He made a point of not letting Margaret see him talk to Kenny with the new radio. He had told her it was installed as an idea for his work but that he was not too interested in that stuff really. Which kind of rang true.

Chapter 8 Disguise

February turned into March with its many winds. Kenny had to balance whatever work he had with his other endeavor, which he hoped would lead to the pivotal moment of his life. But everything felt like it was in slow motion as he tended to his job at the airline and he used it to keep in touch and monitor the lie of the land.

One Friday morning on a day when he was, for a change,

thankful to have no work, he heard the doorbell ring in his apartment in Sumner. It was a parcel delivery from a mail ordering service. He had been expecting it. On opening it he found that it was a bit disappointing. He had ordered a hairpiece (or Toupee) of the type that was fairly common in the sixties and seventies. This was not too thick as he did not want to look like a hippie. Rather it was wavy in style and reasonably short, dark brown in color.

He tried it on and looked in the mirror. Well, maybe it might be used for the forthcoming job but he was a bit doubtful. He wanted to make sure it was seamless from the point of view of the public looking at him. Yet, on the airplane and at the airport he wanted to be disguised. He was not impressed by this. The color difference with his skin was not really convincing. Perhaps when he was young it might have been. But not now really. He already had another piece that he sometimes wore which was the same but with gray hairs streaked through it. That might be more realistic but then he might be less disguised. He didn't know which to pick.

He had always had these ears that stuck out a good bit from his head and he wished he had a tidier pair that did not protrude so much at the top. Apart from not being pretty, if people were giving his description to the police it might be nice if they had the wrong ear profile. But he could not cut them off . . . Might there be a way to keep them tied back? It seemed comical.

For the rest of his outfit he did not want to wear any standard garment that would be traceable to commercial shop outlets. So he had a black coat that he got secondhand but had never worn. It might have been slightly dated. He was not sure but he had looked in the main clothes stores and did not really see one exactly like it in detail.

It was a similar story with the pants. He picked them up at a flea market and though they were black overall they were odd. They had a vague gray fleck going through them when you looked closely in order to tone down the black a bit. The shoes he had were dark brown in color and from years ago. A pair of slip-ons he never wore. He never liked them as they looked terribly plain but they had rubber soles (higher than normal) and would function just fine for his purpose.

The following morning Bernie dropped in with a little something for him. "I managed to come by some tinted contact lenses – polarized I think. I guess they might be the same as what the pilots wear. These are flexible and come with a gel for insertion purposes. They're not very dark I reckon but should change the color of your eyes. You wanted them brown, right?"
His buddy was well pleased. "Yeah. If they work out it would give me peace of mind."
Bernie agreed. He knew how important that would be. "You might need to get used to wearing them. See how dark they are for the inside of a plane at night. You will want to test them for that. So what else will you be wearing?" he was looking round the room.
"This" said Kenny, putting on the black coat "Over a plain white shirt. Like so."
Bernie looked on "ok, are you going to wear a cap or something?"
"Oh I have two of these." was the response as his comrade put on the gray hairpiece.
"Christ!" Bernie bit his lip before a grin broke through. "Man, you look like a slime-ball I would not trust."
"Would you recognize me?" asked Kenny.

"Not really, no. You look like a bad guy in a badly directed movie. If I saw you on the plane I'd get a chill. I swear to god, you look like one of those Kray-twin guys."

Kenny thought about that for a moment "Thanks!" He looked in the mirror. "So, maybe, with a false tan and those contact lenses fitted I might look like something from down Mexico way."

Bernie's eyes widened "Yeah, maybe. But I gotta say , you look pretty convincing right now. Will the Toupee stay on properly?"

"Oh yeah – no problem. Until I take my jump of course. I can say goodbye to it then. The blast of the air will take it. Get yourself a cup of coffee while I put on these."

When he was in the kitchen Bernie raised his voice to be heard "Did you think about that wet-suit thing I mentioned?"

Kenny gave it the thumbs down "I reckon it's a non-runner. With a bit of luck I will avoid landing in rivers – even though the Columbia river does get fairly wide in places. I have been in cold water before. I think I will survive. Also, it would be far too hot for wearing on a plane under all the gear. And too awkward. Besides, it's another trace of evidence we would have to deal with before and after the event. We will have enough stuff to bury or destroy."

Kenny sensed that this kind of talk made Bernie nervous - that he did not like to get too close to the monster. It was not that he would not break a rule. He broke more than Kenny ever did from day to day. He just did not perform so well in the eye of the storm – so to speak. He did not lie very well. He seemed to be either uncomfortable with it or too comfortable with it.

"Have you decided about the fingerprints?" he asked.

Kenny had another idea for that. "I reckon there is a good

industrial barrier cream for hands that will obscure them when it's rubbed on. I don't want to complicate it by mixing it with false-tan lotion though. I heard it said in the canteen one day that it obscures fingerprints. Worth a try. Why not?"

Inserting the contact lenses proved a bit of a struggle at first but he learned how to do it.

Bernie was getting excited by what he was seeing standing in front of the mirror.

They took the blue-gray color out of Kenny's eyes, giving them more of a chestnut color. "That looks pretty good.

Are they very dark to see through?"

"No. I don't think so. I guess I will have to check them for a bit at night. Now I need to try this false-tan lotion."

He removed his shirt and rubbed the cream into his hands, neck and face. He removed the hairpiece and covered his fairly bald head with this olive-colored lotion.

Bernie watched in silence as the shirt went back on along with the black coat and then the other hairpiece – the new one with its darker, more youthful color. "Wow!" he said. This really worked and they both agreed. "You look like something out of El Salvador. ¡Perfecto!"

Chapter 9 Briefcase

Spring was sweeping in and it seemed to have such buoyancy the memories of November's dark days were banished from Kenny's mind. Oh he knew winter would return to have a further say but he was determined that it would be on his terms. He felt he was stepping across a threshold into the brighter place of his dreams. It would be against his every heartbeat to go back and a betrayal of his character.

He was pleased with the work so far but he needed to nail down a suitable bag for transporting the CB radio onto the plane along with various utensils: batteries, the homing device, flashlights (there would be two small ones included), a good penknife, some spare rope or canvas harness in case he needed it.
A shoulder bag might be a possibility but he did not fancy fishing around in it for things. A briefcase was perhaps better in order to anchor things down properly inside. But which one? It would need to be secure in its locking , sturdy and with a good handle. He would reinforce it if necessary as he would need to harness it to himself for jumping off the plane. In order to survive the rigors of the blast and landing it would have to be tough.
Then came the issue of size. Most briefcases were about sixteen inches by twelve inches by three or four inches in depth. Something deeper was needed, like six or eight

inches. Curiously, briefcases made for pilots offered some of the best design. But they were a bit specialized and he did not feel comfortable about making a purchase of some distinct item which could be traced by the police if they were doing due diligence. Maybe a Doctor's bag or some of those cases he had seen for carrying LP records might be suitable. He could take some industrial case for specific tools and paint it if necessary to give it a different appearance. As ever, secondhand might be better. He already had one that was a bit small, Charcoal in color and maybe too distinctive looking.

But after looking in various junk shops, what should he come across? A perfect black one in terms of geometry, six inches deep internally and well made. It only cost him a few dollars. It had two combination-style spring locks either side of the handle though none in the middle under the handle. The only thing that was a bit non-standard was perhaps the black plastic wear-protectors fitted to each corner. Usually they were only seen on traditional suitcases. But this closed over making a tight seal as with a good briefcase. It was a sturdy looking item.

On the inside there was red and gray cloth lining and a folder insert in the top half for paperwork. He would decide later what to do with that. But this case was lovely and deep. He checked it all-round for strength and was fairly happy with it. Exactly what he wanted.

Now he needed to mount the various bits and pieces inside the case. The CB radio would sit to the right on the floor of the case and toward the back, In addition, two large 12 Volt batteries would be placed to the left side of that at the rear. So when he carried the case by the handle, these bigger, heavier items would rest at bottom and all would be strapped into place.

To accomplish this he needed to make up a metal frame that complemented the shape of these items and would be bolted into the back end of the case, internally. In this way they could be anchored to the back wall of the case - or bottom when the case stood upright. So he got Bernie to supply some Aluminum sheet metal from the boating company. He managed to bend and cut this accordingly to create a frame inside the case. So what he fitted was a horizontal partition or, more correctly, a false floor. This floor sat on top of the CB radio which came about 3 inches up from the bottom of the case. At the rear six inches was another compartment which housed the batteries, the homing device and was the full six inches in height of the case. So the false floor could hinge if he wanted access to the radio, hand-held microphone or anything else he needed to get at. Into this he could strap down knives, flashlights and various wires that interconnected the equipment with the batteries.

Also, from the inside back plate he mounted sturdy metal semi-circular hooks which protruded out through the bottom of the case. He mounted four of these, two on the end of the top cover and two onto the bottom part. These made it look strange but only if you got a glimpse of the bottom of the case. He would paint them black to make them disappear. It did mean that when he stood the case on the floor as normal, these protrusions were being used as feet. But he was not worried about that either. Much more important was the fact that this enabled him to run rope through these rings and secure the whole briefcase before jumping. Far better than just relying on the handle while flying through the air at two hundred miles per hour.

He would also have space for an antenna inside the case and on top of the false floor he would fit a large red single-throw switch with a guard cover. This could be connected to the whole circuit and would enable fast action when he landed with the parachute. So the transmitter could be switched on immediately and the signal doing its job. Meantime he could be occupied with getting everything together to get on the move. He had decided at this point to gather everything up and throw them into the parachute, briefcase, bags, the lot would go into the parachute. Then simply sling it over his shoulder and make his way on foot out of whatever forest or field he landed in.

On top of the false floor he would also tie coin slots in order to house coins for use with the roadside Pay-phones in case he had to resort to that.

Bernie and himself sat looking at the handiwork of his briefcase. It was now beginning to take shape.

At this stage they had driven all over the roads around the landing zone that Kenny had marked on his map. Confidence was high provided Kenny actually managed to get down in that zone.

But he was not clear on everything. "I am pretty happy with things within that zone on your map, I know the area well and all that. But what happens if you drop far beyond it? I mean, how does that play out exactly?”

Kenny straightened up in his seat "Well, you have farther to go and I have longer to wait. Like, what's another hour if all is going ok! But I understand we need to get out of there early. This will be in the night, in the dark, in the woods. I need to get to a road for you to pick me up. You need to get word of where I am. Hopefully the radio gear will do its thing. I will have it all wired up well and soldered.”

"You know,” said Bernie "After the 727 takes off in Seattle it is doing about 500 miles per hour. It will be in the region of Portland in minutes flat. So you will need to jump pretty fast – like as soon as you can."

Kenny gave a vague smile "Oh I know. You're right, I will need to act quickly. But I think I might have a way to slow her down. Nice and easy does it . . . "

This drew a shadow over Bernie's face. What the hell did he mean by that? "But generally, Jet aircraft cannot be in the air by doing much slower speeds. They are designed for that speed. They don't function too good at lower speeds, if at all. They have to accelerate like hell. They're all about speed – that's how they go!"

Kenny insisted "Oh I know, I know! Let's just say, I have a certain technique. These aircraft were tested for paratroopers for the likes of Vietnam. You don't think they jumped at 500 miles per hour do you? Can you imagine – the cold at that speed . . . It would rip your face off, let alone your parachute."

Bernie was in deep thought "I guess I never considered it too much."

"Well," reassured Kenny "Somebody has. People whose lives depended on it. I reckon I'll get that big bird trimmed back."

Bernie looked surprised "By how much?"

"By a lot!" was Kenny's reply. "You see, the experiment has already been done. In raw terms."

Chapter 10 Air-Stream

Summer arrived, coming in punctually at its platform in June, like it always had and the whole of the North West region seemed to be on song. Like everyone else, the two fellows came out to greet it, enjoying the drives in the sunshine, down the highways of Washington state and toward Oregon. Even the shaded back-roads between all the forests were so lovely and enjoyable. Everything seemed so

perfect.
For Kenny, he still had to grind on with the crumby job and his work was patchy as usual. But he felt that the light at the end of his tunnel was indeed bright with promise. He just hoped it would not turn out to be a train . . .

They had debated about when it might be best to pull off their big stunt. The 4th of July was of course a big holiday period when all kinds of people might be a bit relaxed and off guard. The whole world, after all, grew toward the sun. It was known as the silly season. But Kenny felt that a different holiday - one in winter would favor them more. This was for a number of reasons.
Firstly it gave them more time to refine and rehearse their plan. It was really important that they master every aspect of it in order to deal with every possible complication that might arise and be able to adapt to the situation.
In addition, the shorter days of winter would be a great help. The nights were so much longer and that gave them more time on the ground to make good with the operation on hand. Also, there was more probability of adverse weather conditions. This point could actually be a bit dicey for them, potentially at least. But they were willing to take their chances.
In particular, they both agreed that a fall of heavy snow would be detrimental for them. This could create tracks, cause them to be broken down or stuck in the car – needing to be rescued as well as apprehended and imprisoned. That would be disastrous. Too unpredictable and also too slow-moving from the point of view of clearing the-hell out of dodge. Snow was taboo.
So they would monitor the weather forecast carefully. If a heavy snowfall was promised for that day they would have

to call it off.
After some discussion, they came to the conclusion that Thanksgiving would be the optimal time to pull it off – November 24th. There was not a family in America who did not want to sit down round the table and celebrate that night of the year. This was probably the one thing all Americans agreed on, except that in this case our two friends would manufacture, well . . . an exception.
So at nightfall on Thanksgiving airports were generally emptying out as were flights with passengers in many cases having already made it home by then. Just as they would want it. The fewer people around the better. And they knew from many years of experience this was how things went at that time of year.

While on one of their excursions through what they hoped would be their landing zone, south of Washington state and north of the Columbia river, Kenny brought up a little point that was still unresolved in his mind.
"Hey Bernie, have you thought about how you will explain away your absence from the table on Thanksgiving? I mean to Margaret and everyone. We normally go to Helen's also, right?"
Previously he, Bernie and Margaret all went over to Helen's house for the holiday dinner. Helen Jones was a friend of the Geestmans and she always seemed to have great time for Kenny. It was, in truth, evenings like those which so endeared him so much to the area of Seattle. His adopted city.
He could tell from the bored look on Bernie's face that the answer to his question was no.
The 1950s had passed where a woman was brushed aside by the man in the house and told to run along. Oh there was

still bullying and abuse going on in households across America and there would be for a long time to come but Kenny felt that Bernie might be misreading that situation in his own case. Margaret had always been so great and sweet toward Kenny even giving him cheap rent on a shack on her farm while he was trying to make ends meet and get a place himself. She rented out the place to him for just fifty dollars a month. They got on like a house on fire having so many conversations together with so much common ground in their thinking.

But in his reckoning, if you tried to insult her intelligence she could pull your fingernails out before breakfast. He was very clear on that but who was going to tell Bernie? He was, after all, her husband. He really had not married a regular old girl. She was a lovely person but sharp as a razor. And she was nobody's idea of an idiot.

Although Kenny valued her so much as a friend this was one time in his life he would have settled for her being a simple girl who was easily distracted and fobbed off. Yet he knew that was not the way this would pan out. In reality, this cookie would not likely crumble at all. It was as hard as the hob of hell. To be blunt, she did not fit his narrative.

He turned to Bernie "Well look, whatever story we come up with it has to be a solid one. And we need to be united on it. I would suggest it be along the lines of – you know, we were drinking with the gang from work or something and the party dragged on etc. It needs to be simple and believable. If it's far-fetched she will smell a rat."

Kenny felt he would have to tread this one very carefully. He certainly did not wish to damage his relationship with Margaret Geestman. More importantly, he did not want to arouse suspicion in any way. Everything would have to come off seamless, natural and genuine in terms of why

they would not be showing up for Thanksgiving. Maybe they would find a way of tying the alibi in with either Bernie's work or his own job.
Bernie responded "Tell her nothing. She will be just fine – don't worry!"
Kenny thought to himself how that approach was answering nothing and would not go down well with a caustic Margaret the day after the event when she demanded explanations. Of course it would be Bernie's doghouse situation as such and not his. Bernie was the one who was involved in the marriage, not Kenny. Yet it seemed that Bernie had this blind spot with people and how he thought he could get away with deceit. Up to a point this was good in that it fueled self-confidence and in this case he was motivated by dollar signs. But he needed to know and be aware of moments when he did not manage to fool someone. Kenny was concerned about that. It was like he knew Margaret better than her own husband knew her.
He would have to keep his fingers crossed on this issue of mollifying her. He contemplated telling her about their operation, letting her in on the secret but then felt it would be a bad idea. There was no guarantee how she would react. No no. He must not go there - ever. Even with her approval which he was not at all optimistic of, she might inadvertently tell somebody sometime and who knows where that could lead to. No thanks!

A while later they pulled into a diner at the roadside and after eating dinner they sat outside under a shaded area out of the sun, sipping beer. Across the car park and over the other side of the motorway there was a side entrance signposted for a trailer park site, one of the many in Washington state.

They watched a car pull out of their car park with an Air-stream holiday trailer being towed by a car.
Bernie leaned forward "Hey Kenny, you think it would be a good idea to get one of those trailers?"
Kenny did not properly connect at first. "How do you mean? You fancy -"
He turned and looked at Bernie squarely. "Oh of course." His jaw dropped. "Jesus yeah. That would mean we would have a base here somewhere. That could be great."
Bernie added "It might give us more options. We could park it up somewhere, like over in that trailer park for example."
Kenny was not sure why hadn't thought of it before. "We could use it as a base down here or if we had some unforeseen difficulty. It could get us off the road quickly in the event that there were complications."
They sat there contemplating for a few moments.
Kenny broke the silence "You reckon you could swing it? I am totally broke as you know . . . "
Bernie was not fazed by the notion. "Yeah, they are cheap enough to buy second-hand. There's loads of them to be had."
Kenny was visibly thrilled "Man that could be a real good addition. It would also be a help in concocting a suitable story for Margaret . . . "
At that instant the idea gelled and they both knew it. Only too well.

Later that evening while driving back they chatted more about it. It was decided that Bernie would try to get a trailer somewhere second-hand.
Kenny as ever was cautious "maybe don't buy one locally. See if you can pick one up farther afield. Doesn't have to be like New York but in some neighboring state. Also, we best

make sure Margaret and the crew at home do not see any radio gear installed in it. We don't want them to put two and two together in the aftermath. The story is that we are just two guys hanging out drinking beer in a crappy holiday trailer in the woods."

So, over the next few weeks, in between his work Bernie went shopping through the adverts for a secondhand Air-stream trailer. Credit where it's due, we cannot fault him for his effort. After a few unsuitable adverts that he had answered he went to buy one from a couple living near Albany, south of the city of Portland. It was a bit far down from Seattle but it was cheap. Still, being a cheapskate he ended up going cheaper still at a sale in Arizona where he did the deal. On the way back he realized he would need some new tires for the trailer, the ones on it were a bit perished. So he pulled into a place to get it done.

Although it was on the big side it was fairly old. Just what they wanted. They could stay in it, sleep in it, whatever they needed. Kenny knew he was on the way back as he had radioed him successfully from Albany with the news. So that evening he drove across to Bernie's place to check it out.

Man did he get a surprise! A big trailer, full of chrome on the outside, like a mirror. Flashy as hell. Bernie was there to greet him, polishing his baby and looking pretty pleased with his day's work. Kenny got out of the car with his jaw dropped taking it in.

After a few seconds he gathered himself and turned to Bernie "Say, you couldn't maybe get one that's a bit more flamboyant could you?! Something that might attract more attention maybe! I mean ya wouldn't want to make the mistake of being discreet or anything . . . "

Bernie looked dismayed at his reaction "This is the norm, man. Every dog in the street has a chrome trailer. Where the hell have you been? Farm-boy from Minnesota!"

Kenny looked at him. "You're serious . . . "

"Yeah I'm serious. Wake up. If you want to stand out from the crowd you get one that isn't full of chrome on the outside. This is as common as muck!"

"Really?" Kenny began to absorb what he was saying and found himself laughing at his own ignorance of holiday trailer trends.

At that very moment they heard an engine revving at the entrance to the driveway. It was Margaret. She stepped out of the car and brightly enthused about this cool looking mirrored box outside her home.

"Wow" she looked at Bernie. "You were talking about getting one but I didn't expect you to land up with this thing from the future. Gee it's pretty big too . . . "

Bernie evidently decided to spin off the first thing that came into his head, "Yeah, I reckon it would be great for going golfing and whatnot."

This set off an alarm bell ringing in Kenny's head. He shot his companion a glance as if to say "Shut up you moron and get in the goddamn house. She sees right through you."

Thankfully and perhaps because he was feeling awkward Bernie stretched his arms saying that he was tired and humbly buzzed off indoors.

Kenny and Margaret remained around the trailer for a further inspection.

She turned to him "He doesn't play Golf. Is he taking it up?"

Kenny could not help but laugh "Not at all. Are you kidding me? He's joking. You should know him by now."

He opened the door and stepped inside. She followed him

in. He could feel that her mental cogs were turning, trying to figure it all out about Bernie getting the trailer. It was like she was on his case.

Kenny decided to be his good moderate self to diffuse it a little. "Wow, this is pretty comfy you know. Not so new looking inside." He sat on the bench seat and looked around. "Nothing that could not be fixed up a bit."

She agreed. It was comfortable.

They sat chatting in the trailer as the day drew to a close. She mentioned again how she was a bit puzzled at why Bernie decided to get this trailer. She did not think it was his cup of tea, really.

Kenny managed this no problem. "Ah he just wants to let his hair down I guess. Relax and have a few beers. Can't blame him with all the hours at work he puts in. And anyway, he can always sell it on. I don't think it cost a lot exactly."

"No." she replied. "Let him get it out of his system."

A few days later Bernie gave his newly acquired trailer a more permanent home, right back down near Portland. Just north-east of the city. They could move it later if need be. But overall this was a very strategic location for their operation. Kenny stressed that it would be a good idea to head down to it frequently between now and Thanksgiving to 'normalize' things in terms of appearances and behavior. It was tucked away nicely in the trailer park in a wooded area along with lots of other holiday trailers. As the year advanced into the autumn it would hopefully quieten down a little with less holiday goers.

Bernie told Margaret he was keeping the trailer at his shop rental property in Oakville, the news of which pleased her not. She raised her concerns as he was getting ready to go out to work. "Do you think that's a good idea, leaving it all the way down there, unsupervised. I mean it might be destroyed by vandalism."

"I know what I'm doing. Don't lecture me!" was the reply over his shoulder as he marched out the door in a huff.

In fact, Bernie would move his trailer to a number of locations within 40 miles north-east of Portland, in the direction of Mount St. Helens. While Margaret had some idea of the general region where he was bringing the Air-streamer he made a point of not letting her know precisely where it was or when he changed its location. He figured he did not want her suddenly turning up at a critical moment of the operation just like she might be apt to do, knowing her! He wanted to rule out that possibility. Perhaps wisely.

At any rate, she more or less bought Kenny's interpretation of the new trailer episode, that her husband was just a regular guy who wanted some free space the odd weekend.

Kenny and Bernie met up occasionally at the trailer site near the end of August.

After changing the location over and back as well as a bit of discussion they settled on a trailer park near the edge of the Silverstar Scenic area and a few miles east of Hockinson. This was a rugged wooded area, very quiet and off the beaten track a little. Still it was only about eight miles from Route 500 at the north-east suburb of Portland which in turn fed onto the 503 heading north. It was shaded heavily under trees and hopefully the place would be fairly quiet by Thanksgiving.

Chapter 11 Reconnaissance

With all that had been accomplished up to now Kenny was keen to cover all aspects in terms of preparation. He wanted to tidy up odd ends and felt he would never be able to forgive himself if he did not take some flights in a 727 along the target routes of NWO.

For the flight between Seattle and Portland he toyed with the idea of employing another transmitter, to be placed in the trailer. This would transmit a signal while he was in the air. Now, with a portable receiver in an inside pocket and connected to an ear-piece he would be able to listen for the signal. When it gets to a certain strength he would have a good idea of when to jump.

That was the theory of it. He was not so sure it would work

out in practice. On the flight he would be occupied with getting ready to jump. There would already be enough to carry and strap in with parachutes and everything. And he was skeptical that he would receive much of a signal inside the aircraft as its fuselage acted like a shield unless you were connected to the outer antenna like the pilots were. That was his understanding from the guys talking in the hangar though he had never tried it.

Still, out of curiosity he decided to put the transmitter in the trailer, switching it on in the briefcase and connecting it up to a 12 Volt car battery which Bernie had got for general purposes. There he left it transmitting for the day. He would now make his way to Portland International Airport and get on the short flight to Seattle. Bernie might be coming by the trailer that night so he could disconnect it or else he would be there himself again tomorrow to pick it up.

When it came to the big event, both he and Bernie had agreed that no incriminating evidence should be left in the trailer. No radio equipment or anything unusual. At the same time lots of empty beer bottles might be a good idea – something to show that these were just two piss-heads having a good time and hanging out at weekends, in the (hopefully) unlikely event of any police raid.

There was some distance to walk to the highway where he located a bus stop which enabled him to catch public transport on a short ride into the city. He preferred not to mingle with locals and hitch-hike or anything like that, being mindful of anybody making connections in the aftermath of a crime. The less interaction with folk the better. Small communities talked, not because they were nosy but because they had nothing to do. He wanted to keep all tracks covered.

Dressed in a hooded jacket, jeans and baseball cap he made his way to the airport desk. He needed to make sure he looked very different from how he would look on Thanksgiving.

It was an early September afternoon. The airport was moderately busy. That was one thing he needed to check, to see just how many passengers there would be. The fewer the better. But he already knew that by this hour on November 24th it would slacken off.

He went up to the desk and booked a flight for Seattle. This would only be a short hop, thirty or forty minutes away. He was able to pay for it without giving his passport or any identification. That would turn out to be important. In those days, no such document was needed for a domestic flight like this. It was as casual as stepping onto a bus.

This particular flight, the 2.30 PM to Seattle was normally done as part of a daily routine for an NWO 727 aircraft which began its day with flights from the midwest, over Minnesota and working its way westward to Portland before hopping north to Seattle. Of course they also provided service in the opposite direction. Kenny had checked schedules and they were invariably equipped for this route with the Boeing 727, now his favorite aircraft.

He hoped to see as few familiar faces as possible with the airline staff. At the same time he did not want to be too heavily disguised. It might serve as a test to see if people recognized him, it being a small world. Still, he was well used to operating on flights near Japan and places like that. So he did not expect to see many people he knew.

So far, none of the staff at the desk were familiar to him. As he looked out from the viewing bay at his awaiting 727, he got a glimpse of two of the cockpit crew – strangers. And then, more importantly perhaps, the three air stewards in their red uniforms, consisting of two women and one man. Still, he knew none of these people. Great, just as he wanted.

Then, as he was in his seat before takeoff he made a point of looking round over his shoulder. Now he saw something that stopped him in his tracks – a bloody Air Marshal !!

He was wearing a dark sleeveless jacket with the federal stamps on the shoulders and a cap. He was sitting in the back row on the aisle seat, armed with a gun in his holster and looking a bit menacing. "God Damn It" thought Kenny. He had completely overlooked those guys.

In fairness, they were not too common, being mainly placed in Florida where trouble on flights had flared up in recent years. He could not know if this guy was just on a connecting flight or regularly posted there, or what . . . He would need to check this situation out to see what was the story. Good job he took this little test flight. He had better take another, he thought. This spooked him no end. Damn!

He was sitting pretty near to the back of the plane at a window. He wanted to look out to recognize landmarks below. You could never be too familiar with them. Observing times would be a good idea for estimating when he was over his target area. Nothing like regular punctual flights in order to plan things.

Before takeoff he popped the ear-piece into his ear and turned the dial on the air-band radio to start listening. Mostly what he picked up was the flight crew up front relaying the usual stuff before takeoff. He also managed to hear the relays from the control tower but a bit more faintly. This did not surprise him due to the close proximity to the aircraft.

As soon as they were airborne he listened and scanned carefully for his ground signal from the trailer. Nothing! As he had expected. So this killed off any debate he was having about using it during the flight on Thanksgiving. So the only signal he would employ was to be the one he would switch on after landing in the woods.

Bernie had always been a bit conservative in his approach to everything. Maybe a bit short-sighted. Not the fastest to move off the couch and embrace an innovative new idea. Still, Kenny knew that if it involved the Yankee dollar he suddenly became a different machine and could perform just as good as any dedicated lab-coat at doing a thorough job. To be fair, his attitude had been great when it came to this project of Kenny's. He had spent money and put in every effort. Of course it was not he whose safety was on the line when it came to the dangers of the forthcoming operation. That would be Kenny's privilege. But the fact that his old buddy was willing to risk so much seemed to resonate with Bernie.

Later that same day Kenny ran over his story about the Air Marshal with Bernie. He had been a while out of the airlines so he was not sure. But he didn't seem to think it was very common to see them in these parts.

When he asked around at work the feeling he got was that Marshals were mainly sent to troubled areas like Florida with some spot checks and random deployment here and there for a show of strength and reassurance for the public. This eased Kenny's mind a bit but he remained wary.

Another day he took a flight in the opposite direction. All looked good with nothing new to observe. No Marshals visible or anyone he knew.

With Bernie and himself driving around all the roads in the area, they had done a reasonable job in writing down items of interest on the roadways for quick reference later on, in the event that they needed to resort to identifying where they were. Big roads and highways were of course lit up. Back roads going through a forest were a different story. And there were a lot of roads. In this case, landing in a dense forest and getting onto an adjacent back road might take some time. Then, seeing signposts or identifying where you were might mean a considerable walk. So they were prepared for a wait even though they would be anxious to vacate the zone in a hurry. All the more reason why landing in their target zone would help so much to increase their chances of a quick pickup and exit.

Chapter 12 Private hire

Between forests and rivers and volcanic mountains the landscape of the north-west is hardly boring. They were at this stage well used to looking at it on various maps. There was the standard fold-out tourist map and a whole variety of survey-style maps that were officially produced, showing elevation contours as well as all kinds of detail that for the most part was not needed. Then you even had aviation maps showing flight routes and vectors.

Kenny had hoped to reconcile the map view with the aerial

views he had when he flew over the region between Seattle and Portland. However, he found that while this was ok for identifying large items here and there when you looked through a 727 window, you were getting an incomplete glimpse. This was in part because the narrow window on an air-liner restricted your view.

Ideally, what he wished to see were satellite photos. But even if they had been properly archived by 1971, unless you were NASA you were not going to gain access to such things.

He suspected that what he needed was some aerial photography taken from a small aircraft which would fly only at a fifth of the speed of a jet. Also, the views from such planes were more open providing far better panoramas for the passenger. He felt he needed this not so much for something in particular he was looking for but for whatever reasons he failed to think of. Perhaps something he did not foresee. Besides, who knew what he might see that could be beneficial - for the sake of a bit of effort. It was a kind of a net test strategy.

At any rate, he was still recovering from the shock of seeing Mr. Air Marshal on that flight. He did not need any more surprises. Why leave anything to chance?

So, he would put the case to Bernie for hiring a light aircraft for an hour or two from one of the flying clubs. This would be as a regular sightseeing tourist with a camera in hand. Kenny's camera. A few rolls of Kodak color film ran off over an hour or two while out over the region might do a lot to clarify things.

What was more, he could revise his long forgotten techniques of E6 film processing. This was photo development for positive film which was better than that used for color negatives, the C41 process. The latter would involve a dark room which he did not have. In the early years when he was based up on Shemya island, one of the guys there introduced him to it. It involved getting chemical kits which were easily available from good photography stores as well as some plastic basins, containers, a thermometer and not a whole lot more. He would have to revisit the process but he already knew it was not difficult although he had never actually done it himself. He already had the 35mm camera.

The advantage of processing at home was the all-important privacy, not to mention that it could be done in a hurry. Like a few hours.

Now to get uncle Bernie to provide the aircraft.

Later, when they were both in his apartment looking over maps and the like, Kenny asked him. "Hey, does Margaret have one of those slide projectors?"

"I think she actually does. You wanna do a slide-show?"

Kenny proceeded with caution. "Well, I might need to develop some film and have a look."

Bernie removed the unlit cigarette from his mouth "Why do I find it hard to believe that there isn't more to this, somehow?"

"Ah" said Kenny "that's because I haven't told you yet."

"Oh. So it's not really about a projector? . . . "

"Ah no. No . . . not really . . . Well yes, we would need a projector also. But there is another machine involved."

Bernie simply could not wait to hear more.

Kenny went ahead and got the explanation out about how that other machine would be an aircraft. To his mild surprise, Bernie seemed to see the sense in it. Probably because he trusted Kenny as an overall strategist.

"How much is a joyride in a private plane?"

"I'm not going to lie to you. It's probably something like

fifty bucks an hour." Kenny knew it was probably more. "A helicopter could also be used but I think a fixed wing craft is cheaper."

He continued, "And I can show you how to use my camera – nothing to it."

"What do you mean *you*? I'm not going up. You're the one who needs to see it."

"That's true. Except that later, when they publish descriptions that vaguely look like me – or my disguise, people at the flying club might make a connection."

Bernie looked like he was check-mated. "You have an answer for everything, don't you?"

Kenny felt awkward. "Well I do what I can, that's all."

Anyway, Bernie was persuaded at this point. "Is there any other aspect of this venture that I need to know about?"

"I really don't think so." was the reply. "We're nearly done."

Looking over maps of the target zone, Kenny explained what Bernie would need to do when he was in the air.

"So, what we're most interested in is what's called Victor 23. That's the route that planes take when heading directly south after departing from Seattle. It's pretty much a straight line south though you don't need to come quite as far as the Columbia river. But at the Flying club you don't mention Victor 23. Just say "Go directly south and turn back up along these Volcanoes". You pretend you are a casual tourist with his camera."

He continued "Now, you can bring 5 or 6 reels of E6 film with 36 shots per reel. So you might be busy snapping photos and changing out film. But at the same time I guess you want to make it look like you're an enthusiastic holiday maker and not like a guy who is on a mission of some sort. So be sure to get every area you go over. You are not really interested in volcanic mountains but of course take the odd shot of it."

"By the way," he added "Some of these pilot guys have backgrounds in the military and all sorts of stuff. So if you think you see any familiar faces take note but I wouldn't get locked in too much conversation with them."

Bernie was beginning to smile "Thanks dad!"

Kenny could see the funny side. "I'm just saying now would be a good time to play the hillbilly a bit - "Wow, that's fantastic", "Gee I never been in a small plane before." Also you need to do the flight in daylight of course."

He hoped that Bernie would keep nice and quiet for this trip. He knew he was well capable of being calculating. He just needed to learn the art of silence.

It was early November and the two guys found the pressure coming on a bit though they managed to stay composed and focused about everything. While the light aircraft was being organized Kenny found himself over in Bernie's place quite a bit. It was warmer than his own apartment now that the winter was coming in but the main reason was that out the back in Bernie's shed there was a proper bench with a pretty good set of tools and lighting. This was just what he needed to finish off his briefcase – his flight bag as it were.

He had some more wiring and soldering to do as well as more anchoring of brackets within the case. He was using the heat-shrink gun to wrap some of these coin tubes in red wrapping. He had already done a few at this stage. They looked very good and would hold plenty of coins. He would strap these onto the upper side of the false floor using clench-style nylon straps like the type used for bundling of commercial pallets. These were provided by the NWO hangars as were the coin dispenser tubes - straight from the aircraft flight crew.

As he sat at the bench absorbed in his work he heard the door of the shed click open behind him and felt the cold air coming in. The door had a habit of clicking open when it had not been properly closed. As he turned round to attend it he got a fright.
Bernie's thirteen year old niece was standing there staring at the case on the bench and the glaring red color of the shrouded coin tubes.
In a near-panic Kenny got himself into gear "Ah honey, you're not supposed to be here!!"
"Oh ok . . . I'm sorry." was her reply as she turned to retreat out of the door. Kenny followed in her footsteps to try patch it up as gracefully as he could. "Yeah, Bernie goes mad if he sees people coming into this place."
He closed the door properly behind her. Alarmed as hell, he swung around to look at the bench. What had she seen? He put his hands to his head as he took stock. The open briefcase, attractive red in the inside and the red coin tubes. It would be obvious he was working on something.
But that could be anything now that he thought about it.
She had stood rooted to the spot staring at the red tubes. Just as anyone would do, instinctively, especially when they did not understand what they were seeing. It did, after all, look really interesting.
Leaving tales to be told was not something to be happy about. Especially with a breaking news story of a crime in the area. "Jesus" he thought. "I need to be more careful."

Bernie went through the motions of hiring a private small plane from one of the flying schools. This was near Puget Sound, south of Seattle. The plane was a typical two-seater affair, the Cessna 172. A fixed wing aircraft with a high placed wing which made it ideal for aerial photography.

So he explained to the pilot he wanted to go directly south for a bit then maybe turning back up sometime before reaching Portland in order to make their way back up by the volcanoes. So going down south they might catch the river and coming back they would view the mountains. Something like that. And they duly set off on the clear November day. It was a day with perfect conditions but he was not sure if he had departed early enough. Being late in the afternoon it might be getting dark in a while, which may or may not be beneficial to them.

Though it was not the kind of thing he relished he took out the camera and got stuck in. He shot plenty of film and hoped he was doing things fairly ok. He had six reels of film in all so he figured to use three on the way down and three on the way back. He was a bit dubious about this excursion being of much benefit in the end but he agreed that it was something they should make the effort with. Just to be sure.

He knew that the target landing zone was shortly below Seattle and this was a chance to study things in slow motion. The 727 would be much faster even if Kenny did manage to slow it down as he had promised to. The little Cessna was doing about 100 miles per hour. He recognized most things he saw below him having become familiar from the maps he had grown so tired of looking at. But this was a fresher view and more interesting. Off to the right as they headed south he could see the Columbia river widening as it did on the maps.

A little north of Vancouver (the northern suburb of Portland) they banked left toward the volcanoes and began the return back up north. At one point he was really struck by crazy dense forests. It put fear and dread in him to try to imagine landing in that in a parachute. What's more, it

would be at night. Better Kenny than him for that stuff. He knew his old comrade was fit and would need to be. Fingers crossed . . .
He suddenly wondered if it would have been more valuable if this trip had been at night. That may be, but he did not know if the camera would really perform in the dark. He figured they just needed to settle for what they had, for better or worse.
In the end he used just four and a half reels when it was time to pull into the airfield. Whatever his buddy would think of his day's work.

Chapter 13 Look before you leap!

Kenny had collected the various bits and pieces that he would need from some round-town photography suppliers. The E6 development kit with all the chemicals and immersion box to take the reel of film while it was being processed. Then there were various plastic containers. Most important was the instruction document. He had a record of following instructions and finding success. The more he did it the more successful he got. Instruction sets were a vehicle for getting people to try new things and be accomplished. And even if you did not succeed you always learned something from the attempt.
He decided to first try with the half-shot film reel that was still in the camera. He went through the process, changing out chemicals and monitoring his clock. Eventually when he wiped down the strip of film and held it up to the light

he was pleased to see clearly developed images.

More of the same please! He went through the other four reels that were used up by Bernie as fast as he could. It took patience. Finally he had them all.

So it was time to go through them on Margaret's projector. He did not have any slide mounts done so he would just run the strip of film straight through, frame by frame. With the curtains drawn over to bring down the light he proceeded. And as he went through the images projected onto the wall what did he see? Initially, there were no surprises. These pictures were taken at an altitude of two or three thousand feet. He would be jumping from something like ten thousand feet.

If he could memorize big landmarks and be able to recognize them below, he should be able to steer the parachute, not so much as to accurately land in a small area but to steer away from disastrous areas like the wide parts of the Columbia river and of course cities or urbanization.

Kenny studied it all carefully for hours, referring back to the map constantly. It was awkward because he could not conveniently get prints of these pictures and pin them to relevant locations on the large unfolded map. Nonetheless he was able to process it in his mind and a pattern emerged.

Looking at the map, if you drew a line directly south from the center of Seattle you would intersect the Mount St. Helens volcano. Actually the line ran just east of the edge of the volcano but too close for comfort. If you ran another parallel line a little east of Seattle you would go between St. Helens and Mount Adams and even brush with Mount Rainier which lay to the north of these two. Bad idea. For this reason aviation authorities normally advised an air route to the west of Seattle when heading south. This headed out of the volcanic region but stayed east of the

Columbia river.
Happily for Kenny, this terrain was half forest and half normal flat area with a fair share of open fields. It did not really matter where along this strip, from south of Tacoma to north of Portland. He could deal with it all. Little patches of forest interspersed with fields. So he could use forests to stay out of sight if need be (though it would be in darkness anyway) while at the same time he did not have really dense forest to get out of. And he was less likely to get stuck on the top of a tree in the dark.
At the same time he would have to avoid that lake area around Ariel, Lake Mervin. It would be just smooth black in the darkness. He would have to be aware of it. It was very large. And on examining it, for the very first time he made a connection – the lights of the Merwin Dam. He had seen this often from commercial flights but had never really paid attention to it. It sort of floated somewhere in his sub-consciousness. But now, even in the early lighting-up hours that Bernie had taken the photos he recognized its semi-circular shape. It was a useful landmark and could be a visual identifier for the dam and also a reminder of when to jump from the plane.
Kenny called up Bernie and showed him this. On reflection they were both really glad they had taken the private plane. They could see how it helped crystallize a strategy for landing and it settled their nerves a bit. They were feeling the benefit of tinkering and going the extra mile, even when it had no clear goal. Looking at designated forest areas on maps was one thing, But seeing the photographs was a big addition. It somehow had an settling effect on both of them. So long as Kenny now managed to jump at the correct time.

In 1971, the November 24th Thanksgiving holiday fell on a

Wednesday. On the Monday before, Bernie told Margaret that he would not be around for it as he wanted to head off in the trailer for a change. She held her tongue but was not exactly happy. No doubt she might have found it a bit depressing as it was a first for them in their marriage when they would not be together at this time and perhaps even a signal that their union was beginning to suffer or at least not be what it had been. Bernie departed the house on Tuesday.
Kenny and himself made some final arrangements at Bernie's shop property to make double sure they had everything before heading off to the Trailer site. As they drove they went through the list of things to check. Even having Bernie's station wagon fueled up was on the list of things to check off.
Kenny was leaving a change of clothes in the back seat of the car. He knew he would need them. He could be wet and cold after coming down through the air but also because it would be a good time to completely change colors and outfit. Forever after he would never again wear that black trench-coat outfit. The same would apply to the hair-piece.
He also left a few black plastic refuse sacks rolled up and ready for use. These would be great for concealing all kinds of things later as they moved stuff out of the car.
They reached the trailer which they had tucked away near the Skyline Trailer Head in the south west of Washington state. This was on a flat trailer park in a hilly rugged area. It was about fifteen miles from Portland as the crow flies.
It had been more or less emptied out by this time of year. They only saw one other trailer down the way as they were pulling in. It felt really quiet and remote. It was getting dark and was feeling chilly. There were the usual gaslights for these trailers which were great. But there were plenty of bedclothes and blankets so they could battle the cold for

one night.
With great concentration they went over the plan, both aware that if there was anything amiss they would have to abort. So Kenny would have checks to do on board the 2.30 flight from Portland. For example, the sight of an Air Marshal would be a show-stopper. The plane being unexpectedly full of passengers would be another.
For Bernie to be listening in on the Air-band radio would be very important. He had gotten used to Air Traffic Control from Portland and Seattle. The flight in question would be NWO 305 and he knew the jargon enough to tell him if the plane was taking off or if there was a delay.
It was normally a half hour flight to Seattle. According to Kenny's agenda, if the plan is not aborted it would mean there would be a definite 'mechanical' delay of arrival in SEATAC - maybe an hour or more. So in that case the plane would be doing circuits around the airspace while problems were being sorted out. But if it arrived punctually at 15:00 then that would likely mean he had called it off.
It was also a good idea for Bernie to note the time of departure from Seattle which of course would be much later than 15:00 – probably more like 18:00. Kenny expected to be jumping more or less 20-25 minutes after that moment. It would take another 10 minutes to land on the ground. So a total of about 35 minutes after takeoff from Seattle heading south.
At that point Bernie should expect to hear a signal on the CB radio. The agreed radio handles for use were simply John and Jimmy meaning Bernie and Kenny respectively. It would be a bad idea to use their real names but they wanted to stay off the radio as much as possible saying only the minimum.
After a spell of no communication Bernie would move off

slowly in the car onto Route 503 while continuing to listen for a signal. If there was no joy after a while – no signal, no radio call, he would head to the shop in Oakville and simply wait for the phone to ring, assuming at that point the radio gear failed.

In the (hopefully) unlikely event that Bernie was to be left sitting in the shop for hours waiting with no word and those hours turning into a day - that would be unbearably grim and eerie. Bernie perhaps did not really dwell on that but Kenny was as ever the type of person who would have.

Kenny mentioned it to him at one point "By the way, if after a long time, like 2 days, there is no contact from me and there is no definitive word over the media about what happened, keep off the radio at that point. It will likely have gotten into the wrong hands. Unless you actually recognize my voice. The same goes for the signal. Proceed very cautiously. Careful not to be incriminated."

Having explored all the roads over these last few months they fairly quickly realized just how plentiful public Pay-phones were. When you had never used them you would not know but it's only when you go looking for them you find that they are installed at probably every gas station or diner. So they could relax the criteria for paperwork and road markings and the like. That was assuming they did not hang around in the area for too long.

With all in place on the eve of what was to be the strangest day of their lives, the two set to bed early in their windswept trailer in the woods.

They had put in much work and felt confident.

To Bernie it was a wild and crazy criminal involvement for sure.

But to Kenny it was so much more. On a platform of truth and decency he had struggled under-foot all of his life with

the whole world of mediocrity flying high above him. But while in the gutter he had managed to invent a new world in which the situation would be reversed. The plan was now founded and forged, the iron was hot and he was determined to stamp it onto the forehead of the beast.
And NWO would pay for it. All of it!

* * * * *

Act 2 The Deed Indeed

Chapter 14 Early morning

Next day, Kenny and Bernie were up before dawn.
As quiet as could be, they each went through the checklist of everything they needed. Basically it had all been prepared. It was just a matter of going through it again to see if anything was left out. Kenny with the case and everything included, radios, batteries and two little flashlights, flattened in profile, they were ideal for carrying. Two sharp penknives. He had a knife and a flashlight stashed into a coat pocket. Their two comrades were strapped into the lower level in the briefcase. On the upper layer he had installed, among other things, an altimeter to track his height and of course that all-important kill switch for the radios.
In addition he would carry a white department-store shopping bag which had two handle straps and was made of heavy paper. This could carry extra items such as his hairpiece and disguise as well as a useful canvas strap that he had picked up which had a locking harness. He felt it would be useful for strapping things up on the plane before he jumped. Being made of paper, the bag was biodegradable, all the better for self-dissolving evidence.

Bernie for his part was concentrating on checking his car tires as well as the radios on board. Everything was in order. He had filled it up with gas already and was raring to go. Also, the clocks were synchronized – his watch and

Kenny's as well as the clock in his car and one in the trailer. But he was a bit nervous at times.

He opened the door of the trailer before daybreak and felt the chill of the air sweeping in. It had been raining on and off during the night. They both agreed to hit the road before there would be any activity in the trailer park or in any of the surrounding neighborhoods. The plan was to make it into Portland early before many people were up where Kenny would be dropped off at the edge of the city.

With everything in order they checked the contents of the trailer for any possible tell-tale signs. Other than some empty beer bottles and some clothes there was nothing out of the ordinary. Just as you would expect from two guys who were away for a few days, chilling out.

With the V8 engine of the station wagon started up they slipped off down the hill and out of the trailer park. Making their way through the forest roads they were both quiet and pensive.

Past the little rivers round the roads they went until finally they pulled onto Route 500 at the north-eastern corner of Portland. The airport was not far.

Soon they had turned onto the 205 and were crossing the broad Columbia River with Government Island sprawled out to their left. After crossing over the river and island they were coming onto the end of the beltway with the airport to the right. Low-flying jets could be seen and heard. This indeed was the place.

Kenny pointed to an exit, "Pull off here, There's a gas station down there we can slip into."

As they pulled into the station there was just one other car moving out. Kenny beckoned to a lane-way at the back of the building to the car wash. Bernie moved into an unoccupied side bay and switched off the engine. He lit up a cigarette and rolled his window down a little. Kenny could see the tension on his face. The lights were just going out in the city as at the start of day.

Kenny was wearing a baseball cap and a light wind-breaker over his white shirt. The specially picked black coat was in the white bag wrapped up neatly. He did not want to be recognizable to anyone who might see him around in places like this, coffee shops etc.
He turned to Bernie. "All you gotta do is watch your clocks and listen to the radio. If for any reason I need to abort the operation and call it off I will try to reach you on the CB. So it could be a good idea to have it on before the flight departs, just in case."
He continued, "Now the flight to Seattle takes off at 14:30, so if you're listening in on that Air-band radio set you have you should get that confirmed, no problem."
Bernie was in the know. "Yeah, I got that - Flight 305, I been listening to it every day, it's nearly always on time. So, normally, it only takes about half an hour to reach Seattle. It's what happens after that, that's what bothers me."
"As I said before," replied Kenny "There will certainly be some delays. Listen out for departure from SEATAC directly south – Victor 23 is the air lane normally used but there is no guarantee you will hear that term used over the radio for a given flight announcement. Anyway, twenty minutes to half an hour after that departure, there should be the jump. From that point on listen to the CB and be prepared to move. If you get no call or signal for still another hour after that, just head up to your shop and wait for a phone call."
He continued "The important thing is not to be seen to do anything out of the ordinary. Stay indoors and be alert. No

drinking or sleeping."

"Are you kidding?" Bernie looked at him "Yeah right, like I'm gonna nod off."

This drew a burst of laughter from the two of them. They were both wary of the elephant in the room here (death or imprisonment to Kenny) and neither wanted to give way to it. Rather, they kept the chin up and stayed focused, as if they both knew they had no option. There was just no other way to get this done.

After some small talk Kenny gathered his things which included the loaded briefcase. Stepping out of the car he turned and offered his hand to Bernie as he did so he saw a shadowed expression move across his face. His partner shook his hand and did his best to stay composed.

Kenny met this with a slightly reflective but super-confident sparkle in his eye. "See ya soon!"

As Bernie watched him walk away from the car in the early morning light he started the engine and pulled into the traffic.

He decided to head back north, up the 503 toward his shop. This would give him a chance to monitor the radios before making his way back to the trailer in the afternoon. And anyway it would look fairly normal to pull back into the trailer park around midday. He did not want to arouse any suspicion.

As he drove, he thought about that conversation he just had. It was almost like an out-of-body experience. Saying goodbye to a guy before he could possibly meet his death. He wondered if he had done the right thing by embarking on this strange adventure given that it could yet turn tragic. But for now he managed to stay positive. Kenny knew parachutes and was very competent in all matters.

Making his way on foot through the cold morning, Kenny also thought about that conversation and goodbye he just had with Bernie. Why was he able to deliver an excited and upbeat smile? Because it was real. And why was it real, going into such a perilous operation? A nightmarish quagmire of uncertainty and dread, where the actual most probable outcome was pretty dark. Why of course because he was motivated to settle a score, not just because of its everyday consequences but also because of the sense of accomplishment. Attempting the impossible and achieving it was at the core of who he was even if it seemed to lie dormant for so long, he who had so little to show for it. And it was in defense of principle, a fight against corporate enslavement as he saw it. He had under-delivered on this aspiration recently. Success was overdue.

Be that as it may, there were no guarantees about anything. Still, even if he faced prison he would tell the tale and make his stand. He relished it all – success or failure. The tricky part of course was avoiding death. Death was the one thing he did not fancy. He would have to watch out for that.

Chapter 15 Getting on board

It being Thanksgiving, the early morning was fairly pedestrian in terms of airport activity. There were the usual flights landing and departing but the traffic and people were down in comparison with a regular weekday. Just as Kenny had hoped. He had checked the weather forecast all week and there seemed to be no snow in sight. Perfect!

After crossing the 205 onto the Airport side he stopped into a little drug store and got coffee and a sandwich. He was not all that hungry for whatever reason but he knew he should have something. It might be a long day but he had endured long days in the past without much food. After that he went into a quiet public toilet and locked himself into a cubicle in order to change into his disguise.

He set to work. First came the contact lenses that gave him a brown-eyed appearance. They went in fairly easily as he had been used to them lately. But he also kept a pair of dark glasses in his pocket in case of complications.

The barrier cream for the palms of his hands were applied then to help obscure fingerprint detection. Next came the false tan which he rubbed on well under the neckline, all over his face, even round his fairly bald head. Everywhere. He also put some in the back of his hands and up his forearms a little.

He then fitted the hair in place, preferring the brown colored one making him look slightly younger. Making sure there was nobody in the main area of the restrooms he stepped out of the cubicle to check his appearance in the mirror. He scarcely recognized himself. It transformed him, especially with the olive skin color against the white shirt. And yet it did not look out of place really. It looked fairly convincing.

He fixed the black clip-on tie he got from JC Penneys shop at Sumners in early autumn. Pretty sharp looking. Finally the coat came out of the bag. All was ready.

As soon as he was outside he tossed the windbreaker into a large rubbish bin near a cafe and the baseball cap into another. With a briefcase in one hand and a paper bag in the other he was on his way. Just like in the movies.

Kenny still had plenty of time to kill before the 2:30 flight. He bought a morning paper at a newsstand on the way to the terminal building though he knew he was in no mood for reading. This was to make him look normal and casual while he was observing things around the check-in area. But first he would take a casual walk through the greater public area just to have a gawk and watch for any familiar faces in the staff. Normally with his work on the airlines he got South Pacific and the Orient. So that meant dealing with different company staff members from those who worked on US Domestic routes. Still, there was always the possibility of meeting someone who got posted elsewhere or even had some temporary arrangement. He had already checked all the rosters as best he could and there did not seem to be anything out of the ordinary in that regard. No unexpected faces at Northwest check-in desks or with any support staff. The same down on the ramp when he looked out of the window onto the tarmac. Nothing unusual and all quiet. Casual, even sleepy. It was just past 12:00 midday. Time to sit and read his paper before buying a ticket.

At that very moment just a few miles away Bernie was driving back into the trailer park. He had spent the morning listening to airport proceedings with the various flights. As Kenny had advised, he kept the CB on and was combing it frequently in case of a call. There was still another two and a half hours to go until takeoff. Part of him wanted to get a call from his buddy saying that there was a problem and that he would have to call it off. But something told him that was not going to be. Besides, he had disrupted his regular Thanksgiving arrangements and would have to face the wrath of his wife at some point. It had better not be called off . . . whatever. Right now he was feeling nervous.

After waiting back and watching everything Kenny's time had come quickly. He had seen from the departure gate that it did not look too busy as far as he could tell. No major lines of people for the flight, just a few sitting around waiting for the call to board. He felt pretty sure there would be no more, giving the usual pattern with passengers just twenty minutes before boarding. So he would approach the desk of Northwest Airlines and buy a ticket.

Up he went to the desk assistant.

"Hi, could I get a ticket for Seattle please – the 2:30?"

A friendly reply came from the official "Sure, is that one way?"

"Yep. That's a short flight normally right? What's it, a 727 or something smaller?"

"Ah yeah, I think it's nearly always a 727. So, that will be – with tax, $20 please."

Kenny gave him a $20 bill. Before the day was out he would see a lot more of them.

The desk official proceeded to issue the ticket, filling in the boarding pass. "Your name sir?"

"Dan Cooper" was the reply from Kenny. That was his good luck charm. And why not? His old comic book friend.

Back then, airport security for internal flights in the USA was very laid back. Absent was the rigorous checking that would one day become the norm. Especially on Thanksgiving when everybody was just keen to get home. So he could easily get away with giving any name for his flight ticket.

He received his boarding pass "Thank you very much. Gates will be open shortly for boarding. I think it's running a bit late today, actually. Probably a delay of 25 minutes or something like that. Happy Thanksgiving!"

Turning to the gate he saw two air hostesses in their

splendid red outfits. Trolley Dollies as some of the hangar staff called them. He gazed through the viewing glass down at the Northwest 727 awaiting. He was wondering briefly about that delay and if it would matter. Not really. As he saw it, delays like that were to be expected on a holiday like this. Sometimes the airlines or airports would be short-staffed leading to little operational hold-ups. This aircraft normally made its way through the mid-west during the first part of the day before arriving at Portland. So there were no surprises really.

He had seen some of the pilot crew coming through a little earlier. He peered at the cockpit window of the aircraft and saw two of them inside. Strangers. Nobody he knew. He moved over to a corner of the area and sat waiting for people to board with his coat over his arm. Often in an airport lounge he might hear a familiar voice "Hey Kenny man. How are ya?" But not today. He was doubly sure of that. He had checked repeatedly in the bathroom mirror. He looked nothing like his normal self.

A few passengers had gathered. Just a handful of people traveling so far. He lit up a cigarette and waited patiently.

Only a few minutes later there was a PA call to board Flight 305 to Seattle. Passengers promptly lined up in the usual manner. Kenny did a quick head count. About thirty five or so. A nice tidy crowd.

He wanted a back seat on the aircraft, so he held back to let all the passengers go through before boarding. Seeing that he was the last, he put on his coat and went through with his ticket. The lady staff member checked it and let him make his way to the now empty gangway to the plane. He felt very calm.

Chapter 16 Excuse me, Miss

Inside the Boeing 727 everything looked as though a normal flight was getting underway. Except that in this case the aircraft was not so full. The tired crew were no doubt in a relaxed mood coming to the end of their shift and would be as eager to get home to their families as everyone else. Just what the doc ordered.

Kenny was about the last to step on board and he made his way down to the rear of the plane, picking a center seat in row 18. The closest passenger to him was in the same row and at the other side gazing out the window.

He kept his coat on and placed the briefcase on the window seat next to him, opening the two latches, ready for action. It was almost as if he could feel the power of the briefcase – the power of his work gone into it would pay dividends. The white bag was tossed onto the floor for later when it was needed.

With a cigarette lit up, he noticed only a little activity by the three air hostesses up front. They seemed pretty casual in all respects. As it was coming up to 14:30 the usual announcement came across the PA system - "Ladies and gentlemen, this is your Captain, William Scott and along with me is First Officer Bill Rataczak. We welcome you on board for this short flight to Seattle. We will be departing shortly and we wish you a comfortable flight and a very happy Thanksgiving. Thank you."

Kenny buckled in as the aircraft began moving, taxiing

down the runway. He knew he would not make a move before takeoff.

Back in the woods Bernie was listening intently for everything in his car parked up by the trailer. He had no call from Kenny on the CB. It was just past the stroke of 14:30 and the winter's day already looked dull from the clouds overhead. Rain and thunderstorms were promised on the weather forecast for the Northwest region for Thanksgiving. Why had he heard nothing yet for the Seattle NWO flight? It should have taken off quite some time ago. Was it delayed or did he miss it?

"Northwest 305 you're free to proceed" - ah there it was now. Pretty much on time. His heart began to race a bit as the time had arrived. So now that takeoff was about to get underway he would be none the wiser about the status of the operation until after it landed in SEATAC. There would be nothing to indicate whether or not Kenny was put off by something during the flight and decided to abort and just be a normal passenger. He would not know about that until later. He would have to wait. That would be a minimum of 30 minutes . . . more. "Jesus" he thought "The waiting is already unbearable." He had better grab a coffee right now when he had a chance. He dreaded being away from the radios in the car in case he missed anything vital.

Down the runway hammered the Boeing 727 as though she was in as much a rush for Thanksgiving as anyone. Like a goose in a mad hurry, she would lay the golden egg by the end of the day according to Kenny's plan. As Flight 305 took off he felt the excitement in his chest as they started to gain height. Some aspects of danger were really enjoyable. There was no doubt.

He wanted to put things in motion so he signaled to the hostess for service, as planned. He ordered a Bourbon and 7up as usual. This particular hostess was Florence according to her uniform lapel identification. A cute looking slip of a thing with a pout and a Vidal Sassoon type hair cut that had been so common throughout the late 60s. When she arrived with his drink he thanked her warmly and paid for it. "Keep the change and this is also for you" slipping her a small folded piece of paper he had prepared. She calmly put it into her pocket and moved on up the plane without reading it. Kenny's eyes tracked her up the aisle to see if she was going to read it.

She did not. She tended to another passenger along the way. "Damn" thought Kenny. He really did not have the time for inaction like this. He wanted her to get cracking straight away.

He raised his hand for her attention "Excuse me, Miss!" Luckily she saw him immediately and came down to him.

"OK?"

"I gave you a note, Miss. You better read it!" He finished with a firm stare making full eye contact. Her facial expression acknowledged his urgency and she turned briskly and made her way up the aisle to the front of the craft. He saw her taking the note out of her pocket, reading it while her steps slowed to a standstill.

Miss -

> *I have a bomb in my briefcase and will use it if necessary. I want you to come sit with me.*
> *You are being hijacked.*

He saw her looking up when she had read it and moving slowly toward the pilot's area. She was moving very slowly as though she was stunned. He knew the signs – lack of motion in the feet.
He watched as she managed to move inside to the cockpit without creating a scene. "Finally," he thought, "Steady yourself girl."

Inside the cockpit the Captain actually had control of the plane when Florence walked in. The cabin crew settled in as normal as could be. Nearly asleep, except that they actually had a job to do.
As soon as Scott noticed she had a note for him he reached back with one hand to take it. He read it quickly
and immediately jumped from the fright, losing grip of the steering. The plane wobbled momentarily but the co-pilot instantly grabbed the controls to recover. The passengers no doubt thought it was air turbulence but back in the rear seat Kenny might just about have known better.
The Captain scrambled to catch his breath and take hold of the situation looking round at Florence to consolidate the story. She was struggling, herself, to get words out "He's down the back. Back row sitting alone."
Scott got on the intercom "Ah . . . Alicia to crew please."
Alicia was the Senior Stewardess. The captain gathered his thoughts as she entered the cockpit. He put his forefinger to his lip in a stern gesture of "Hush" giving her the note. Her jaw dropped. "He is down the back. We need to keep quiet and act normal while at the same time keeping an eye on the other passengers to make sure that all is well."
They both had a riveting look of concentration. "Get Tina in here!"
Scott leaned over to Rataczak in the co-pilot seat putting his

hand on his shoulder "We got a 7500. Man the radio!"
By now the flight engineer over in the rear corner woke up from his day-dream and sprung to his feet. He was all over Captain Scott "Did I hear you right?"
Scott answered "Correct. Squawk a 7500 stress call immediately!" He turned back to the co-pilot "Bill, when the tower calls back tell them we are getting further details."
The international air code for aviation stress calls had a value of 7500 reserved for Hijacking. This meant that if this numeric value was transmitted the Air Traffic Control tower would immediately know the plane was being hijacked, even if the crew did not get a chance to reach the radio or if for any reason the normal radio equipment was tampered with by the Hijackers.
Tina arrived in the cockpit. As soon as the door was shut, the Captain spoke to all three stewardesses "Ok, so we have a hijacker on board, down at the last row, right? Alicia, you please tend to passengers up front. We want to keep as calm as possible and not let any passengers know."
Turning to Tina and Florence "Go down to him calmly without making a fuss and ask him what he needs etc. Bring pen and paper. Write stuff down and get the information back so we can relay it to the tower."
At this point Florence looked really shocked but was recovering somewhat.
Captain Scott double checked both of them for composure. "Ok? Just stay calm and ask him how can you help him. Try and observe as much detail as you can. Try and see if he has a bomb or what but co-operate with him and be courteous. Remember to act normal. No over-reactions or anything like that. OK?" He gave them a nod to proceed and off they went.

Meantime, back at the control tower in Portland, nobody liked to be working for Thanksgiving. Like with hospitals and Fire Service it was necessary to have staff scheduled in to work the most unpopular shift of the year. But everyone knew that it would be very quiet in terms of air traffic and some kind of food was usually on order for these hours, like pizza or hamburgers or the like. Or maybe some Black Cherry ice cream. Really, it was a pleasant hour of the year to be in the office.

Until it wasn't. As soon as the words '7500 Hijacking' was uttered the whole place jump-started into a tense headless chicken scramble. Background pop stations were turned off. All the ice cream was instantly melted. Who would ever do something like this? No sane person in this office.

Of course the control tower got on the radio to the crew, to be as professional as they could. "Ah . . . NWO 305 you receiving properly? We got a 7500 squawk. Can you give us an update?"

Rataczak replied promptly "305 here. Yes squawk 7500 is confirmed. We are just awaiting some details. Please stand by for more."

A look of dread swept round the control tower staff. The emergency protocol was put into gear as best as people could remember what to do and how to do it.

The police would be contacted as well as more and more people by the minute. Right now all they could do was wait. They were all spellbound.

Who the hell needed this on such a day of the year?!

Chapter 17 Enter Tina

Considering how many times an air stewardess walks up the aisle of the passenger aircraft, this walk to the hijacker in Row 18 must have seemed like it would last forever for Florence and Tina. The thirty seven passengers on board were generally sitting and scattered round the middle of the plane as on any normal flight. The hijacker (Kenny) was sitting in the aisle seat of the last row and smoking a cigarette. He eyed the two carefully as they approached. They looked dead serious. There was a steady exchange of glances.

Tina spoke in as composed a voice as she could "You have some information for us? Something you want to show us?"

Kenny kept his eyes on them with a firm expression. He nodded and without turning his head moved his left hand to the briefcase on the middle seat. He saw how the two women were glued to it intently, taking it all in. He continued to watch them while lifting the lid on the case to make his exposure – the Bomb!

They both gave a controlled gasp and drew deep breaths, chests heaving all round making it look like terminal breath . . .

Small wonder when we consider what it was they saw.

Those coin tubes really delivered some visual punch after they had been wrapped extensively in red tape – eight of them. Each six inches long strapped together and wired up to look like dynamite, anchored onto the red false floor of the briefcase . . . Across the other side sat the altimeter. And near center stage was the menacing red cover guard for the big deadly switch. Better than anything Hollywood ever turned out. Kenny had been tickled by how realistic and engaging it all looked.

He continued to watch them and gave a squint of discomfort, knitting his eyebrows while putting his thumb over the cover of the switch. With a flick it sprang open to reveal the switch itself, a metal single-throw type. One toggle and it would be over for everyone on board.

The two girls were as white as a sheet. They understood what they were looking at. They had seen enough movies by now. They felt it. Florence's mouth quivered with near panic, looking like she wanted her mommy. She was not taking this well. To calm their nerves Kenny closed the switch cover to safety once again. He swallowed hard as he did, as though he was mindful of the danger of this device. They looked momentarily relieved. A micro smirk flashed on his face. He was doing his level best to stop laughing. Luckily he was pretty good at that. He was well aware that he had a codger of a smile making him look like an old fool that nobody ever respected. That had been proven to him time and time again in all those years. But there would be no soft smile today.

He spoke calmly. "I need you to sit and take some notes, please."

Tina made the first step toward restoring normality by saying to Florence "It's all right, I can do this. Why don't you go up front and I'll be up shortly."

Florence said nothing but at least had the wherewithal to go along with it. She needed to do her job and not faint.

Gladly, she turned round and walked in the direction of the cockpit.
Kenny looked at Tina and gave a brief but sincere grin to acknowledge her hands-on approach. He knew how important it was to achieve visual impact with the bomb he had made so that the air staff would relay the seriousness of it back to the authorities. He was glad that episode went so well. After all, being taken seriously was the order of the day.
Tina spoke "Ok, let me call the captain on the phone here and confirm the situation." There was a phone on the wall back a few feet behind Kenny's seat. She picked it up and promptly got hold of Captain Scott. Kenny could hear her confirm the bomb was real with out using the B word. She told him she would be in touch soon and hung up.
She then turned to Kenny and waited for what was next.
He now produced another note from his pocket which he had written. He handed it to her "You need to bring this to the crew. Transcribe details if you want. I need to have this back please as well as the other note I gave earlier."
She took the note and looked at him for a second as though she was trying to process the new developments.
"Go ahead," said Kenny. "Hand it in up there. They need to get a move on with this. It needs to be organized by five o'clock. Thanks!"
He was concerned about time and progress. They needed to get things in motion and meet his demands before the plane landed, this being only a short flight. So far things were on track.

This girl Tina had an earthly aspect about her. Kenny felt he could relate to her and depend on her. She seemed to have the ability to keep her head in a situation and perhaps to relate to things better than her slightly younger colleague. In reality he did not like giving anybody heart attacks, especially fellow workers on the crappy North West Orient airlines. He knew well that they had enough hardship everyday. So this operation was something of a compromise to his principles in that regard. He might be pressing them a little and trying their nerves. They would have to forgive him in exchange for him sparing their lives. Well, he hoped they would look at it that way.

When Tina walked into the front cockpit Florence was in the middle of explaining the Bomb. The Captain instantly saw the new note in Tina's hand and grabbed it anxiously to see what it said.

I need $200,000 (in $20 bills) delivered to Seattle when we land, in canvas or other suitable carrier bags.
In addition, 4 parachutes – 2 front packs and 2 back packs, civilian type not military.

When that is delivered I will let the passengers off.
We will also need to refuel.
No funny business.

He took a few seconds to absorb the meaning of it and turned to Bill in the co-pilot's seat "Right, let the tower have this right away. It's ransom time. No," He paused "I will do it on second thoughts."
He sat back in his chair and reached for the radio "305 to control. We have demands received." The reply came immediately from the tower "Go ahead 305."
Scott proceeded to relay the details of the demand as best he could. The tower double checked all relevant points

"That's 200,000 in $20 bills for SEATAC?"
"Roger!" replied the captain.

Miles away in the wilderness of the trailer park sat Bernie in the car anxiously listening to his Air-band. The flight had been late taking off which did not help matters. It was nearing the half hour mark into the short flight 305 and he still had not heard anything out of the ordinary or special reference to it. It would soon be time to land. Suddenly a bolt out of the blue from the control tower "That's 200,000 in $20 bills for SEATAC?" This was unmistakable. It was surreal since he never heard the corresponding pilot's transmission. But the mention of the money was crystal clear. Wow!

Now he was in it and there was no turning back. A bout of nerves hit him. This would either be the best day of his life or the worst. There was little transmission immediately after that except some talk about bags and the like which he was not paying attention to. He had been so shocked by the money line it eclipsed the other details in his mind. But he got the important bit. Kenny had struck.

He switched on the AM radio briefly to listen for any newsflash. Too early maybe. Now he would have to wait for the next update. But for how long? He put both hands to his head and took a deep breath while he tried to take stock of the situation. The Air-band went quiet for a bit. All he could hear was the wind and rain outside his car. And all he could do was wait.

Soon after the details of the ransom were conveyed the control tower got back to Flight 305 to double check that the aircraft had enough fuel on-board to do some circles at

SEATAC before landing. The reason for this is that everyone anticipated delays before the authorities had everything in place to cope with the ransom demands, not to mention the coordination of all things on the ground for handling this now highly exceptional flight.
Scott conferred with the flight engineer about the fuel situation. There was plenty stored in the tanks for doing circuits and the like. For a couple of hours if need be.

Back on Row 18 Kenny was smoking a cigarette when he heard over the intercom "Ladies and Gentlemen, this is Captain Scott. Unfortunately we are having difficulties with electro-mechanical systems which we are trying to resolve. Also, there are operational and congestion problems at Seattle International Airport so we anticipate some delays with landing. My apologies for this. We will give you an update as soon as possible."
Kenny was pleased to know that things were in progress. Good to hear it. By now he had put on his glasses in order to assist his disguise. He had already disclosed his eye color falsely as brown. That was enough to put out the wrong information. They would be reporting him as brown-eyes because of course this was the color of the contact lenses. They did not need to be looking at him any more. Besides, if one of the little lenses were to fall out, as had happened to him recently, there might be a slip-up. Better this way.
He saw Tina approaching. She sat into the seat beside him.
"Everything good?" he asked.
"Yes, the details were sent on. Here are those two notes you mentioned." handing him back the two pieces of paper.
Kenny responded with a pleasant grin. "Thanks for that. There will be some things on the ground to take care of. So it will probably take a while. They need to try and have

everything ready in SEATAC by about 5pm."
That Tina had sat into the seat and was chatting with him did not escape the attention of the closest passenger to them. In the same row on the far side at the window the guy sitting there, in his late twenties, threw them a glance as if to say "Wow, what a good looking chick! What on earth does she see in such an old guy?" We can only imagine what might have been going through his mind, "Man . . . and his hair piece is a joke. Obviously dyed or something. She seems quite taken with him. God, how sad is that . . . "
Kenny noticed him looking over and suggested to Tina "It might be a good idea to ask some of these passengers at the back to kindly move up the front a bit. You could say there are some difficulties with the electronics and there is an engineer trying to resolve it."
She could see the sense in this as they just wanted the operation to be as smooth as possible. So she followed through with it and got several of the rear-most passengers to move up the plane. Nicely. That way he now had the back area all to himself. As any self-respecting hijacker would want.

Chapter 18 A rattle in Seattle

For all those involved, the reaction to the hijacker's demands was one of confusion, shock and people were generally panic flooded. There was scarcely a chance to discuss all the aspects of this crisis in real-time let alone handle the situation on the ground. To say that everyone

was caught off guard would be an understatement.
Coming on the eve of Thanksgiving was in itself a sting to the authorities but there were two elements of the demands that seemed so sinister and almost alien filling everyone with fear and dread.

The first was the presence of the bomb. Normally, with hostage takers using firearms in these standoff situations law enforcement officers would deploy a team of armed staff to surround the situation and possibly storm the vehicle if the opportunity arose. But if the incident were to result in detonation there would surely be more loss of life than that of the hijacker's. And so the prospect of an explosion on board colored things very differently and would take the wind out of the sails for any attempt at storming the plane.
The second strange thing that really bewildered all concerned was the demand for four parachutes and a refueling of the aircraft. What was this hijacker planning to do? Where was the plane going to fly to after it departed Seattle? And why did he want four parachutes? Obviously the second set was intended for a second person. Was he planning to take someone as hostage for a further ordeal in order to ensure his escape?
Meanwhile everyone had to scramble at breakneck speeds to comply with these demands while the Boeing 727 did circuits around Seattle aerospace, her passengers cursing the delay for Thanksgiving celebrations while being completely unaware of the actual reality on board.

The city of Seattle did indeed have reserves of cash to deal with emergencies like this. But before any such decision was made to co-operate with a hijacker the acting chief of

Law Enforcement had the presence of mind to call the CEO of Northwest Airlines for approval to pay the hijackers.
Even in Seattle the Yankee dollar was the Yankee dollar. Being in America, "How ya gonna pay for it?" would always be the first question asked. If the head of the Airlines sanctioned the payment of ransom money then it would make things so much easier for police handling red tape in the aftermath.
The order was sent to Seafirst Bank in Seattle to process and prepare the cash regardless of anything else. This was done as a matter of form in such emergencies. Deep in the money vaults the emergency cash had been prepared – up to $250,000 of every variety of note in fact and the serial numbers of every bill had been recorded on microfiche. Blocks of every type of Dollar bills were stocked and blocked accordingly, 10s, 20s and 50s. Kenny knew about this well and he felt that $20 was the optimal choice for his ransom demand. Each bill weighed 1 gram, $200,000 paid out in $20 meant 10,000 bills each with a weight of 1 gram. This made a total weight of 22lbs. Kenny had tested that weight from the point of view of physically carrying it. The 20s would be manageable whereas the 50s would be harder to circulate in the community.
So, according to the hijacker's demands the blocks of $20 bills were squared away into canvas bags, ready for shipping.
Meanwhile back at police quarters the chief was on his feet pacing over and back the floor. His mind was racing. He had been trying to reach the head of NWA with no success as yet. The phone rang. He picked it up. It was the airline CEO returning his call. He explained the situation quickly, getting to the point. "Sir, there has been a ransom demand from the hijacker on board one of your aircraft here in

Seattle - $200,000 in cash."
This was met with silence. The airline chief already had the bones of it explained to him in the earlier message. His breath was audible over the phone while he gave it a moment's thought.
"Do you have it in cash reserves?"
"Yes sir, we do. What I need is your approval from the airline. Is NWA prepared to reimburse the city of Seattle for this sum?"
"Absolutely! We'll take no chances. We have insurance policies for this kind of thing. Go ahead and do what you have to do, officer."
"Thank you sir!"
He continued "Listen, Officer, above all, we want nobody coming to any harm and to try and have our plane back in one piece. The last thing we want here is some violent scene that gets out of hand and who knows how much tragedy might ensue. So, please don't hesitate with any payment!"
He hung up.
Now it was all systems go. A military force and swat team was getting ready at the airport. He needed to be making his way there right now. But first he needed to check what the story was with the four parachutes.

And oh those parachutes . . . They gave everybody the runaround. Not everyone in the police knew who to ask for such items. The military it was assumed but who exactly and where to ask at this hour? Also, as the hijacker had specified 'civilian' and not military. This led to some head-scratching and in a panic the authorities just started making phone calls to the armed forces. After some struggle and false starts they managed to reel in the interest and concern of some hard-working people at the other end of the line who made some inquiries on behalf of law enforcement. Word got back, though not before time that it was the flight schools that might be the best bet to call given the hour of need.

It fell upon George Harrison, the NWO official working on the ramp at SEATAC that day, to oversee this crisis operation. Acting on a tip off he called Norman Hayden who had a parachute supply and machine shop just near the airport. Norman had the back chutes and they were promptly dispatched by taxi, being the first to arrive in Harrison's ramp area.

Success breeds success. It turned out that the man who packed those parachutes for Hayden was Earl Gossey who was based in Sky Sports and was a well known paratrooper and rigger. After a call from Harrison it was established that he could supply the front chutes. These would normally be used as a reserve parachute in the event that the main chute did not open. It was his job to make sure all parachutes were properly packed with the canopies neatly inserted into the retainers and with the rip cord ready for quick release. The fact that these were being organized for a criminal did not impact on this critical requirement. And besides, there was a real possibility that one set would be used for a hostage. So if ever protocol was important it was right at this moment. However, the rigger did not actually have two completely standard front chutes to hand – only one. The other he had was a modified affair but he felt that he had no other option but to include it. So with that, he jumped into action and the front chutes were on the way to SEATAC.

Back on the plane Kenny had ordered his second Bourbon whiskey for which he paid. Tina was in and out and at times relaxed looking and perhaps inclined to be a bit chatty. He might have been delighted to talk to her but, really, he felt he could not get too friendly and anyway he had to concentrate on the situation at hand. And it was indeed a situation so this was not the time to get cozy. After he sipped on the whiskey she very politely lit his cigarette. No doubt, in the back of her mind the more spirits he drank the less chance there might be of detonating that dreadful bomb. But a second Whiskey was not going to dent our Kenny. At that point he was still getting warmed up being well able to handle such matters easily.

By now it was well past the official landing time of the normal half-hour flight and the plane was doing circuits round Seattle which agitated one or two of the passengers, patient as they were, about having to postpone Thanksgiving celebrations. Looking up the aisle Kenny noticed a bit of commotion developing toward the front of the plane. One passenger in particular was making a bit of noise and complaining about all the delays in the air. From what he could tell from a distance he suspected the guy might have had too much drink. Perfectly understandable given the situation everyone was in.

This gentleman was now standing in the aisle and having an altercation with Alicia, the chief Stewardess. This went on for another minute or two, which in a heated exchange like this can seem forever. Judging from the rising volume of his voice he sounded irate and was not backing down.

After another minute of this it started to escalate and another passenger intervened. The first guy was now getting a bit rowdy and the incident did not look like it was going to be solved. With that a third man got out of his seat and intervened, seemingly with more grip and authority about him. From what could be observed from the back row this appeared to have worked as the noisemaker became less verbal and sank into his seat. Whatever was said to him in this intervention was out of earshot for Kenny but he could see the guy was being talked to pretty firmly by this new arrival. Nothing like a threat to focus the mind, alcohol or not.

So with things settled up front people got back in their places, the hero passenger was the last to go for his seat. He stood in the aisle casually chatting and shaking hands with an apparent acquaintance he had met, another passenger who was seated. Kenny felt grateful for his intervention.

But at that very moment the hijacker saw something that cast a cloud of dread and doubt over everything and horrified him.

Something he had not expected. This heroic passenger was the very same air Marshal he had seen on a previous flight. As Kenny gazed he confirmed his suspicion. This was definitely the same person. He recognized his burly figure and his face.

Kenny's heart was in his mouth and he had the feeling it was all over. A feeling that he had miscalculated and there was nothing he could do now. All the Marshal had to do was take out his gun and fire the life out of Kenny and being so accurate at shooting that would be exactly the thing to do in this hijacking situation.

The seconds of dread wore on with the plane's engines buzzing away and the hijacker in a mentally locked state as though he was in a dream. He gazed at the marshal's smiling face and it seemed like the blackest moment of his life.

From the back of the aircraft he could hear the Marshal laugh out loud from the conversation he was having in the aisle. This seemed to wake Kenny up somewhat and he began to gather his senses. He realized the Marshal was in plain clothes and not in uniform. Presumably he was off duty and traveling home for Thanksgiving. The big question here was if he was carrying a gun in his possession. From what Kenny knew of passenger laws he was forbidden to do so but an off-duty Air Marshal could easily bend the rules and some of them were probably happy to do just that. He could not be sure.

The other question was whether the airline staff knew that he was an off-duty officer or if they had communicated with him that the plane was being hijacked. Kenny's guess was that they likely would have known him but they might not have made the connection especially as he was off-duty and dressed in plainclothes. And of course, the captain up front would have given them certain orders on how to proceed with this crisis. They had enough to deal with besides getting some bright idea about involving a vacationing Air Marshal and, again, did he even have a firearm with him? The airline staff probably did not know either.

So, Kenny began to breathe easier. He had thought the worst but, fingers crossed, the staff would be too busy and with a little luck the guy would not have a gun anyway.

He remembered how with any big accomplishment, those involved nearly always needed some pinch of luck. He decided to press on as normal. Besides, there was not much else he could do.

Time was moving on and winter darkness was drawing near for the early northwest evening. Lights around the cabin came into effect while the staff did their best to keep passengers calm and comfortable. Kenny knew there was no problem for the authorities getting the money. There

should be no problem with the parachutes either but still there was potential for confusion. He knew these aircraft would have enough fuel to do quite a few circuits in the area but at some point they would have to get down.
The Captain came on the air to say that hopefully the problems would be resolved soon and thanks to all for their patience.
In a quiet moment, while lighting his cigarette Tina turned to Kenny and spoke in almost a whisper "Why are you hijacking the airline?"
He had his answer ready "I don't have a grudge against you ma'am, I just have a grudge." She would have to make do with that amount of information.
A little later she spoke about where she was from – Minnesota. Kenny responded by saying how it was a nice place. As well he should know. He did not want to appear cold at all but he needed to monitor all things and now he was getting a bit anxious. He had enough Whiskey and cigarettes and really needed to check the situation.

Chapter 19 Landing prepared

Even in 1971 it was kind of hard to move into emergency mode at a major international airport without the media getting wind of it. But on this occasion the offices of newspaper and TV were wrong-footed for the same reasons as with everyone else. Thanksgiving celebrations were underway in these establishments also and although there were indeed some skeleton staff on hand in the various

Newspaper, TV and Radio networks, invariably they were left wanting in terms of breaking a big sensational story. If only it had been twenty four hours earlier it would have been no trouble. So with limited hands on deck there were going to be delays before these organizations could get a proper handle on this news and frankly, no story would be better than the wrong story.

It seems that in the early stages of this crisis not too many news reporters were on the ground within reach of SEATAC airport. The authorities of course had to prioritize the demands of the hijacker and get through this potential nightmare so they were not exactly taking tea with the press in these moments.

In the meantime the armed forces had sprung into action and were deploying snipers as well as having ground troops on the ready. But with a bomb on board nobody was very hopeful of a tangible point of attack. They felt it would be a game of wait and see, play it by ear and let it develop. They were eager to move in but had to assess a complicated situation. With a bit of luck the hijacker would make some mistake and undo himself under pressure. Still, that had as yet simply not materialized. Right now, it was not in the bag for law enforcement.

The ransom money had been the first thing to be delivered to the airport. This was handed in by a local Homicide unit of the FBI, neatly packed in two canvas bags that were commonly used in the Banking sector.

Next came the two back parachutes from Hayden's machine shop, only a stone's throw away from the airport.

The front chutes however triggered delays as Cossey in his haste had sent them to the wrong place, a local air base instead of the international airport. Eventually, after much grief and anxiety they arrived by private car delivery to the right place. George Harrison at this point was a very relieved man as was the chief of police operations. Finally they were ready.

Word of this reached flight 305 and confirmation was given to Kenny that his demands had been met. At this point he asked Tina to put him through to the captain for a word. Speaking on the inter-phone that she handed him "Captain, please be advised, we need to taxi to an isolated, well-lit area after landing. Please notify the tower of this."

Captain Scott was paying full attention at this point. "That's all right sir, we can do that."

The hijacker continued "In addition, we should use the rear door only for all exit and entry. The passengers leave after Tina brings the all-important item on board. After that she should go down for the parachutes. At that point the refueling truck can move in and do its business. I will send this up with Tina to the cockpit so you can relay it to the tower."

The captain was already making notes.

Kenny continued "Now, all I need for the new departure is yourself, the co-pilot, your flight engineer and Tina. all right? Just the four of you. You can let the other girls go after the passengers get off. Also, be sure to order meals for the crew. I'm sure you have an appetite at this point and will certainly need it over the next few hours. OK. Thank you."

Scott replied "Thank you sir, we will get that sent to the tower straight away."

And he did, though anxiously. Both the crew and authorities were wondering where the plane was heading to after Seattle.

So, with that the tower gave permission to land after a

quick scramble to decide where to put the aircraft exactly. They organized airport staff and ground crew to bring the passengers from the plane quickly, picking a well lit area that was reachable for all. This caused some repositioning of the armed forces not to mention the fuel truck. Nonetheless all was hastily laid on.

Shortly after that Captain Scott's voice came over the intercom "Ladies and Gentlemen, thank you all for your patience, I am happy to inform you that finally we are in a position to land at Seattle Airport. My apologies once again for all delays. We have been experiencing a lot of mechanical difficulties at this time."

This was met by a cheer of relief and a hand-clap from the passengers.

But the captain continued "Please note everyone: Due to the nature of the fault we will need to exit through the door at the rear of the plane after landing. But please, I need all passengers to remain seated after landing with safety belts fastened until notification is received from the ground staff. This additional procedure should only take about three minutes more while the aircraft is being checked externally. It is because of the mechanical trouble we are having. Thank you for your cooperation on this and once again, my apologies on behalf of North West Airlines and I wish you all a very Happy Thanksgiving."

As the flight was preparing in the normal way for approach to landing, Kenny summoned Tina with another instruction "Can you please pull down these window shutters on both sides for the last few rows of seats."

Tina looked puzzled at his request for which he had an explanation.

"They won't take me alive."

This would put a darker mood on things as she carried out

his order blanking out the views from the rear seats on either side. Kenny was mindful of snipers round the airport trying to pick him off if they got the chance. What they did not see might not give them ideas. Still, was he simply expressing determination on his part or was he being cynical and reflecting the attitude of law enforcement? - that they were inclined to shoot first and assassinate him at any opportunity. Of course no airline staff worker ever signed up for that kind of grizzly diabolical spectacle. And who could blame them.

As soon as the authorities got wind of the hijacker's plans to take off with the ransom and remaining crew to a destination as yet unknown, someone hastily decided to get some fighter jets from the military to follow the plane in pursuit. It was as yet unclear as to what the plan was exactly except to follow it and track it for whatever information could be had. Obviously, shooting down a civilian aircraft would not be on the agenda – far from it, especially with crew members being held hostage on board not to mention every other reason. Really, the only benefit would be to provide information in case any strange tricks were attempted by the hijacker. At this point everyone had been handed enough surprises for one evening and the powers that be were beginning to get a grip on things. There was a vague worry that some disappearing act might be carried out with one of the hostages which might go into some missing-person saga and last for heaven knows how long. Also, the jet fighters were much faster and more capable in the air than passenger jets so they could adapt to a variety of situations. Whatever lay ahead in the coming hours it was important that everything was tried in order to bring as swift an end to this situation as possible.

So Captain Scott prepared for landing in the normal way. Flight 305 began its descent toward the allocated runway at SEATAC as the airport lights drew closer.
But that was the end of normality. From the point of view of the crew, ground staff and authorities things could not have been more different and unexpected. They had not bargained for this at Thanksgiving holiday and did not know how it would end. Or when.

Chapter 20 Tension on the tarmac

George Harrison, the ramp manager for Northwest Orient Airlines stood at the edge of the allocated runway for flight 305 and the brightly lit up area which had been set aside for the flight to taxi to in accordance with the hijacker's demands. He was zipped up in his company-issued Hangar jacket to battle the cold and damp. The rain seemed to hold off at this time which at least offered some consolation for the troubled operation on hand.
Although the area was full of people it was unnaturally quiet. You could easily tell something was amiss. A conspicuous baggage handling trolley truck sat nearby with the money and parachutes guarded by a few ground staff and two FBI plain clothes officers. On both sides of the destination zone were armed law enforcement lined up. Then there were the sharp shooters who had just got themselves into strategic locations on rooftops and also behind one or two planted vehicles near the edge of the track.

The brightness of the floodlights proved somewhat annoying to those who would be trying to spot and seek out a target. Moving around were two coordinators from law enforcement, each with walkie-talkies. It was their task to manage operations on the ramp and liaise with a person they had placed in the control tower.
One of them came toward Harrison. He was there to consult in real time with the people in air-traffic control. It was hoped that he might get some information relayed to the ground about the activities and position of the hijacker, in case there was a chance to take a shot at him. There was not too much hope of success but if they got half a chance there was no doubt the snipers would be in with the first bullet they could fire.
Laying back also was the refueling truck ready to go, the usual complement of fire trucks and ambulances to respond to whatever might ensue as well as staff to whisk away the passengers. And there was even a big awkward food freight rig with hot meals for the crew though they knew they would not be given priority.

As the NWO 727 approached SEATAC Kenny felt a little nervous though he had confidence in his plan. He knew about the operational mechanisms, procedures and constraints and also understood the inability of conformist workers to break the mold and do something non-standard. At least that was how airport crew normally operated. Time to put it to the test.
Of course it was in the nature of police and the FBI to break rules, driven so often by a sense of entitlement and sheer intolerance of law-breakers. Especially the likes of a lousy scumbag hijacker. Still that bomb on board could have a very undesirable outcome if it was detonated. Nothing like

the danger of a public screw-up to sharpen those fine minds of law enforcement. Right out on the open runway for all of America to see on Thanksgiving.

A detective approaching Harrison was carrying a holdall. As he got near to him on the ramp "You're Mr. Harrison, NWO right?"

He went on "Alright, look you should put on some of this safety gear – we're not really expecting an incident but just in case." He opened the bag to reveal a bullet-proof vest and a security helmet. Harrison was glad to avail of these. As he was putting them on the officer produced a hand-held walkie-talkie. "Pop this in your pocket. I have it switched on. Just listen for our instructions. You are not likely to want to talk."

As they saw the suitcase flatbed vehicle being moved up he continued "So, of course you will be driving into place in this thing and waiting for the crew member to open the rear door and come down. Now it's important that you don't go too near the rear door of the aircraft so as not to make the hijacker nervous. In fact, you should stop in time so that you still have the rear side windows of the aircraft in view. He may be tempted to look out of the window which in itself would give us more information."

"So" asked Harrison "What do I do at that point, just wait?"

"Yes. When the door drops down from the aircraft, just have the two money bags ready to hand the staff member. At some point they will come out again and you give them the four parachutes, there. At that very second you're out of there – scram!"

This all sounded good to a pensive Harrison "All right, I can live with that!"

There were radios clicking at the edge of the landing area with lots of people scrambling to get a grip on the situation.

This added to the nervousness in the air.
Another officer approached Harrison "She's coming in!"
They waited and watched. The talking and radio clicking simmered down to a silence among everyone as they looked toward the black night sky over the runway in the distance. The familiar aircraft lights appeared, seemingly motionless but getting bigger as the seconds rolled on. Gradually the image grew to something more recognizable as it lowered itself over the runway and touched down. They watched it come to a halt as they had seen thousands of times before. After reducing the speed, Captain Scott wasted no time and began to taxi onto the reserved area. As the aircraft approached the noise levels rose notably from its jet turbines. When it reached the center of the area it stopped and immediately the engines were switched off and could be heard spinning down. A wild wind blew across the tarmac and the surface was still wet from the rain.

Inside Flight 305 Kenny was all agog behind his glasses though calm on the outside. He was more interested than anyone to see how things would go from here.
While the engines were dying down the captain spoke to the passengers "Ladies and gentlemen, once again let me remind you that as this is a non standard exit from the aircraft and we need you to remain in your seats for two or three minutes more. Thank you. Ah . . . cabin crew to the tail door please."
Tina was strapped into the back row seat opposite Kenny and knowing that this was her call was only too happy to respond and get this over with. Kenny watched while she sprang to her feet and went to the back door. Within three seconds it was open and was lowering onto the tarmac outside, the fresh air rushing into the cabin. Kenny gave her

a look over his shoulder with a brief smile. Down the steps she went and could immediately see a baggage truck laid on some forty feet to the right of the craft. As she walked over, George Harrison was there with two weighty bags in hand and a stern look on his face. "ok?" was all he would say as he handed them to her. As quick as she could she immediately legged it back up the stairs of the craft and quietly dumped them on the seat beside Kenny. He whispered "Open up there, please."

She leaned forward and untied the top of both bags to reveal stacks of $20 dollar bills. He did a quick count of the bundles in each bag – there looked to be about fifty in each bag. That was correct. It looked to be all there, just as he had specified.

Wasting no time he beckoned to Tina "Passengers – quick!!"

Tina went to the rear phone and conveyed this news to Captain Scott. His voice came immediately over the P.A. system "Thank you for your patience folks. You can now leave through the stairs at rear where there will be staff to take you to the terminal building. Please make sure you have all your belongings and thank you so much for your cooperation."

The passengers did not need any further prompting at this hour on Thanksgiving and with only thirty seven on board they were easily turfed out of the back stairs, filing past Kenny the engineer as they went and onto the awaiting bus. Included in the crowd was the dreaded Air Marshal who, it seemed after all, was just on vacation. Joining them were Flo and Alicia all coated up and ready for exit in accordance with Kenny's instructions. Tailing them down the steps was Tina to fetch the parachutes as though she was on a mission. For a moment Kenny wondered if she was

expecting a cut of this money as well. She seemed so full of energy.
As the last of the passengers were making their way toward the terminal building she met Harrison at the trolley and took the first two parachutes. With the weight of them he told her she would have to make a second call for the other two. But she decided to grab all four despite the weight. Leaving two at the bottom of the stairs she dropped off the first two with Kenny in the aircraft. By the time she made it up the back steps with the remaining two chutes, Kenny had been checking their comrades and felt fairly happy with what he saw. He gave the signal to Tina "Ok order the refueling of the craft and let's get out of here!"
Word reached Captain Scott and he promptly signaled to the tower for the fuel truck to start its business.

Meantime, with the passengers coming off the plane and being led into a room set aside for the FBI a police officer in plain clothes stood up to speak. "Ladies and gentlemen, I represent a local division of the Police department here in Seattle and I need your attention for one moment. The plane you were on tonight was actually hijacked."
This brought surprise and gasps from everyone present in the room.
He continued "Now I am glad to see you are all well but it is an on-going situation. I would be grateful if you could give us just a few minutes of your time to gather whatever basic details we can. It's just to have any information or descriptions you may have of the passenger down the back row of the aircraft – if anybody got a look at him. If you noticed anything about him or the bags he was carrying, for example. Anything at all we would be much obliged for your help. And please, before you leave the airport tonight

be sure to give us your contact details in case we need to talk to you in the coming days about anything." He felt like such a chump at having to go through with this knowing it was not likely to yield much valuable information. Still, he knew he had to be thorough and do his job.

Kenny stole a look out through the lower part of the window at row 18 by slightly lifting the shutter. He could see the fuel truck with the pipe unraveled and being hooked onto the under-belly of the wing. This looked satisfactory.
Captain Scott's voice came over the P.A. "Sir, the refueling is underway now. We need to make a flight plan. Where do you want to go?"
Tina reached for the wall phone and handed it to Kenny.
"Captain, thank you for your cooperation. Alright, fly me to Mexico!"
Mexico? At this hour? There was a jaw-drop among the four remaining flight crew which included Tina. This would take ages.
Kenny continued in a reassuring manner "Now I will be making drop-offs along the way so it won't be that boring. Plus you will soon have some nice food and you can take it in turns to get some sleep and rest up a bit. If you do as I say, you have nothing to worry about. You will all be safely back with your families soon."
He went on after a brief silence from everyone. "So, please take note of the following flight configuration. Set the flaps to 15°, keep your undercarriage down at all times and leave the stairs at rear open. Do not pressurize the cabin and stay under ten thousand feet at all times. I have an altimeter here and will be monitoring it. This configuration will allow us to fly at not more than two hundred miles per hour – so keep the speed down to that limit."

Kenny repeated all the details again so they were clear.
After an initial gasp of bewilderment all round the co-pilot Rataczak spoke first "So it's Mexico at this hour and he wants to take it nice and easy – like the scenic route. What a god-damn weirdo!"
Scott came back to Kenny with a response. "Ah . . . Sir, we need to check this flight configuration with the tower. I am not sure if it's possible or safe to fly like this. We have never done this before with this type of aircraft."
Kenny persisted "Sure, go ahead and check with the tower, I can assure you the 727 is fine in this configuration. Go ahead!!"
All those years spent by Kenny in lonely places did not go to waste. While on Bikini Island he overheard a conversation with some pilots who flew for the military. One of them was telling how he had actually done test flights in the Boeing 727 with this configuration in order to allow paratroopers to safely jump from the tail end. The tests were easy to do and a success. This enabled the military to earmark the 727 for possible service in war zones if needed.
At the time he heard it, Kenny was only half interested, it being of no real concern to him. But for this operation he had revised all the details and went over them. He was super-confident in it. Even from his own reckoning with aviation it made sense. The 727 was unique in that it was the only jet air-liner that could be flown in this configuration and of course it had a convenient back door. Every other passenger jet had to naturally reach over five hundred miles per hour to stay aloft. But not this strange bird. With its huge tail fin, it might soon go the way of the Dodo but tonight it would do its own thing and party in the air like never before. Yes sir!

When word of Kenny's proposed flight configuration got back to the tower the people there were equally puzzled. Like Scott and his crew they never heard of doing such a thing with a jet liner. It put a different color on things and at this point there were more questions than they had answers for. With a mad dash they went to the phones to try and consult someone in the know. But who? Boeing maybe? The makers of the craft . . . It was perhaps a minor miracle that someone had the wherewithal to consult the military air base and that someone else, who actually knew the answer, was available to pick up the phone at this hour on Thanksgiving.

When hearing about this proposed flight configuration his response was "That is correct. But how the hell does he know about this? This is classified information and top secret. I can verify that we did tests of 727 in this flying formation and it was confirmed to work though I have not done it myself in the air. The military did this to check whether it was possible to drop chutes from 727s. I can't remember the specific details but what he is telling you is correct. Absolutely!"

So, with this information confirmed by the authorities, law enforcement came up with a side-stream strategy for tracking the hijacker in the air. Knowing now that the hijacked 727 would not be flying at high speeds, might it be possible to track it with a helicopter? This would give flexibility as helicopters could, of course, hover in the air. It might open more possibilities in terms of a successful pursuit.

A military chopper was quickly summoned from the air base and getting ready to accompany the pilot in flight was a high-ranking police officer. They would chase the jetliner into the night and see whatever was to be seen.

Back on the plane, while looking at the cash Kenny began to cheer up and smell his success. He reached into a money sack and took out a bundle of $20 bills – quite a bundle. About half of a stack. He held out his hand and offered it to Tina with a warm smile "Here girl, you deserve it."
Tina's response was a bit awkward "Listen I appreciate this, really. But I can't take it, I'm afraid. No tips allowed."
Of course it was possible she could be accused of taking stolen money, strictly speaking but she could also say she was recovering part of the ransom for the authorities. Either way she had enough problems already to deal with.
Kenny momentarily reflected on her refusal "Alright. Suit yourself."

The phone finally rang behind the seats of Row 18. Tina picked up and promptly handed it to Kenny "It's for you."
Captain Scott was on the phone "Ah excuse me Sir. We have checked your proposed flight configuration with the authorities. They are sure it's good. But we do have two immediate concerns. First of all, the door being left open at rear – nobody can verify this for take off. We are worried that it could be dangerous in terms of creating sparks if it drags on the ground. This could cause a fire or explosion. We think this is very risky, Sir."
Kenny bit his lip "Well, it definitely can be done. But alright, we can take off with it closed and open when in the air if you want."
"That's good sir. We'll take note of that. Now the other thing is that with this flying configuration we will be using a lot of fuel and will not be able to reach Mexico without refueling, just to let you know Sir. We would need to stop somewhere."
Kenny had anticipated this. "Well as long as we are flying

directly south of here along Victor 23. Where do you suggest?"

"Well I guess Reno, Nevada, Sir, as a first port of call. The problem is we are not sure exactly how much fuel the craft will use in this configuration. So it's better to be safe."

Kenny paused and breathed in as a way of making it look like he was seriously considering it. "Okay, that's fair enough. Reno it is."

As soon as law enforcement got wind of this modification in plan, they started to feel they were gaining the upper hand and likely to close in on the hijacker. It also turned the heads of the people at SEATAC – not to act in haste but work it out later with the folks at Reno. There might be a better chance to pick him off with a shot or even storm the plane by then. They would have more time to think it through.

But Kenny had been over this situation in his mind many times and despite his relaxed manner with Tina he had made a point of keeping her at the rear end of the plane along with himself. He knew that the control tower would be asking the cabin crew about the situation and whereabouts of everyone on the aircraft. With Tina down the back there was too much at risk to try firing at him with the use of snipers. A stray bullet or ricochet was all too likely and could easily hit her. Really, it was a non-runner. She was being used as a human shield. Successfully.

So, with word being sent through to the airport and police at Reno, the people at SEATAC could really not do much more except conform to the hijacker's demands and see that the flight takes off safely, heading south.

Up front of the 727 in the crew's cabin the co-pilot and engineer, though professional at all times, were growing a bit resentful of this hijacker and his screwball demands. While finalizing the flight path the First Officer turned to Scott saying, "You know I would really love to drop this son of a bitch in ice-cold water somewhere tonight. And with the weather the way it is right now we might just be able to drift off course a little – like east over the ocean somewhere."

The captain considered this for a moment. He rubbed his eyes. "You better do as he has asked Bill. We have quite enough complications to deal with. It seems our boy down the back here might be more knowledgeable about some things than we are. And anyway, if we are only going at two hundred miles per hour we don't have so much scope for trickery. We're a bit of a lame duck in this flight configuration. We'll do exactly as he says."

Down the back Kenny was getting a bit anxious. He was eager to get off the tarmac and into the air, knowing that doing so would greatly increase his chance of success. He had parachutes after all.

He was wondering what exactly was taking the refueling so long. This is something he had performed himself many times on the ramp. Sometimes you might get an airlock so there was that possibility. But he was thinking of the worst – that the authorities were stalling and playing for time. He had noticed a second fuel truck on the tarmac. Was that because the first one froze up or was it something else? He stared over at Tina, listening carefully for faint sounds. He felt a bit spooked. They had already closed up the rear stairs door. "Find out what's keeping them with that fuel!" Then, as she made her way to the wall phone he couldn't wait. At the top of his voice he found himself yelling "LET'S GET THE SHOW ON THE ROAD !!" The thunderous sound he made filled the entire fuselage right as far as the crew up

front. It might have been heard as far away as the terminal building. Being such a soft-spoken guy he never realized he had so much power in his voice . . . Handy that.
At this outburst from the hijacker an already irate Rataczak grabbed the intercom and stormed the tower "305 to control – WHAT THE HELL IS HAPPENING? A LOT OF AGITATION ON BOARD HERE – WE NEED TO FUEL UP AND GET UNDERWAY – IMMEDIATELY!"
"Roger, stand by 305."
The control tower made inquiries and it transpired that the tanks had indeed been giving airlocks but ground crew managed to get past it after a struggle. A third fuel truck was now in attendance. When this word reached Kenny he felt a little better. But he knew he had to stay sharp.
The moments that followed in silence seemed like minutes. Nobody said anything. Suddenly Scott's voice came clicking over the intercom with welcome information "We're ready for take-off sir." At that very instant the engines started to spin up and this rejuvenated Kenny. He knew that this was almost as good as take off in terms of his security. Fingers crossed.

Chapter 21 Troubled Flight 305 for takeoff

By the time the aircraft was getting refueled it was about 7:20. At this stage Bernie had been close to passing out with his nerves rattling. For long periods there was nothing relevant on the radio and he was in dread of the police storming the plane. So he was also checking normal radio for newsflashes – nothing yet. Not a word. It was just like any normal evening.

Then he heard one of the crew yelling anxiously at the tower. That was when he sat up "Wow" he told himself "They must be getting ready to go. It's actually happening!" You would normally never hear a tone of voice like that by any air staff. Gee . . . He wondered if it was a stalling tactic by the authorities to delay things somehow. The problem was while Kenny had said to expect delays he only had a very crude way to gauge progress. All he could do was follow on the air-band. There may have been other transmissions related to 305 but if so he had missed them in all the chat that comes over an Air-band radio. He could hardly wait for takeoff. As long as the plane sat on that tarmac there was some chance of military intervention. The tension was nerve-racking.

If the police stormed the plane it would be a hail of gunshot resulting in death to people – and absolutely to Kenny. At that point it would be over and there would no doubt be some delay before the press was informed and then you would get a newsflash.

So hearing nothing on the public radio was in itself good news. What he needed to hear was takeoff on the air-band. One radio would bring shock and devastation, the other would bring relief. And of course he could not help but go over and back between the two. It was ridiculous.

He opened the car door and stepped out for some air. The wind was howling and it lashed rain in the dark. Still it felt sweet and he welcomed it. He could feel the cooling effect on his boiling hot tension-filled face. He lit a cigarette.

Failure tonight would certainly spell financial disappointment. But he had also invested months of energy in this. He wanted to see it succeed. He despised the likes of NWO and would be gutted to see them come out on the better side after this. Not to mention what would happen to Kenny, a very real chance of death or imprisonment. Then he might also feel some heat himself from the cops. Or perhaps not because they would just be happy to get the main man and anyway he would have his alibi if it came down to it. Kenny and himself were just hanging out in the trailer for a couple of days vacation and he said he was heading into town for the day to go shopping and the like. He knew nothing about any nefarious operation and by the time of any interrogation he would ditch the air-band receiver. He had also made sure to have nothing incriminating in his home or down at the shop property. So he was clean.

But really there was only one possibility he wanted to entertain: a successful night with a good outcome and yet he had the dreadful feeling that it would be just too good to be true.

"All right, stay calm" he heard himself saying. All he could do was keep the head and roll along with whatever happened. Whether it turned out to be a bad day in his life or a good one. He would just handle it, go through the motions as best he could and get back to normal. There was no turning back now. That was all he could do. Just let it play out.

He would try to do what Kenny would do. Keep calm. But he was not Kenny. He would just have to do his best. It was strange how he had always thought of his old companion as something of a soft touch but he had realized from all of this that actually he was a case of still waters running deep. He had never exactly looked down on Kenny but now he was definitely looking up to him.

As soon as Kenny felt the airplane beginning to move on the tarmac he felt safe. At that point all doors were closed up and it was clear there would be no tricks played by law enforcement. As they taxied to the start of the runway for takeoff he turned to Tina "After we are airborne I will need you to pull up these window shutters all round. Thanks."
She was strapped into her seat and still looking a bit concerned, no doubt over uncertainty about what lay ahead in the coming hours.
Kenny went on "After that, call the captain and get him to flick the switch for the back door here. No point in delaying."
"Oh no" she said "It just operates from here directly. It doesn't need to be enabled from the cockpit."
"Really?"
She glanced round as she spoke "Yeah, just turn that handle right there and give a small push. That's it!"
"Oh, I see. Right." It came as a surprise to him that they allowed that arrangement in a civilian jet.

With that, the note of the engines came up in the aircraft and the 727 leaped forward with the surge. In no time at all they were airborne and Tina sprung to her feet while they were still climbing, pulling up the window shutters on either side. She looked anxious.
The plane banked a little and having got a glimpse out of the right window Kenny asked Tina "Is that Puget Sound, down there on the right?"
"Yep. We're heading south."
All was good in Kenny's book. Exactly the way he wanted. He looked at her as he spoke "I have to check the altimeter. Don't be nervous now if I open the case." He was smiling politely but her face turned to stone as she heard him

undoing the latches. Looking at the instrument on the right revealed they were climbing still but slowly and at about the 8000 feet mark. Of course the plane was going slower and very much in takeoff mode, burning lots of fuel as she went. With the gain in altitude they hit rain and clouds fairly quickly which blanked out any views they had of the night-lit terrain below. Kenny was prepared for this which is why at takeoff he noted the time as 7:37 pm. So, at this speed, he would be hitting his target jump zone after about twenty minutes.

Over at McChord air base just south of Seattle, the two specially reserved Corvair F-106 jet fighters were on standby and had been ordered to wait until after Flight 305 took off. Everyone was mindful of these aerobatic aircraft being much faster and articulate than a passenger Jetliner. Their goal was to track the craft as best they could and ultimately provide information to the authorities about the location of any drop-offs that the hijacker would make. A recovered ransom would indeed be a good piece of work not to mention whatever else it might yield such as the identity of an accomplice on the ground.

Generally people were feeling a bit more confident and given that the plane was bound for Mexico and stopping over in Reno there was a growing feeling the hijacker's exit from the plane would not come anytime soon. If at all. They would be in this for the long haul. It would take a while but inevitably law enforcement would turn the screws and gain the upper hand.

This was perhaps based on some psychologically generated feeling, the authorities gaining some measure of control on the situation without concrete evidence. But in this changing nightmare nobody could really be sure of anything.

A short time after Flight 305's take off and just as the airliner had bypassed McChord air base, both fighter jets roared into the air in pursuit and were greeted by cloud and rainstorm.

With two or more aircraft flying in the same vicinity, each traveling at speeds of hundreds of miles per hour, that area becomes very small, very quickly. This is why Air Traffic Controllers are constantly under stress and can never relax. Even on Thanksgiving.

The most critical thing for the tower was to ensure that all aircraft in the same area were allocated different altitudes to occupy in the air. This is how mid-air collisions are avoided. From tracking 305 on radar (though it took some time for the tracking data to come through) the tower was able to advise one of the jet fighters in pursuit to fly below the airliner, placing the second one above her in the air.

Now the problems were two-fold. The Corvairs were far faster than the 727 flying in her modified snail-pace configuration. Therefore the jet fighters had to do circles around the zone at higher speeds. This made it complicated in flight and even on a clear frosty night with the difference in speeds it would not have been easy.

The other thing was that the 727 was now shrouded in a thunderstorm. Dense clouds in the night meant zero visibility making it impossible to glimpse the airliner let alone keep track of her.

After some minutes of trying out this circular technique it was dawning on everyone involved that this search by the Corvairs would be fruitless. Most of their preoccupation was with taking information from the tower about flight trajectories, leaving very little scope for actually getting a visual on the passenger jet. It proved a pointless task with no prospect.

The police chief on duty had made it his business to get a helicopter ready and left the airfield in hot pursuit of flight 305. Unlike with the Corvairs he and his pilot had some ground for optimism as, like with the 727, the chopper was a relatively slow affair. In fact they managed to keep a visual on the aircraft for some time after it took off, its red blinking light at the tail being seen for some time. The rain pelted on the chopper's glass and the noise was tremendous all round. When the aircraft disappeared into the storm cloud the police officer turned to the pilot over the intercom "Can we continue for a bit? She might come out of the cloud after a while."

They did just that, occasionally seeing the tail light of the craft. The problem here was that it was in darkness. Even with a break in the clouds, if the rear door should open, they were not likely to see any paratrooper exiting from the plane. Sure, the aircraft's tail-light was bright but not much else.

On they went through the storm. A few minutes passed when they got another glimpse of the hijacked airplane. Now it was farther ahead. The chopper had been lagging. There was even less to see. The pilot did not sound hopeful "It's getting harder to keep up. I'm not sure if this is going to work out."

The police officer in the passenger seat was, at this point, very sure. He had seen enough. "Come on" he said. "I think we can call it off and get back."

He rubbed his eyes in disappointment. "Not in these conditions, I'm afraid."

Well, they had tried.

On board the 727, Kenny was now in very good form. Knowing nothing about any aircraft pursuit he was having a great time. Buzzing along like a millionaire in his own jet aircraft and a pretty girl for company. Who could ask for more!

He had been eyeing the parachutes and figuring out how to proceed. They looked good. After some minutes of flight he had kept an eye on the altimeter. All was good. But the rain clouds kept visibility down and he could not see where he was. He had to stick with the old reliable watch.

It was now 7:55. Time to say goodbye. A tiny part of him was sad to be leaving.

For the last time he turned to Tina "All right, I need you to go ahead into the front and join the crew. If I need any help I will call you. Thanks!"

Only too glad to get away Tina moved promptly up front. This would be so much better than being sucked out of the back door. Not something your average air hostess was geared up for. As she turned to close the cabin door behind her she caught a glimpse of Kenny who was now on his feet and working on one of the parachutes.

Chapter 22 Into the Sacred Black

As Tina was retreating toward the crew area upfront Kenny started examining the parachute bags. He was anxious to get to work. Out came his harness that he had brought along and he fastened it round himself quickly. The two back chutes were big and pretty much clear cut. One of these he would wear. Looking at the two smaller front loaded chutes he noticed that there was no harness to hook them into the back chutes. This was typical of the kind of thing that happened and amid all the confusion it did not surprise him much. Already he was glad he brought his own harness which was a strong canvas with steel hooks at various points.

From out of the side window he saw some lights on land through a break in the clouds. He paused his activity to have a closer look as to where he actually was before he jumped . . . The lights from the Merwin Dam. Perfect! Exactly as he had reckoned.

As he heard the door closing out up front from the cockpit area he noticed that one of the frontal chutes was a bit non-standard looking. He could not see the rip-cord anywhere. It looked like something modified and he thought that this one might be good to cannibalize as a source for spare rope. He took out his knife and opened it up, reefing the magenta colored parachute canopy out of the retainer bag. It quickly sprawled all over the floor. He had to hurry. He felt anxious even though he knew he was going according to schedule. Five of the canopy cords were quickly severed with the aid of the knife. These he would use as various makeshift ropes for everything else. He decided to insert the two money sacks straight into the empty canopy. He ripped off the tie he was wearing and tossed it on the seat. The overcoat was fastened up. On went the harness onto which was mounted the all-important money sacks on the front.

He fixed the second front chute onto his chest and fastened it in. Hopefully, he would not need to use this as he would be depending on his hastily made knots being tugged on. Still he was confident they would withstand the task if called upon. There was always something forgiving about rigging parachutes. It was part of what made him feel relaxed as a paratrooper.

On went the back chute without any modifications. Fastening it in he could feel the rip-cord in place and it was ready to roll. He could feel the weight coming on now with the money weighing over twenty pounds as well as the two mounted chutes front and back.

Now he slipped a cord through the handle of the briefcase and round through the metal eye-hooks at bottom as planned.

All this still left one of the back parachutes to be used. He stared down at it for a second and thought to himself "You're coming with me sonny!" If there were complications in the air with the other parachutes it was not much good to him sitting here in the aisle. Generally, he knew that parachute packers took their job seriously and would not try any dirty tricks, especially as they were supplying a double set – maybe one for a hostage. So he was pretty confident that with three chutes he would have at least one perform successfully. But of course this was more weight to attach to himself. He didn't care. He hooked it into some free metal clips round the waist. It was at arms length if he needed it.

It was important that when he stepped off the plane he made a clean departure from the craft and that nothing got caught and hooked onto the end of the stairs or anything of that nature. Being dragged along at 200 miles per hour in the dark could be a bit tragic. So he gave a visual check on all the knots and ropes as far as he could see. All was tight. He had to be sure that he walked clear of everything even if he did not have far to walk.

With all this ridiculous burden attached to himself he was not exactly slick and macho. Not quite like Dan Cooper. He would just have to do.

But cometh the hour cometh the man.

He turned to the rear stairs.

Finally, after all this time, he was stepping toward the back door to put his hand on the lever which opened the stairs. As he moved it he could hear the air noise level increasing. With the cabin already depressurized he knew he would not simply be sucked out dangerously.

Sensing a great moment, the threshold of his life, he was thinking of NWO, all their two-faced corporate lies and nonsense that they pedaled and their sheer aversion to decency whenever the opportunity arose.

He could feel the satisfaction circulating through his veins. "You are what you do" he thought to himself. With the lever pushed fully over, the stairs dropped open causing the plane to rock dramatically at the tail end, dipping due to a changing air-stream. This was instantly felt in the cockpit by the crew. The rear stairs-open indicator light came on and the co-pilot had to steady the craft in flight and correct it. The crew all looked at each other. They now knew the door was open but what else?

Kenny did his best to keep all his baggage as tidy as he could while he stepped down the open stairs. The force of the air outside had partially retracted the stairs to a near closed position again. Now his weight would draw it back open a little. He made his way down a few steps until, suddenly, it gave way and collapsed beneath him and was gone. Before he even realized it, the airplane vanished in the wink of an eye, he had been flung off the stairs instantly. Tossed into the black void, tumbling in the darkness and immediately drenched in a wet and cold blast. Boy that cold! What a shock. As for the plane, he could not even tell which way it was gone – at 200 miles per hour. He could not even hear it now – just as well. For a bare millisecond the sound from the Jet engines was thunderous and would have wrecked his hearing had it hung around for long. He had stepped from one world into another. It was like a birth. His life had begun.

The sheer blast of air took him back a bit. Sure he had done it before but it had been a while and not in the dark like this. He was pelted by cold water and rain as he plunged down through the clouds, an assault to the senses. Pitch black, freezing and as yet not a thing in sight below in terms of land structures and lighting. The only light he could see was flashes of lightning some distance away behind the clouds, this being a thunderstorm.

Within the cold air stream he was recovering from his initial tumble. So he reached for the rip-cord of the back chute and gave it a pull. Nothing. He gave a second pull, becoming more alert now after the shock. This time it opened. Wow – he had forgotten the thrill of it but it was all now coming back to him like in a slow dream sequence as though he had been re-educated, to feel a parachute open at this moment.

Up it came while exerting a pull on his chest and shoulders. and his speed slowed down immediately leaving him comfortable with all his baggage. Straight away, he could feel himself breathe fairly normally. He could see the canopy opened out above him with the lightning flashes all round. That long-lost feeling of relaxation had returned. He felt as if he had betrayed it for so long. Like he had walked out on it all those years ago. Like he had made a mistake. He felt the money sack secured to him keeping him warm. Everything was intact after the tumble. He found himself overcome with anger and rage – like an animal -

"I HAVE ya. … YA BASTAARDS !!"

The new world he had created had just risen up and taken shape. His time had come. And he was never going back.

Kenny had his fists clenched and was determined there and then to never let North West Orient ever see that money again. Even if he had to burn every note of it - it would be his pleasure. Not man nor nature would stop him. And heaven help those who stood in his way.

He knew that in another few minutes all hell could break lose but this was no time to countenance failure. This was his baby he was carrying and it would live!

His eyes were looking down to see features from the ground. At that very moment he didn't give a damn where he landed. He felt like he was ready for anything. He continually searched for breaks in the cloud . . . There! He was coming out now. He could see some lights from cities or towns. Gradually a bigger picture emerged. But where was he exactly? He stared and stared for what seemed like a long time. Was his mind slowing down with the cold?. It had happened to him before when he had to walk through a flooded area in winter up to his waist. He clenched the parachute cords with his two hands to try to stay alert. He could see a large city or town toward his horizon but he did not recognize it.

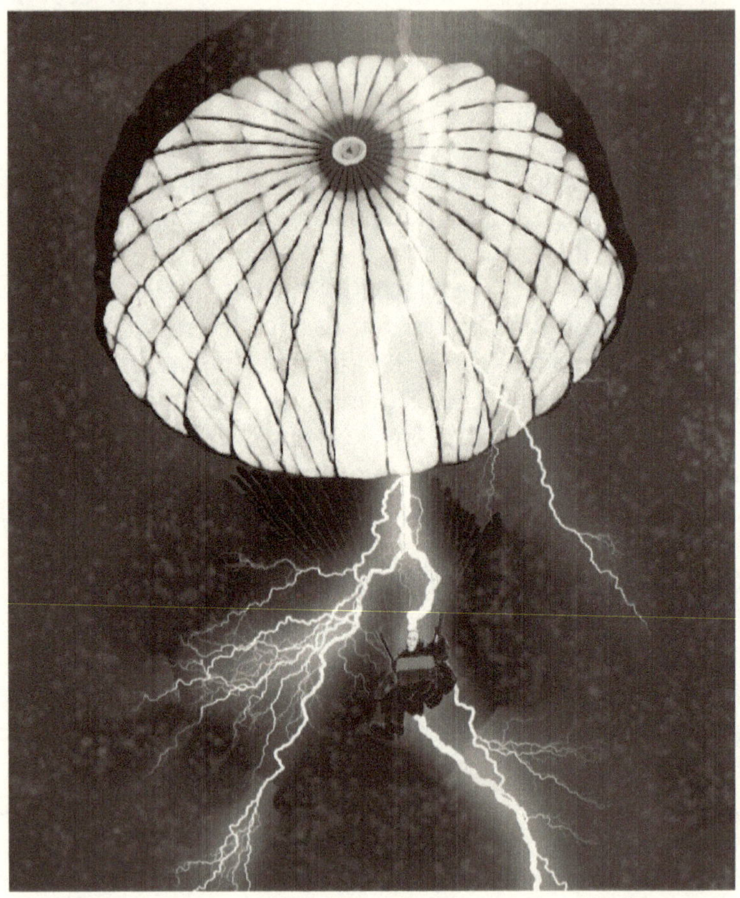

The orange-yellow glow against the blackness of the night. Suddenly he wondered if he had been facing due south. He turned himself round to see in the other direction. The big lighted city was now behind him and ahead lay dark land areas for the most part. He could see occasional patches of light strewn along the landscape from left to right. He thought this might be the quiet road toward the two lakes Mervin and Yale which he needed to avoid. A look to his left confirmed this. He could see the shape of the Columbia River outlined by lights and Longview, north of Portland. That was Portland and Vancouver he had seen first and was now behind him. He was exactly where he was hoping to be – somewhere over the area of Battleground. Excellent.

Hopefully he would not drift too much though there were definitely winds about his chute. He certainly did not want to end up in the cold waters of the Columbia at this hour in darkness. Anywhere west or north-west of where he now was would be just fine. He steered the parachute by pulling on the front canopy lines to create some drift. It was not really a suitable rig for steering but he was drifting already with the wind a little. He was coming down fairly fast as the moments ticked away. The lights he had seen along the Columbia looked more oblique now toward his horizon. He began to see one or two building lights approaching and the occasional car lights moving on roads. He did not want to encounter any of these really. What he needed was darkness for landing. Remote areas to allow him to attend to the business on hand, quietly.

So far so good. There was plenty of darkness below him. He had studied the lie of the land well from those maps and photos. Now to get down without hitting water or other obstacles. He knew he was well south of the lakes.

One or two clusters of light grew clearer – houses by the looks of it but not too many in this area. The parachute was heading askew in the breeze, like to the North-east.

Kenny was a little anxious about the presence of trees. To have come this far was great but it could end in tragedy with a final 50 foot drop from a tree top in the dark. He could not spot any trees or elongated silhouettes. Yet he was moving pretty fast at something like a 60 degree angle toward the ground. If he did hit a tree the trick was to grab onto a branch and not fall to the ground. If you fell from as little as 10 feet you could break your neck in the dark but if you held on you could slowly work your way out of it. This was always dicey . . .

But now there was a lit-up house in the distance coming toward his horizon. He was closing fast. It looked like a field below him. No trees, seemingly. What a relief. Bracing for impact, the thud still took him by surprise a bit. He felt briers, bushes and wet mud under foot with the baggage he had breaking the physical knock somewhat. All the motion came to a silent stop. He was down!

The parachute canopy came down over him like a tent obscuring his vision. He felt around for the silky soft material in the dark, grabbing hold of it and quickly dragged it in from around himself to reveal where he was. He scrambled to cut things loose as he wanted to tidy up the white color of the chute quickly in order to avoid being seen in the darkness. With his eyes still adjusting a bit he looked around in the pitch black and listened. Not a sound. He could see over the fields a light from a house or building of some sort. Probably a farmhouse. He quickly wrapped the chute and stuffed it into the retainer
as best as he could manage.

Time for the signal – immediately. He reached into the briefcase and felt for the rocker switch cover. He sprung it open and flicked that same big bad switch. Far from being a bomb this was now enabling the signal for Bernie to receive.

All the main items were still roped together but he needed

to check for everything before he moved from this location. The little flashlight in his pocket showed that he had landed in the dirt track of tractor wheels – a mucky affair with all the rain. With everything gathered he now wanted to get into the shelter of the woods which he could see across the field. He felt a bit uneasy out here. Two more minutes of following the tracks led him to a thicket of trees. All the time the money was safely strapped onto his chest. He had warmed up nicely but was fairly wet overall and it being a wet night another shower would not be far away. Dumping everything on the ground he took out his knife. Now for some surgery.

Kenny had quickly got to work on all his baggage he wanted to tidy up. He wanted to use a parachute canopy to insert everything into and use as a big carrying sack. But he did not fancy using either of the back chutes for this. They were white in color whereas the front chute in its retainer sack was a not-so-bright pink. Plus it was smaller and a bit easier to handle.

Really, he wanted to dump the extra back chute which was unopened. That would lighten his burden. Yet he was not all that happy about leaving any evidence for the FBI. As a compromise he decided to cut the canopy off the back chute he had used and dump that instead. This was flexible and over time would be weather-beaten and not grab so much attention as a complete chute that was packed in its container. Also, this would leave him with a usable container sack on his back if needed.

In the dark he cut the strands to the open chute he had used. With it balled up as best he could he needed to find a place where he could bury it somehow.

Conveniently, there was a large embankment at the trunk of a big tree which dropped some ten to fifteen feet with a mass of bushes and briers overgrown within. A real no-man's land. This would be perfect to dump the severed canopy which would be one thing less to worry about. It might, hopefully, be a long while before it would be discovered by anyone.

Being wary of making a noise he was also mindful that the vast majority of people were sitting down to dinner right now – just as he had rigged it.

He tossed the chute clear into the bank and down it went, a good bit down. Shining the lamp down into bushes, there looked to be no trace of it. He glanced over at the light from the farmhouse in the distance. He was leaving them a souvenir.

Miles away, in a different part of the woods, knowing that the plane had taken off some half hour before, at a little before 8:00 pm, the suspense was killing Bernie. He had been listening to the air traffic, listening for news on the radio and listening for the signal sound over his CB set. Nothing to report. He was spending the time moving up and down the channels carefully. Generally, it was quiet except for the odd trucker. Especially quiet now with Thanksgiving dinners being held across the nation. No celebrations for him. This was the weirdest November 24th he had ever experienced. And the worst. With no clear outcome it would likely impact his marriage at the very least.

On the one hand he had to be alert and think on his feet. On the other hand he was nervous, worried and could not concentrate.

At the moment when he eventually did encounter the signal from Kenny he stumbled past it in an unfocused daze. Did he just hear it? He stopped turning the dial and rolled back

a couple of clicks. There it was - wow!
He was beside himself. Kenny had actually jumped. And as yet, no word of anything reported in the media. He couldn't quite believe what was happening. There was no mistaking that signal and Kenny had to switch it on very deliberately – only when he had reached the ground.
He had to steady himself. So he knew Kenny was down.
What to do next? Kenny had instructed him not to make a call on the CB but rather wait for a call and respond. This was dictated by Kenny's situation and whether he was out of earshot or in a safe place so that he could talk. Bernie checked the strength of the signal - not all that strong. Maybe thirty or forty miles off judging from previous experience with it. The rain was spilling down outside his car in the darkness. He decided to wait a little bit longer to see if Kenny called. Give him time to find his feet after landing. This was surreal. He was anxious to get out of here and get going. Even if it was all in the plan he still, somehow, could not believe that Kenny had jumped out of a passenger jet aircraft. Christ!
Although Bernie had decided to wait for a little while he only lasted about two more minutes. He felt so nervous his anxiety to move got the better of him. He started up the engine and wanted to head up the motorway somewhere north to see if the signal would increase or decrease.
He headed off in the general direction of West toward the 503 highway, north of Vancouver before turning up north. During these minutes going west the signal actually did not change much in quality. The roads were generally quiet but a fair amount of surface water had fallen during the storm and the rain was not done yet by the looks of it. Really, it was not a night that anyone would want to be out driving.
After moving some miles through back roads he heard a

static blip interrupting the signal. But no voice. He slowed down the car and pulled over at the edge of a wooded area. He switched off his headlights and listened carefully with the engine running. There was another static blip. Suddenly Kenny's voice came on.

To a casual eavesdropper the conversation would have come off as fairly humdrum.

"Hey John. Happy thanksgiving!"

"Oh - hey, hi ya doing man. What's happening?"

"Oh just getting dinner ready here. Hey listen, remember that guy you were asking about? I think he might be up near Battle Ground somewhere. Maybe a little to the north or North-east of that place."

"Oh, OK . . . right. Not too far from me actually."

"So look I gotta go. I'll check back with you later, all right?"

"Ok – out"

Kenny had often pointed out Battle Ground to him on the maps as a central point of interest. So he knew it pretty well in terms of where he was at this moment.

He turned right down a side road to go in the direction of it. While the roads were quiet he was nervous of being stopped by routine police checks. He did not know as yet the status of any law enforcement operations with regard to Kenny's mad jump. In fact he knew damn all at this point. Kenny really had sounded like he was sitting down to dinner. Relaxed as ever. For a second Bernie wondered if he was actually having dinner somewhere. He wouldn't put it past him. Never mind any involvement in a crime of this scale. And here was the poor old driver, behind the wheel and about to have a hernia.

He had been heading down the back roads and the progress was a bit slow without much change in signal strength.

"Screw it" he thought. With this rain so bad he might just hit the 503 and go north for a few miles. That way it would be quick and he could detect the change in signal quicker as he bypassed the Battleground area.

This he did and to good effect. After just a few miles on the 503 the signal became slightly louder. This settled his nerves a bit though he was anxious as ever to find Kenny and end this crazy unthinkable excursion.

Back in the woods, Kenny had been moving toward what looked like a main road, judging from the occasional car he saw passing. He crossed a forested area following the silhouettes here and there as he passed through the trees. He had been thoroughly pissed on by the rain at this stage. He wondered if he might catch pneumonia. Having come this far how ironic it would be to catch his death from exposure to the elements like this. The parachute over his shoulder as a holdall had been effective. He remembered seeing it done years ago in the army.

The problem now was to get to the side of a road and wait while not being seen. The battery running the signal and the CB radio was still okay, he hoped. But there might be a danger that some of the apparatus would be damp somehow. Of course he had stacked a load of quarter dollar coins inside those coin slots which he dressed up to look like dynamite so he could call Bernie from a pay-phone if need be. But he did not want to resort to that as it would mean delays and Bernie having to make it back to the shop and wait for the call. Plus, the less time he was seen out on the road by anyone the better, though the night was still young and with plenty of darkness around to help them get their job done. Still, carrying this makeshift sack he would no doubt look a bit non-standard out in the rain on such a night as this. He needed to get collected – to get out of sight and out of mind.

There was so much soggy land under foot from all the rain it was difficult to walk through. With the occasional help of the flashlight to pick his steps, he made his way up a slope and through ditches onto what looked like the main road in the dark. He had to be careful he was not seen out like this so he tried to keep in near the trees. He could see a lighted house down the way at the far side of the road. What he needed to do now was identify this road he was on. He thought he saw a road sign farther down so he tipped on down a hundred yards more. As he approached the sign he tried the flash light to see what it said – Route 503 – great! Although he was no longer in the air he felt he knew which way was North.

He moved in behind a tree in the darkness and reached for the radio.

Bernie was doing a steady 40 miles per hour and listening for changes in the signal when he heard Kenny's voice.

"Hey man, how you doin?"

"Ok – you got your dinner already?"

"Yeah, listen I think that guy was on the 503, you know."

"Really? Ok what part of it?"

"I think it's up the north part of it. You know when it turns and starts heading over East. Along there. Give it a try I guess. But I'm not entirely sure where."

"Ok, thanks for that. Talk to ya!"

A minute later Kenny saw a sign which read "Fargher Lake – two and a half miles." So now he knew where he was approximately, east of the turning point of the 503 where it changes direction and heads east. He reported this to Bernie who was now a couple of miles before this point so it would only be a few minutes before he got there.

Kenny got back behind a tree and waited in the welcome, glorious, protective dark. In the wet. It was not a night for man or beast. It was the perfect night for their operation.
The occasional car went up and down the road but this was really the quiet hour. The quietest hour of the year.
It seemed like an age before he heard a car coming from the west some half a mile away. This could be him, he thought . . . He grabbed the radio "What's going down man? You going east?"
"Yep. After the Fargher turn."
To Bernie, the signal was nice and strong. The car approached a chicane on the road and as soon as it appeared Kenny knew the square station wagon headlights only too well. He flicked his flashlight toward it. It was slowing down. It had arrived. Like magic!

Chapter 23 Home and not so dry

Surely never in his life was Kenny so glad to step into a car out of the rain and the elements. Bundled with his sacks and the money still snugly strapped close to the trunk of his body, he climbed into the back seat of Bernie's station wagon. As soon as the door was slammed the driver did not need to be prompted and took off into the night.
Kenny spoke, "Better head for my place." But his companion had a different notion "Would the shop unit not be a better idea? I mean we would have space and privacy there."
"Yes but we want to look as normal as possible. Who

spends this hour on Thanksgiving moving in and out of a commercial real-estate unit?! Besides, we can do everything we need to in my place. And more."

Bernie's shop property was a bit closer than Kenny's apartment in Sumner but that was not that much of an advantage. To go back to the trailer of course would be quicker than both but they were then loaded with all the evidence they had to deal with. In a cramped space things might become visible in such a trailer park site. That might leave them vulnerable. Kenny's idea was probably best.

Anyway, Bernie was not going to argue. He was still doing all of this with dread in his mind and wanted to finish this episode, like with nothing he had ever been involved in before. He swore there and then that if he got through this with no reprimand he would rather spend the rest of his life poor and shoveling shit than go through the agony of the last few hours.

Kenny quickly got busy unpacking and taking off his wet clothes. "I need to check everything now."

Of course Bernie had to ask about the big prize "How much did you manage to get?" as he drove through the puddles.

Kenny leaned forward putting his hand on his driver's shoulder "Bern, not a word. Concentrate on getting us home. Nice and easy!"

He had to beaver away in the back seat with everything, getting all into those black garbage sacks and out of immediate sight in case of a roadblock or something unexpected like a flat tire. The top priority now for him was to go over all sacks supplied by the authorities carefully. He had to check more thoroughly for electronic bugging devices being planted in the lining of the sacks or stitched into the seams somewhere. Earlier he had done a quick check but now he needed to go through the money more thoroughly. It had occurred to him earlier that the cops might just quickly have tossed a device in with the money bundle at the last second. He filed through all the bundles of twenties flicking at the ends and feeling for anything irregular. This took a few minutes. There were so many bundles to look at. All kept nice and dry despite the wet blast they had come through. Never before had he handled so much money and certainly not money that was now his. That would take some getting used to. He was relieved to find nothing implanted anywhere. That was an oversight on his part. Luckily, law enforcement was caught off guard on this occasion but it might have been so different. So far so good.

With his mind at ease he changed his clothes, putting on a fresh vest and pullover as well as a pair of jeans. The black and now wet fugitive outfit went into the plastic sacks. His hair piece of course was now gone, having vanished into the blast of the air coming down. As did that white paper bag.

Having checked the money sack which was now tucked into a plastic garbage bag he now went over the retainers of the parachutes he had left. Now was the time to be real sure they were not fitted with any bugs. He used his knife and the flash light, wanting to avoid the use of the car's internal light thereby attracting attention.

He methodically shredded everything he saw that was going to be for dumping. Canvas straps, parachute lining – all into smaller pieces for later disposal. As the rain hammered down on the roof of the car with the wipers at full belt he did not quite understand where he got all his energy from, this had not been a restful day with square meals exactly.

At some point he realized he had forgotten to turn off the

transmitter in the briefcase. He quickly reached in and switched it off. He had originally thought the radio to be an optional idea yet it had made so much difference. It was hard to imagine now that, had he been without it, he would have had to go on foot to pay-phones – doable but in the interests of making a quick exit from the scene, not a good idea given what he had just come through. Now that they had used the radio and transmitter with such success, no way! It would have been asking for trouble to just rely on getting to a phone.

They both were aware that the horrible weather and wet roads were an ally to their enterprise. The roads were unusually quiet and who was going to be observing anything in this rain?! Just a few trucks were seen coming and going as well as the odd car. Floods were one thing that needed to be guarded against and could potentially cause detours but that was only going to be a problem on smaller roads. The distance from the landing point near Amboy to Seattle was roughly one hundred miles. They were now out of the woods but in no mood for celebrations just yet.

For Bernie behind the wheel, the journey back to Sumners took ages and he was nervous all the way. He was hyper-sensitive about hearing police sirens and knew he would not handle such a situation well. At the same time he had to control his speed. The roads were wet and he had to be careful. Slow was sure.

For Kenny in the back seat, time went by quickly as he was so busy with all the baggage re-organization. Now that everything was wrapped away in plastic bags he did not dare to spark any chat with Bernie until they were safely indoors. They needed to stay alert and concentrate.

Bernie had headed north up Route 503 through Amboy and

then left, north of Lake Merwin before continuing northwards for Seattle. It was not the preferred route but at least it would keep them off the main road between Portland and Seattle in case the police were searching.

It was hoped that at this hour on Thanksgiving law enforcement were caught off guard and in this weather would not get a proper search underway until daybreak, ideally.

As they neared Sumners Bernie switched on the radio for a bit to see if they had hit the news. Local headlines at 11.00 pm did not mention anything. Kenny reckoned this might be a good sign as it suggested that Authorities were still grappling with the situation and not wanting to make any statements yet.

Everything on the streets in the southern suburb looked normal and a bit sleepy. Maybe even too quiet . . . Bernie steered into the familiar car park outside Kenny's apartment complex in Sumner and switched off the engine in between two other parked cars.

Silently they carried two plastic bags into the building, one with Kenny's wet hijacker outfit which he had not cut up in addition to the briefcase. And the other with the money. At the entrance door Kenny suddenly wondered where he left his keys. Drawing a blank he looked at Bernie under the orange colored public lighting. Well this was almost comical having done so good with everything up till now to be caught at the last hurl. Bernie tapped his pockets and produced a key. He had held a key to this place for the last few months. Just as well.

They went in and were greeted by a lovely smell of food cooking and a cheerful sounding party down the corridor. The wreath for Thanksgiving was hanging on Kenny's apartment door. They slipped inside to a cold and dark

apartment, switched on the side-lamp and closed the curtains.
For a brief second they looked at each other in silence.
Neither of them could wait another second to see the money, partly thrilled and partly nervous about being caught. They still did not feel safe about what would happen next.
In silence, Kenny uncovered the cloth money sack and emptied it out onto the living room table. Scattered about were dozens of bundles of twenty dollar bills, each clipped together by the paper retainers provided by the bank. Just like in the movies. The second sack doubled the takings with some of the bundles of dollars dropping on the floor.
"Christmas has come early" whispered Kenny with a stern look on his face and looking like a man who still had work to do.
As for Bernie, he put his two hands up to his face and looked like a man who was in a world of trouble. Lowering himself into the chair he was now seeing the fruits of his labors, or, realizing what he had done depending on how one viewed it.
Kenny spoke in a clear whisper "Two hundred thousand dollars! Bernie we had better never mention this to anyone, as long as we live. If we are ever caught they will put us away for a thousand years." He looked dead serious.
They counted the stacks which came to a total of one hundred in all. On counting further each stack was revealed to contain one hundred $20 bills. That made two thousand dollars per stack totaling $200,000 in all. An astonishing day's work. They had never seen anything like it.
They had both agreed they would split the loot 2:1, Kenny getting two thirds and Bernie getting the remainder which rounded up to $67,000. That might be about a decade's

worth of his salary in one lump. Tax free.
"So," said Kenny, "that's about thirty three of these bundles to you. Make it thirty five as I owe you at this stage." As he spoke he separated out thirty five stacks.
Bernie's nerves were still rattling. "I can't touch this now while things are still so hot. Where the hell are we going to put all this and keep it safe? So that nobody lays eyes on it."
This had not crossed his mind until now.
But Kenny had his answer with his facial expression brightening up "Oh, about that. I came up with a little something."
At this point Bernie was inclined to believe him, his eyes following Kenny as he walked out to the kitchen and summoned a chair for elevation. As he stood up on the chair he carefully took out a couple of the lightweight ceiling tiles which were installed as part of the suspended ceiling. This in turn exposed the usual array of central heating and water pipes wrapped in glass wool insulation. Lots of them.
Kenny reached his hand up to one of the pipes and with a careful stir it came away free.
He took it down to examine it. It was about four feet long and with screw-on caps at each end.
"Good old Gun-barrel plumbing, complements of NWO hangars." He smiled while he unscrewed the cap at one end. "Carefully secured by yours truly. I brought enough of them for both of us." He held up the end that he had opened showing an inch of deep screwing thread on the barrel. The pipe was over an inch and a half in diameter. "Dark, dry and safe" was his description with a beaming smile.
This cheer seemed to be contagious as Bernie's face lit up for the first time today. He may not have been self-assured but after what had happened this Thanksgiving his

confidence in Kenny was sky high. The latter had thought of everything apparently.

As he moved toward the table of money Kenny explained "It's best if we roll them up and put them in sideways – like this. That way they fit better."

He reached for a box of rubber bands near the television. He singled out one of the bundles and rolled it up. He was able to wrap a rubber band round it and roll it nicely to fit it inside the pipe end. "Eighteen of those fit in each four foot pipe."

They proceeded to put the rest of the cash in the pipes, managing to stuff Bernie's lot into two pipes and closing them up. They decided to slip these two into a roll of insulation to mark them clearly. Four more pipes were needed to take Kenny's fortune. They were both rich men now.

After the loaded pipes were reinstalled neatly above the ceiling and now just looking like regular plumbing, the slabs were put back into place and dust material was cleaned up neatly from the kitchen floor to give no hint of anything unusual.

They were both now more at ease. As he lit up his first cigarette in hours Kenny reflected on this little kitchen innovation "Well look, at least it gives us an immediate place to keep our hard-earned dollars. I reckon they might even survive a fire up there."

In the air coming close to Reno, Nevada were the crew of Flight 305. Huddled together in the cold they were a bit grim and in the dark about the situation. Chugging along at a very slow 200 miles per hour with the undercarriage down, this was surely the slowest trip from Seattle ever made by a passenger airliner. None of them knew quite what happened in the back at Row 18 since the opening of the tail-end stairs. From what Tina had reported, the hijacker must have jumped. She claimed that the last she saw of him was when he put on a back parachute. That was before she closed out the cabin crew door. They had spoken very little for the past while among themselves, half expecting a call over the inter-phone from the hijacker.

Captain Scott looked at his watch "We are coming near Reno soon. We have to land according to what's been agreed. But what then?"

He looked around at the others.

"Is he even still on board?" For once the answer was not on their faces.

He cautiously reached forward to address him over the PA system. "Ah, Sir, are you there? We are coming in to land at Reno shortly. We need further instructions."

No answer. Not a sound.

Gazing straight ahead at the black night through his wind visor he clicked on the radio to report to Reno "Ah, 305 to Reno checking in for pre-planned emergency landing."

The reply came promptly "Go ahead 305."

"Ah, we are due for landing on schedule. Please note, we suspect that the assailant may have departed the craft."

"Gotcha 305. Can you give any more details on that?"

Scott elaborated "Well, there has been no contact since before 20.05 hrs when the back door was opened. There has been no response over the intercom and under my instruction we are not going back there for safety reasons. So please note that this is our assumption – that he may have departed the aircraft. But we cannot confirm for sure."

There was about a minute delay in response from the tower.

"Roger 305, we have passed that on. Bring her in as and when you can. Thank you."

At this point all decks had been cleared for 305 to land at Reno airport. The military and fire brigade were on hand at both flanks. The authorities were inclined to raid the craft but this news changed their strategy somewhat. They were less prepared for a gun battle and more for a disappointment or a routine investigation. Still they had to stick to protocol and take no chances. After clearance everyone watched the plane come in for landing with its tail door down as it scraped a little off the runway. Other than that it was an easy landing having very little speed to begin with. Scott brought it to a halt on the tarmac in a fairly well lit area as soon as he could.

To be sure of everything he called again to the rear of the aircraft on the intercom. All was silent.

He notified the tower of this. A gangway was quickly dispatched to the front door. The cabin crew eagerly exited and within a few more minutes the military stormed the plane, from the side and through the back staircase which was in the fully open position. Soon, there was no doubt that the fugitive had left the plane. It seemed to them he must have been long gone.

The tired crew members were led into nearby rooms for questioning by police and of course the media were waiting for whatever information they could get their hands on at this ungodly hour.

In Kenny's living room in Sumners, Seattle the two amigos were still trying to process what had happened. It was well after midnight when it suddenly dawned on them to check the TV. So dazzled had they been by the sight of all that money.

By now it had finally got out over the air, about the hijacking that took place. It was all over the news but the descriptions were still sketchy and repetitive though there was enough information to clarify that the plane had landed in Reno. They sat for another bit with the various channels regurgitating the same information.

Kenny knocked off the TV.

"All right. You are going to have to get used to it over the next while and practice looking numb and blank when you hear about it."

He turned away from the window he was gazing out of and stared dreamily across the room.

"Tomorrow will be an easier day, I think. We just get up and wander back to that trailer in the woods while we talk about the rest of our boring lives." He spoke with a delicious smile sweeping over his face. With the two ears protruding as ever, this was his wholesome and awkward self. Like the sun coming out from behind a cloud. The real Kenny Christiansen had come out to play. Gone was the stern and hardened face of a criminal – the Kenny of the grudge. And who would ever have known?

The answer to that question was Bernie. At that very moment he was the only person who witnessed and understood. He looked across at his companion, still in amazement, as if to say "Are you serious?" But he knew he was. He had stopped doubting him quite some time ago. A few hours ago in fact.

But for Kenny it was different. He was not your regular underdog. He had been stepped on all his life, walked into the pavement, almost fossilized. And all done by those he knew very often to be lesser than himself in integrity and sheer ability. Lacking these qualities had just cost North West Orient dearly. He put it up to the airline and it got its nose bloodied. Best of all, nobody would ever even find out who it was that had dealt the blow. Or so he hoped.

Act 3 After The Deed

Chapter 24 Vanished!

Although they had earned a good night's sleep with the undertakings and exertions of the day before, both Kenny and Bernie woke up early on the morning of the 25th November. No doubt, while the nation slept in, the two might have had a touch of nervousness in the aftermath of what they had done.

Kenny was first on his feet and went to pull back the curtains to see if he would dare to invite this new day into his life. Looking out of the window and down on the car park below, it was about half full. Colors were beginning to halfheartedly emerge as the darkness gave way to the winter's morning. Not a stir as yet from anyone. All was quiet.

When he turned round in the room Bernie was sitting up on the sofa bed and rubbing his eyes. They looked at each other as though for a reality check. Bernie cleared his throat "Was I just dreaming or did all that crazy stuff actually happen last night?"

This drew a bright smile from Kenny as he managed to keep his voice to a whisper "Every last dollar of it sonny! Every bend on the road. Every drop of rain. It's all true."

As they both glanced out toward the kitchen in acknowledgment of where they stashed the money, he continued "We're both bad guys now. We're in that club. We're just not as dishonest as slimy company execs and

politicians. But we proved that we have far more raw talent than most of them."
Bernie looked a little uneasy. His comrade moved toward the television "Time to face the music." Switching it on, it did not take long to find reports on events the night before as the whole of the North West district were shocked and stunned by what had happened. The airways were lit up.

CBS News reported it like this -

When he got on a plane in Portland, Oregon last night he was just another passenger who gave his name as D.A. Cooper. But today, after hijacking a Northwest Orient Airlines jet, ransoming the passengers in Seattle, then making a getaway by parachute somewhere between there and Reno, Nevada, the description on one wire service -"Master criminal". Noel Curtis reports.

Thirty six passengers got off the jetliner in Seattle last night. Left aboard – four crew members and the hijacker. Dressed in a business suit, demanding $200,000 and carrying a plain briefcase, which, he told the crew, held explosives. With the full ransom collected from the Seattle banks and four parachutes aboard, the plane headed for Reno. It took three and a half hours- slow for a jet but the hijacker had given detailed flight instructions. The rear stairwell was opened all the way. It arrived at Reno in shreds.

The crew, here being debriefed by the FBI, was told to fly low over Oregon's flat-lands with the flaps down, the speed dropped to two hundred miles per hour. Somewhere, the hijacker parachuted away with the money. The crew had little to say.

Captain William Scott: *Well ah, I gave information to the authorities. We just don't want to discuss it any further.*
Reporter: *Have you been told by the FBI not to discuss?*
Captain William Scott: *No, they handle their investigation and my company would rather have it released through them.*
Reporter (to Tina Mucklow): *Tina, were you with the rest of the crew during the flight, when you left the ground the last time?*
Tina Mucklow: *Yes I went up to the cockpit.*
Reporter: *None of you were in sight of the hijacker, right?*
Tina Mucklow: *We all talked about it and the captain, you know . . .*
Reporter (to Harold Campbell, FBI Agent): *How did you surmise that he was not on the plane when it landed in Reno?*
Harold Campbell: *Well, a search was made of the plane immediately ah, after landing.*
Reporter: *As we understood it he could have gotten off as the plane taxied before it came up here. How did the crew know he was -*
Harold Campbell: *No, the crew couldn't know that but we at the airport covered it.*

Snow covers the mountains in Northern California and Nevada, a hostile terrain for any parachute drop, especially at night. Police believe he left the 727 in the flat-lands of Oregon or Washington but they are still looking in four states, even around the airport.
Authorities began their search here thinking that the hijacker may have jumped off at the end of the runway as the plane touched down but the problem is more complex. A daring parachute escape from a flying 727 somewhere

between Reno and Seattle, Washington.

Bill Curtis, CBS News, Reno.

The TV was simply awash with reports like this. Kenny recognized Tina of course as she shied away from reporters. He felt a little concerned and he hoped that all was well with her. Certainly, she had handled everything well on the plane. Viewing her now on the TV he thought how she seemed like she was just a girl. And such a very sweet girl. He had the sudden urge to hold her and give her a hug. She would surely be on his mind for a long time to come.

After spending quite a while going through the channels the message was clear. The whole region had been set spinning by their actions and they would need to be prepared as they eased back into everyday life. Part of the public seemed overjoyed at pulling off this incredible act. The other aspect was one of apprehension, a fear they might not be out of the woods yet, that at any moment the FBI would storm the apartment and the game would be up, spelling doom for them, life behind bars and all of its grinding wheels of injustice. The never-ending gray world that it would represent.

But how long would it take before they were properly clear? When would they be able to breathe easily? Kenny fancied he had those answers. He had thought of all that too. He had never regarded himself as a 'Master Criminal' nor even an ordinary criminal. He was, at his core, just a guy who thought of stuff, having come up with an unusual plan to bring about change in order that he might have something of a normal life. And, as may be inevitable with such people, he liked to be honest. Thinking people are as such, processors. They process the truth. Just as bankers possess money, the likes of Kenny possessed a few nuggets of wisdom. Maybe even more than his share.

Kenny explained to Bernie how it had been Tina's role to stay back with him on the plane and run the operation. This brought a typically shallow response from his companion "Nice chic. Did you get to make a move on her?" He then awkwardly realized that he might have miss-spoken.

They waited for a while until normal daylight arrived before venturing down to the car park to clean out the car. They did not want to be too conspicuous with activity too early. At about 10 am Kenny set about giving the car a scrub on the inside. He could not believe the amount of dirt from the night before that he had carried in from the fields. All dried up now, it looked to be everywhere round the back seat. They fetched soap and water to wipe it down as well as bringing everything indoors in black plastic bags. They noticed just one neighbor out and about at this hour as she drove out of the car park. The puddles on the surface served as a reminder of events of last night.

Back inside the apartment, they sat about listening for more news coverage, not saying much as they were still half nervous of anyone being within earshot. But Kenny had a mischievous grin now as he turned to Bernie "Here, let's get a souvenir photo" handing him the camera. Bernie did not look too amused "You serious?"

But Kenny insisted "Now that we have everything to hand, why not?" Grabbing his black coat together with the mighty briefcase and a white paper bag he now looked like that infamous hijacker again. Opening up the entrance door of the apartment he stuck his nose into the corridor to see that all was quiet. By the time he turned around Bernie had gotten into the Thanksgiving spirit and was getting the camera focused. He took a shot of Kenny coming in the doorway with the wreath hung on the door showing clearly

it was taken during festivities.
Kenny now sported light colored pants but it was unmistakable in the information revealed and this photograph would play a critical role for historians many years from now.

Now that their hair was being let down a little, they opened up the bags with the parachutes and took a knife and scissors to all, shredding everything to smithereens. This would all be dispersed into small garbage bags and disposed of here and there on their travels. The same treatment was given to the briefcase internals. All was disassembled including the circuitry and battery. This device, having served them so well, would be cast to the four winds in similar fashion - never to be seen again. They decided to leave the CB radio installed in Bernie´s car so as not to arouse any suspicion with his wife or family. That would be casually removed in due course to convey apparent waning interest on his part.

It would be important that none of this evidence was brought near the trailer site and that it was disposed of in different garbage outlets at various opportunities, preferably after dark. So they devised a set of small paper bags to take all the junk and put them inside the larger refuse sacks. But even with all this precaution they would feel a bit wary of driving around with conspicuous sacks of shredded evidence in the car, particularly given the day

that was in it. There was every indication from news reports that police would be looking and searching everywhere. A routine roadside check by law enforcement was not something they relished and volumes of mysterious bags in the back was sure to arouse the interest of any organized manhunt.

They thought about this problem in silence. They did not want to be bringing all these bags but where to leave them exactly? "What about the kitchen?" was Bernie´s idea. "Check for space amid those pipes up there."

With further inspection they found space over the suspended ceiling in the kitchen. In behind Kenny´s amazing pipework all would fit. And they did, awaiting garbage collection of a future time when the dust had settled a bit and they would be more ready.

With all that sorted they were a little more at ease not least with regard to anyone suddenly stopping them and asking about anything. As long as a fire did not break out and go rampant in the building . . .

They soaked up more news reports on radio and TV until the afternoon and it looked like the whole place was sensationalized with the hijacking story. Details were coming in of police searches and manhunts taking place from Reno to Seattle and beyond. But there was no clear mention if police were only searching along Victor 23, the route of Flight 305 or elsewhere. The reports had said everywhere but that could mean anywhere.

They discussed this at length and Kenny reckoned that it may take a day or two for the search to lose steam a bit. "That's another good reason why this holiday period was the best time to pull it off. Everybody is lying low. Everyone is out of gear. We need to do likewise and act with no sudden movements outside of normal holiday stuff."

As he lit up a cigarette he felt that now might be a good time to school Bernie on how to act calm in front of people whenever the hijacking story would come up. And he knew that Bernie was inclined to be all over the place when telling a lie. So he ventured forth "Listen man, there are going to be a few times when this is mentioned in your presence so you have to get used to not reacting - like be calm as if you were almost absent minded. My advice is to never bring it up and always look to kill it off in conversation. Just don′t go there and always have your answer ready like saying they will catch that guy who did the hijacking without a doubt. What a moron etc."

Bernie was riveted by what he was hearing.

Kenny continued "It's important to never get involved in even a slight discussion about it. Just keep a bored look on your face and be distracted by some other topic as soon as you can."

At that point an interjection from Bernie was very revealing "Yeah, I guess I could say that I was having a beer up at the trailer when I heard about it on the radio-"
This brought a raised finger from Kenny "No Bernie, that's exactly what you don′t do man. Nobody is ever going to casually ask you where you were on the night of the hijacking - it's not exactly the JFK assassination. They are not asking so if you tell them they might think you find it important to explain yourself about it. That will raise suspicion with even the most casual customer."
He went on "You will always need to stay sharp about this stuff. Even beware of having a few beers with a crowd – like with the guys at work for example. Don′t let your guard down. Steer clear of situations and don′t talk shop with anyone if it might lead to this topic. Over time of course it will die down and you will hear about it less and less. But in the coming days and weeks you will hear about it a lot so be ready."
Judging by the look on Bernie′s face he was seeing the light. His mentor continued "There's nothing like having your standard comments ready - three or four of them - the cops have ways and means of finding that guy. That money will be traced, he probably died in the jump and they will find the body - and so forth. Simple one-liners. But never say any more. Don't offer to elaborate on anything. Let the conversation die as quick as you can."
This drew an anxious look from his companion "What are we going to do with this?" glancing toward the kitchen ceiling. "I mean what's the story with regard to traceability for that cash? How are we gonna be able to circulate that?"
Kenny assured him "We take our sweet time. Right now it's going to be hot as hell and we can't touch it. We are going to have to let it blow over for a bit and play it by ear. From

what I know the cops will have recorded all those serial numbers of every single $20 bill. So we need to take it real easy. Meantime we just carry on with life as normal."

He knew that the only thing keeping Bernie from wanting to grab it and stash it away was his sheer nervousness. While Kenny himself was a guy who was happy to just have a roof over his head and food on the table, that was not the stuff of his comrade. He was a different creature. Bernie would be there at the crack of doom with the hand out looking to add the dime to the dollar. In Bernie's world, much always wanted more. A down-the-line replication of corporate greed all over again. There was no end to it and Kenny had always understood this about him. At the same time, he was aware that on a certain level he had impressed his companion. So if he was ever going to persuade him to take heed of his advice and tow the line it would be right now.

By late afternoon they both realized they had not eaten in so long. So they choose to head out to locate a diner. Kenny knew one nearby that he had been to before and as they pulled into the car park he put his hand up to his face in sudden revelation. He was broke because of the work situation and had not a cent in his pocket. They both burst out laughing with a sense of irony. All that money that Kenny had, literally, 'piped up', was useless to him. It was like stolen money had already burned a hole in his pocket. Well not quite yet but the two found it so funny that with all that cash they had got, here they were scraping as before with Kenny borrowing from Bernie.

Same as ever.

"I'll make it up to you" were Kenny's words while trying to keep a straight face as his companion pulled out his wallet. This drew more laughter from the latter "Somehow I

believe ya."
Walking into the diner they were still chuckling and giggling at the situation. As before, Uncle Bernie picked up the cheque.
As they drove round later on there appeared to be very little activity with regard to police checks or anything else on the road and so they decided they might as well do a little of what they were officially supposed to be doing. They would head out to the camping site and stay over in Bernie´s air-stream trailer. Making sure to shop for food and beer before getting on their way, they headed down the road toward the trailer park. By now darkness was already falling. A few miles south of Sumner they came upon a traffic jam and had no choice but to join the tailback. After a minute it became clear that it was the police doing a spot check, no doubt as part of their dragnet searching for the hijacker. Kenny could detect some nervousness from his partner. He decided he should play it super cool. He stretched back on the seat and laughed "Relax man, you're on holiday. Besides, there is nothing strange for them to report here. All is good. Smile and be nice and friendly."
Bernie seemed to be doing his best but Kenny decided to wear his big stupid smile as they neared the police car with the traffic lining up in the queue. Just as the car in the line ahead was pulling away he mused "Hey, you think these idiots give a hoot in hell about you or me? The likes of this slob in uniform here - are you kiddin?" This brought a loud laugh from the two just as Bernie, who was driving, pulled the car up to the officer and rolled his window down.
"Happy Thanksgiving sir. May I see your driver's license please?"
"Sure." Bernie handed him the license through the window.
At this point there were about three other police officers

walking round the station wagon with flashlights shining through the windows of the car at rear. All they had to see was stacks of beer and the like.

The officer spoke again "Where are you heading to sir?"

Bernie replied "Down near Portland. We have a holiday camp there."

The officer was at that moment distracted by one of his colleagues calling to him near the roadside. At that point he went to have some words with him and went out of earshot. After about a minute he returned with a slightly bothered facial expression and handed back the license to Bernie "Ok, take care now. Safe driving."

With that they moved off politely and were on their way again. Kenny spoke matter-of-factly "And that's about as complicated as it will get for you. If they are not on to me they won´t be talking to you. And they are nowhere near me right now." This made him laugh a little. "They have a long way to go yet." He made a point of sounding self-assured and relaxed. And with what they had accomplished the previous day, who was Bernie to argue?!

There was a silence for a little while as they reflected on the events of the previous day. Kenny spoke "Listen Bernie, I just gotta say, let me take this opportunity to thank you. I could never have done it without you. You were rock solid all the way!"

Bernie's reply was "Oh well, you did all the difficult bits. It was your idea."

Kenny knew that however different they were as individual people, Bernie was due a world of credit for his contribution. "Anyway you took part in something really amazing. I guess you can tell your grandchildren one day."

This idea gave Bernie a scare. "Damn . . . not likely."

Later they climbed the hill in the woods and finally rolled

up to their little silver trailer, glittering once again in the headlights of the car as if to say that it had been waiting for them. As they stepped out the wind swept through the trees in the dark. The memories of this sweet little holiday home would forever hold a special place in their hearts.

Chapter 25 Watching the dust settle

The FBI ruled America by fear. That was not exactly spoken of too often but it was kind of true. A bit like a large village you find somewhere in the heart of China with 20,000 population and maybe one police station. Not too much would ever happen, mainly because the public understood there would be terrible consequences if they stepped out of line in a criminal sense. The USA was the same with a long punitive history and a highly organized prison sentence that came with the irreversible stigma to match. If you did jail in America even for something minor you would have a near-impossible task to escape the consequences of your bad record. Getting back on the ladder of success would be compounded in difficulty. It was like a permanent shameful stain. Just for good measure.

But in most states the Police Force offered a career, at least if you were a certain type of person. Not to generalize but sometimes men of low morality were attracted to Law Enforcement as it gave them a reliable measure of power. Commanding respect on the street and of course, sharp practice and corruption often came into it at precinct level. That was the public perception at least.

Other, more studious types, worked their way up the ladder and carved out office jobs as investigative staff and forensics. Over the decades the force had become large and bureaucratic. But they liked their time off for Thanksgiving as much as anyone else. So we can imagine their inertia when they got the call to respond to this upstart incident in Seattle.

After the initial chase party had failed to locate Cooper amid the storm the natural thing to do was to organize a wide ground search come daylight. But while stating to the press that a search was being carried out in four states, there was no immediate detail on how comprehensive this was. It wasn't. At least not initially. It took some time for the big machine to get into gear.

Based out of FBI offices in Portland, Ralph Himmelsbach was a special agent who had a reputation for gritty detail and digging his heels into cases. A man who was typically on the ball when many others might not be. The morning after the event, with the media all over the story, he headed into the office to do, as it were, due diligence. After some calls and conversations he was coming to grips on the situation and the lie of the land. Literally.

The search party being deployed was initially along the Victor 23 route and west of it toward the Columbia river which included its southerly forks as it approached Portland.

The general approach was to see how the search panned out while there was hourly interest from the awaiting public, no doubt many expecting to receive news that the fugitive had been caught or killed. Added to the immediate fascination might have been a degree of apprehension with people locking doors for safety.

After daybreak on Thanksgiving as the hours wore on and with no news of his capture the gossip factor was huge. Reports were coming in from wooded areas which were being searched by police with dogs. TV crews waited up with reporters on hand to make updates along highways, near rivers and forest areas. Police and mountaineers would come and go over the hours. Helicopters swept overhead – even the boys in their camper trailer could hear it occasionally. Reports varied on the radio as the picture of exactly what happened on flight 305 began to consolidate. The early consensus was that Cooper had jumped out between Seattle and Portland. But most of the time the TV and radio were regurgitating what had already been said with no actual news on the situation.

While listening to such a radio report in the trailer with the gas lamp lit Bernie turned to Kenny saying "Yeah, I guess the intensity will ease after a day or two."

Kenny looked over with the cigarette smoke in his eyes "You can be sure they will get stuck in with combing the area though. I think I will be bald from now on and I'll need to be wearing this cap." He tried on the baseball cap. "Yeah . . . no more hair pieces. Goodbye to the toupee."

The following morning Bernie decided to venture out to see if he could pick up a newspaper locally. As he pulled off in the car Kenny sat there looking out the window of the trailer, staring at the volcanic mountains in the distance. How peaceful it all looked.

As a strategy for keeping calm when he spoke with Bernie he was not always saying what was on his mind but he knew the FBI were notorious for pulling in even vague suspects in a case like this. Sometimes, especially if under pressure, they would force people into confessions and use a plea bargain tactic. Every tactic in the book frankly when push came to shove. It was a toss of a coin as to whether a suspect was handled by good cops or bad cops. In the case of a routine narcotics charge they might reduce a jail sentence from fifteen years down to maybe eight years in exchange for an admission of guilt – even if the person was innocent. But in such a major incident as this he reckoned he would go away behind bars forever. No wind in the woods or mountain views there. He was keeping one ear on the radio for updates on the sensational case that was sweeping the Northwest. The trailer was already looking untidy and suggested heedless holiday makers were on the scene. Occasionally some helicopters could be heard in the distance. No doubt that was the police but most of the time they seemed to be over toward the Columbia river in their search. He nodded off for some minutes with the radio blaring but woke with a jolt of the sound of "Photo-fit of the fugitive" in the bulletin. Police supposedly had published a mock-up of what the hijacker looked like and the broadcast went on with the details of physical description as before. This sparked his interest to say the least as he sat upright. He gazed into space as he scrambled to update the situation in his mind.

He wondered if he had taken enough care with his disguise. Suddenly he heard a car approach but to his momentary relief he saw that Bernie had arrived back. As his partner-in-crime stepped up into the trailer carrying some groceries in a brown paper bag, he also had a morning paper. Tossing it across the table-top he spoke with a cheerful voice

"You'll never guess who is in this today."

Kenny looked, partly in dread. There it was! A large artist's impression of the hijacker. Right on the front page. He held his hand up to his mouth in amazement. This was nothing like him. They both broke out in laughter.

"Gee, I never looked that good in my life. If I looked like that I would be in the movies!"
There were artist's impression showing two images of the hijacker, both with and without the sunglasses. But the face shown was petite and refined, perhaps dainty, even cute. They sensed at that moment that this was the image that the public would keep in mind when thinking about this case and that there was no realistic probability that it, in itself, would lead to positively identifying the more raw, plainer face of Kenny. There was also some suggestion that the fugitive was Hispanic in ethnicity.

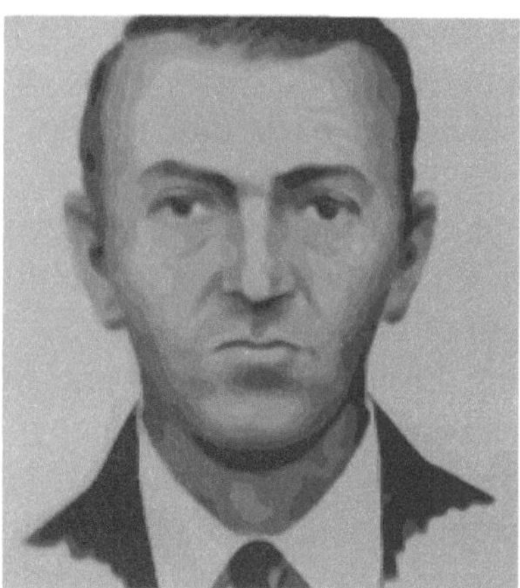

The "Fly to Mexico" order seemed to weigh in as well as Kenny's olive-skin tactics.
So, this error in depiction was reached, no doubt, by shortcomings in descriptions by the Flight staff cascaded to interpretation limits of the FBI staff. This was beautiful from Kenny's point of view as it muddied the waters of the public pool ever further. He felt instinctively that his nice

approach to Tina during the event might have given him a rub of good luck with this, proving for the millionth time that it's nice to be nice.

This was a kind of false meme that had been born (or branded) in the public domain. They both felt it would be a favorable wind in their backs.

Of course he had to guard against another possibility: that the police deliberately put out a less-that-optimal estimated image to lure him into complacency. He would not read too much into that idea given how straightforward and brutish Law Enforcement were inclined to be but he had to be careful.

While the choice of this holiday period to pull their stunt had served them so well they both understood the importance of blending back into normal life as fast as possible.

At any rate, the photo-fit helped to cheer them up a bit and ease their nerves. Bernie opened the trailer door looking out as he took a breath of the fresh forest air.

Kenny was going through the rest of the paper for news. "Hey Bernie, check this out."

It was a picture of their favorite big bird N467US on the tarmac viewed from the rear with a guy looking straight up at the closed staircase above him. "I heard on one of the radio reports that the stair end was damaged from being opened and dragged along the runway while landing at Reno . . . Not a bit from the looks of it."

It was typical of Law Enforcement when talking to the press to exaggerate the bad deeds of criminals and characterize them as nothing but thugs.

They spent their time continuously moving the radio dial from one station to the next for news updates. At one stage there was another little interview excerpt with Tina

Mucklow. She was commenting on how she spent some time with Cooper down the back of the aircraft "He was not nervous. He seemed rather nice, and he was never cruel or nasty."

Most of the time the stuff on the radio consisted of commentary on the search by the police. At this point the first round of searches were done with manhunts in Reno, Oregon and Washington. One reporter had been interviewing some police rangers coming off the edge of a wooded area after a lengthy pursuit in vain. She claimed to overhear an officer saying "If he's that good he can keep it!"

Chapter 26 Bitchin in the kitchen

As the guys moved into the weekend and what was to be a quiet, thrilling and slightly nervous time, tucked away in the little trailer, the nation began to properly come to grips with what had happened on Flight 305 at Thanksgiving. Throughout this time somebody in the newspapers miss-transcribed the name of the fugitive Dan Cooper to DB Cooper. Presumably the 'Da' part of 'Dan' that he left on his boarding pass was the source of the initial mistake. The 'DA' was then changed to 'DB'. Somehow the name stuck and he would forever after be referred to as 'DB' or 'the hijacker DB Cooper' etc. Nobody was bothered to parse the basic data enough to be able to join the dots and recognize that he had the same name as Dan Cooper, the comic book character who made his career jumping out of airplanes.

Kenny felt a bit disappointed at that as he thought of the name to be quite humorous. Anyway, you can't expect a perfect crime. Still, the fact that nobody seemed to notice was a good omen. How much more might they not notice? A lot he hoped.

The police had finally cranked up an extensive search in various surrounding states. Their initial net cast out over cities, suburbs, towns and forest areas, some of which were vast and challenging to cover. Kenny and Bernie went out as little as possible, just once to a diner to break up the monotony and a couple of visits to gas stations and home stores. They were mindful of police activity but apart from the some helicopter noise overhead there did not seem to be much out of the ordinary. At least where they were situated. They of course kept a close ear to the radio for reports of any new developments. Aside from gossip and call-in talk show opinions there did not seem to be too much to digest.

Predictably, the official FBI spokespeople denounced Cooper as a thug and a foolhardy idiot claiming they expected to find his body soon – probably hanging from a tree somewhere or if he did survive the jump he would be apprehended quickly since all the serial numbers were recorded and were bound to be traced in no time.

This particular point caused raised eyebrows in the trailer where the two boys were listening. They glanced at one another. Bernie spoke "I guess that would be right – yes? I mean they probably have them on microfiche assuming they were properly organized in that way."

Kenny agreed. "Yeah, we can assume it. Better safe than sorry. We should take no chances."

Bernie looked a bit wary "They just said that they're gonna publish them. Like, for every single bill? How does that go exactly?"

Kenny kept the cigarette in his mouth as he squinted through a blanket of smoke. "Well, yeah, I guess they will give the serial numbers to the banks. But there's ten thousand of them." He thought about it through some silence. "A pretty big list to go through for one single twenty dollar bill. I mean if a bank clerk gets landed with a whole bunch of twenties – ok, he'd go and check. But for every individual twenty dollar bill that comes in across the counter . . . oh . . . So they might stack them for the end of the day and put someone in charge of checking them in bulk. But that's a pretty thankless task. Unless we were to help them by spending a whole lotta twenties in one place somewhere. That's why it's really critical we lie low with it for a while. But I accept that we need to think a bit about how we want to release it into circulation. Yeah." He smiled "It's like a problem for the Federal Reserve – what a great headache to have. We're bankers now!"

They both laughed at this idea.

The irony was not lost on Kenny. This past summer, President Nixon had decided to detach the beloved Yankee dollar from the Gold Standard. This meant that by disconnecting from a reference value in use for centuries round the world, the administration was now free to print more dollars whenever it wanted. This was of course provided they could manage to mask the extent of its use with the public. So, if they wanted billions for wars and propaganda and all kinds of unethical activities there was now the means to generate it and the action would be bolstered by a congressional machine that did public relations. Meantime people tended not to have enough information available to them to scrutinize things sufficiently as the media went through the motions to be seen to carry it over with hopefully not too much deep

public inquisition. This was how it was rigged. If it didn't make it to the newspapers it didn't happen.
Whoever held the ability to print money held the power. Nice to have a tiny little bit of that mint, however little. The fact that all the loot was in twenty dollar bills would be a good help as it was not too big to off-load.
Next day was Sunday and they decided to head back up to the apartment in Sumner before the vacation came to an end. And what a vacation it had been.
All was intact in the apartment. Nothing disturbed with the pipes and all in place above the kitchen area. That would serve as their mint for the next while. Between them they got their story straight to tell anyone if and whenever they were asked about where they were on Thanksgiving: They had spent two nights over at Kenny's before heading down to the trailer.

The first roll-out of that alibi was done by Bernie early Monday morning as he landed back home for the first time in a week. He was met by Margaret as soon as he entered the door. She did not look like a happy honey. A stern silent stare was all he felt. He couldn't help smirking at his being in the dog house "Well! How did Thanksgiving go?"
She looked like she was already past being furious. He wondered whether the relationship would recover from here. But he frankly cared more about keeping out of jail. He genuinely had to hurry and get ready to go to work. As he raced around some conversation trickled out between them. Her arms were folded as she bitched about having to show up at Helen Jones' place on her own for this holiday invitation. He took a moment to slow down and look her in the eye with some measure of sincerity. "I was up at Kenny's place and we went down to the trailer for a bit.

That's all. We had a few beers." Her facial expression and her silence spoke of deeper problems and mistrust. He felt that was fine but he did not want the conversation to go any further at this moment. He made an effort to speed things up, grab his things and was out the door in record time. As he drove off he thought about how that went all right considering how it could have gone. He was nervous about any talk of the hijacking from anyone. Anything but that.

The more time they had to allow things to blow over the better it was. This would allow both Kenny and Bernie to get back into everyday life after the holiday period with seamless transition. Kenny's work was patchy as usual and for the first time in his life he was genuinely not bothered or motivated to get any work. Freedom at last. Instead he would be anticipating any hazards on the road ahead and managing to steer clear of the law or any possible pitfalls. That would be his occupation now. It was new territory. A different set of headaches. Money changes everything.

They both would have that problem although for Bernie there was an extra buffer of safety since he was not actually on the plane. As long as the police did not have Kenny on their radar, the chances of getting him on it were remote. Still, in the event that the big spotlight ever did come on Kenny his partner would undoubtedly feel some heat. As the weeks would pass their nerves would settle.

After a few more days Kenny decided to touch base with Margaret by means of a casual phone call. He knew he would be better at communication than her husband and it was a good moment to take a reading of how things were going. She sounded a bit cool for sure.

"Well it might have been so nice to have had you both up at Helen's on Thanksgiving but there was not a sight or a trace of either of ye. Gone without a word!".

Kenny stayed composed "Yeah, the stay-over at the trailer would not be my choice if I'm honest. But Bernie was keen on it so I wasn't gonna be awkward so I just went along."

She knew he was that no-fuss obliging type of guy. She expressed her annoyance with Bernie at length. He listened politely at the other end of the line saying that he probably needed some space to himself and he'd be fine. Then came the topic of the hijacking. He responded with his standard answer he had rehearsed in his head "Oh the papers were full of it. Yeah. They had helicopters out and everything. If they don't find a body I'd say they'll get to the bottom of it soon."

This seemed to bring some brightness to her tone which was nice except that it was not his favorite topic for conversation just now. She enthused even more about it and he interjected "Gosh, I never even knew those planes could open up in the back like that. I'm not actually sure if I ever saw one open. That was crazy stuff – what that guy did." Kenny felt a bit awkward in the voice but then again that was in keeping with his usual manner when talking. And of course she would know that about him. She was only too familiar.

So he politely excused himself and agreed to call up to her as soon as he got a chance. As he hung up the phone he thought about whether he let anything slip with his remark about the aircraft. Hopefully not, as it was not really his job to know that stuff since he was normally the purser in his role onboard a flight. And she would not readily be able to tell. Still, it showed just how careful he would have to be.

For most states in America the statute of limitations for an investigation of a criminal case was just five years from the date of the crime. After that period they would get away without ever serving a day for it. But they would never want the police to find out given the fifty ways they might have to "take care of you". Such loose vanity would never be his thing. At any rate these up and coming months could be very tricky.

A couple of weeks had passed with no change in the status of anything. Except to say that in the public domain the outrageous hijacking was holding a fascination rating and at the very least was set to become an historic footnote.

Some days after the event Kenny managed to get his hands on the published list of serial numbers for the ransom money. Printed out in a regional newspaper and spanning over a few pages were the tables of numbers. He felt the urgency to do a spot-check. Taking down one of his Gun-barrel pipes from over the kitchen ceiling, he unscrewed the cap and removed the first roll of banknote that was tied up with a rubber band. He extracted the first few $20 bills and with their serial numbers it took quite some time and patience to locate the corresponding numbers in the list. It was not that he was pleased to find the numbers matched but the prospect of sloppiness from law enforcement was not to be ruled out. He tried a few more from the opposite end of the pipe. With careful searching they matched also. At least he knew where he stood. But this exercise showed him just how tedious it was to manually find a number on the list of ten thousand numbers and identify a given bill as ransom money. The choice of $20 bills had been a good one.

In the middle of the afternoon Kenny wandered into a local launderette in Sumner burdened by a fairly large workload. Just then who should he bump into but Helen and a friend who were leaving.

They were both surprised "Hey Kenny, how are you man?" Of course Kenny normally met her at holiday time in previous years along with Bernie and Margaret. He felt caught off guard but busied himself. Looking around at the tumbler machines he heard her introducing her friend casually "Did you meet Kenny before? He's Bernie's friend – you know Bernie Geestman and Margaret? - Oh hey Kenny, where were you for Thanksgiving? We were expecting you up."

He was not enjoying this "-ah I was with Bernie" as he looked up from his laundry. He decided not to mention the trailer park, keeping it simple.

Helen went on "Where were you guys? I think Margaret was not pleased exactly though she put on a brave face ya know -".

Kenny butted in, hoping to kill off the conversation "Uh I think they might be going through a rough patch, ya know!" She tried again"Where did you go?"

"I was with Bernie." was his reply, spoken a little as if he was running out of oxygen.

She held a look on her face like she was processing something though she kept her composure. Some other thought that occurred to her in parallel with what was being said. Maybe it was Kenny's suggestion of the Geestman's marital difficulties that came as a surprise. It did actually have a grain of truth to it.

Kenny was trying to look like he was preoccupied with his laundry but he feared he was not doing so well. He felt unsettled and ill-at-ease by their presence.

Whatever it was that was running through her mind, it had taken her down a gear and both she and her friend excused themselves politely, saying their goodbyes.

As they left the shop Kenny could see them walking away

through the large front window pane as he slotted coins into the large washing machine. As their voices faded in the distance he thought he heard her friend saying something about hijacking. What it was he could not decipher. He cocked his ear as best he could. Some half utterance he could not make out. Then nothing more. They were gone.
"Man" he thought to himself as he watched the tumble spinner go round. "That was awkward". She definitely seemed a bit spooked. He could only hope it was about Margaret's tribulations and nothing else.

Chapter 27 Meanwhile back at the FBI

J. Edgar Hoover sat at a desk in his home in Washington DC., rubbing his eyes in between paperwork. He felt tired at this hour of his life.
Starting his career in the 1920s he had established and built up the FBI by infiltrating subversives and deviants, identifying communists, and gathering information. No matter what, the FBI needed to have an authorized privilege of breaking rules in order to know the criminal mind and be a step ahead of them. In order to establish the boundary line you sometimes had to step across it. That had always been his modus operandi.
In his role as head of the organization some accused him of being overly intrusive and unethical in his surveillance tactics but as far as he was concerned there would be no America without people like him and the bureau.
For sure he bent a few rules as necessary. This included

keeping checks on presidents or any potential presidents. Many had been on his list like Nixon and of course Martin Luther King who he had regarded as a danger and a threat. He had without apology built a file of information and possible evidence on the latter in pursuit of damning information that could be made public in order to scandalize him and ruin his reputation. That character assassination was entirely appropriate in Hoover's world and indeed actual assassination if need be. King was killed in the end and in Hoover's view he got just about what he deserved.

But if he thought MLK was a danger to the American order he had been frankly terrified by Fred Hampton. Hoover had watched and listened to Hampton and saw clearly that he was a mercurial and genial narrator and speaker who could engage and captivate the public. Worse, his whole mantra was to unite people on the left and the right – the poor on both sides of the political divide regardless of their color or creed. Hampton had possessed the power to convince ordinary Americans that they were victims of the system which preserved the elites in society, that the real fight was actually between super-rich and everyone else, not between Left and Right. This looming political vista had given Hoover nightmares and he did not have to think twice about having him killed. Which he promptly did in Chicago. When his people barged into Hampton's home in the dead of night and shot him in his bed it had been a load off Hoover's mind.

The likes of Hampton were, thankfully, rare. It would always need to be kept that way. Even if it meant keeping the education system dumb or spreading false propaganda through the media. Call it what you like, it would always have to be done. And hence the ever-growing need to monitor those who might begin to beat to a different drum.

So the perceived divisions in America were serving him well. Black versus White, Unions versus Company and so on. This weave-work of tension from state to state allowed the FBI to mingle between all these subdivisions, plant evidence, collect information, arrest and round up, deport, coerce people in Washington and generate favorable publicity. The bureau had a decent rating with the public that served as leverage against presidents wanting to fire him as head. They would feel intimidated through public pressure and private pressure against doing that. Especially after what happened to John F. Kennedy. Not that a given politician would know whether he was going to just suffer political ruin or actual assassination. But most slimy senators just kept well safe of the red line while happy to ride their own gravy train. This often explained their falsity and lack of sincerity in the public arena. They were nervous behind the scenes and mindful of stepping on the wrong toes. Whatever brought them to conformity would get the thumbs up from Hoover. The FBI was really about the preservation of power structures in order to prevent sliding into the chaos of the Wild West. So it had to continuously appear as a tower of strength to the public. Even if that was not always the case. Appearances were everything.

But in May 1971 there had been a break-in by Left wing radicals at the FBI office in Pennsylvania which revealed secret files that showed the bureau was conducting widespread spying on Americans. This was another of the stories that had got out that Hoover felt did not need to be in the public domain. In fact they had no business knowing of it. It put him under increased pressure following

allegations about his other activities that were getting some public monitoring in recent years.
Although Hoover kept a good rap with the public these recent problems weighed considerably on his shoulders.
Now this Cooper hijacking that happened on Thanksgiving was compounding his problems. He had been outraged when he received reports of it and then disquieted at having no trace of the fugitive nor any ransom recovered. There had been no body found in any forest or river. No trace of anything anywhere. It was evidently well planned. He was not happy at the way law enforcement had been seemingly toyed with by this lousy scoundrel in Washington State and at Reno. They were made to look like lame fools. The official line would have to be that the FBI always gets its man – even if it was not quite the right man – if they had to forge a story in the public then so be it.

The problem here was that the crime was unprecedented in nature and execution. The bureau had dealt with hijackings often enough but normally those were done for political motives. But the public optics on this were different. Here was someone who had tried something bold and got away with it. Not only did this reflect badly on the bureau but others might be tempted to try the same thing. Most frustrating was the inability to simply target political movements or organizations with his network. Who was behind it? An individual acting on his own? There was, as yet, no clue.
Retrospectively, what grated his nerves was the way that Cooper had waited on the runway at SEATAC for all that time while no efforts were made to storm the plane. Then at Reno airport, when they stormed the plane it was too late. The Nevada wild horse had bolted.

He sat back from the table biting his bottom lip. "Goddamn idiots. They gifted it to him."
Hoover felt that every effort should be made to get the message out that this type of high criminality would not pay. Also, the story had made the top news headlines in the North East where it happened. Its spread was somewhat diffused throughout the rest of the nation. He would see to it that it remained that way by use of his henchmen and their media influence to kill it off a bit. Especially while they had not captured the perpetrator. It was embarrassing.

Across the country Ralph Himmelsbach and colleagues were busy wading their way into evidence that had been gathered. At Reno, after the 727 had been stormed the forensics crew moved in and took fingerprints and everything else they laid eyes on. As it was a crime scene, the parachute that had been opened and cut, the tie that Cooper had thrown aside, the boarding pass, the ash trays with his eight cigarette butts – all would be sacked and packed to be brought back to the labs for examination. Of course what complicated matters in such cases was to separate out passenger related traces from those of the perpetrator's, since the crime scene was such a public place. But they did their best. The same rigors were also executed back at the Portland Airport terminal where the fugitive had spent some time before the flight but there were not much pickings for law enforcement there. The main concentration of scrutiny was onboard the aircraft.
While the parachutes were examined and kept for records, they were not so powerful as evidence since Cooper had ordered them with the ransom. So it was not like Himmelsbach could start tracing the recent purchase of all parachutes in the region. That would be no valuable source

of information. Clever.

In addition, the crime scene was, as such, split between the inside of the 727 and some spot in a vast forest hundreds of miles away – somewhere in that thicket of trees wherever the hijacker landed. But which spot? Where? And if they could ever identify it, what evidence might they have? Footprints in a forest? Really? Being washed away in the night by the rain. There was always the possibility of some ransom money or a dead body of course but that would be a real bonus. A careful crime like this was not likely to hold such a large imperfection. He feared the FBI might be in for the long haul here. That search was not too enticing in his mind but you had to be seen to go through the motions. You had to do the basics.

They did however communicate with the suppliers of the parachutes and took note of the fact that one of the chutes the hijacker used in the jump was a dummy that was intended for training. This was a mistake by those involved and a bad one at that but as there were no hostages made to jump out of the plane the only life put at risk was the hijacker's. So the exact types and descriptions of the two missing chutes were recorded.

The clip-on tie was supplied by Cooper and with some tracing it was found to be sold by JCPenny. Which exact store and when was another matter but they would look to monitor all possibilities for valuable clues. They did establish that it was a perfectly common tie. Also, they noted that the fugitive might be left-handed according to the way the tie was removed. Not great information but it would be filed.

A better prospect in the long run was fingerprinting evidence. Everything that Cooper had touched was sampled by the labs and this included things like the boarding pass and tie. Separating out partial fingerprints was something you did in order to match future detainees for questioning. This was done but without suspects on hand it would be a long and frustrating wait.

Trying to pinpoint exactly where Cooper might have jumped was a messy task. This was addressed more after the initial searches had turned up nothing. The NWO airline staff members were questioned again and after some double-checking and correction, the bureau suspected they might have been searching perhaps as much as twenty miles east of the real landing zone. But they could not really be so sure. The flight crew had done their best to impart accurate information but with the chaos after the event and unusual nature of it, the best strategy was to move forward searching all possible areas.

With regard to Cooper's escape on the ground, the theories varied. Some thought he must have had an accomplice waiting in a car to pick him up. Others suggested he might have had a hideout where he simply laid low for a time. But nobody was sure and no hard evidence came through. As to whether he had a getaway vehicle planned or not, it was anyone's guess. And at this point they would only be guessing. The FBI was simply in the dark.

However, two things did start happening that kept the investigation team busy. Information from the public began to trickle in as the weeks wore on. Most of them led to nowhere but officers knew that even the slightest scrap of evidence could crack a case wide open overnight. And so they were compelled to check out all calls and information from the public. Most of the time it was claims like "I know a guy who looks like your photo-fit" or "My neighbor pulled into his driveway at a strange hour on Thanksgiving". All reports would be logged in the usual

manner and checked through.
The second thing that arose from these reports and other cross-checking done by the bureau: suspects were being lined up. This was typical of net testing that police would normally carry out. Criminals with known records were checked out and questioned if need be. Also, anyone who appeared to have suddenly come into larger sums of money than expected would be looked at closely.
The narrative that the hijacker landed in the Columbia river and was killed was the one most favored by law enforcement. Proof of that would shorten the case and kill off the story in the press, putting an end to the manhunt. The big problem was the absence of any body being washed up on the river banks or money or parachutes or briefcase or anything else. Any one of these items of evidence would be a big turning point for Ralph Himmelsbach but without anything being retrieved the emerging sub-conscious message to the public mind was "He Got Away !!"

Chapter 28 When crime meets grime

While both Kenny and Bernie got back to normal life as quickly as possible, the question of how to put large amounts of loot to use was something they would quietly discuss throughout the Christmas period and beyond. We are talking of course about money laundering – illegally hiding stolen money.

Originally they had agreed to be cautious about spending it but they also realized that in the real world it was hard to take care of. Not to mention it could be a liability for them if the physical stuff was ever discovered in their possession. Ideally they would like to exchange it out to ten, fifty and hundred dollar bills. But who could they exchange it with? Certainly never with the banks or any other financial organization, foreign exchange bureau or anything of that kind. Not even a single bill. There was always a chance that someone in the bank might remember to put it through routine checks with the ransom list. Worse still, they might have an automatic policy of sending all twenty dollar bills back to a central bank specially for checking. Whatever system the boys deployed, it must function to avoid all official systems.

The obvious thing for Kenny to do was buy a house or some land. He proposed to do this by some kind of mortgage or bank loan that he would 'service' over a ten or twenty year period in the normal way by monthly repayments. In order to be approved by the Seafirst Bank where he had an account, he would need to show some kind of capacity to repay. Holding a position at North West Orient Airlines would be a benefit in the eyes of the bank officials but as Kenny's account balance had always made poor reading he would need to beef it up a little. So he arranged with Bernie to exchange some loot money for some normal cash which would come from Bernie's bank account, which had always been healthier than Kenny's. Meantime he applied for outline approval for a mortgage to see how much he would be granted so as to allow him to go and eye up some property. At this point he was looking like a more-or-less typical aspiring house buyer starting out.

This activity in turn spawned another idea in Bernie's mind. He would ask Kenny if he could give a personal loan to his sister Dawn to the tune of a few thousand dollars. Dawn Androsko and her four kids had been living with Bernie and Margaret for over a year now. This money would be a great help to her in finding a place of her own and giving her a much needed break. He put the suggestion to her half casually "Listen Kenny is a nice guy. He's got a lot of wise investments ya know! He never spends a dime, being single and all . . . He still has his god-damn childhood savings I'm sure. Why don't I run it by him about giving you a hand with some cash to help you to move out and find your feet."

She looked at him with surprise "Wow. Ya think? How would that work exactly?"

Bernie found his words a bit awkwardly "Well, you could pay him back, ya know. I mean he would be fairly flexible and all. He's kind of a soft touch with people really."

She seemed to warm to the idea "Ah he's lovely. But I wouldn't want to mess him around. How much do you think he could put up?"

Bernie tried to look like he was thinking deep "I dunno. Two or three grand maybe."

"Wow – That much?" Her face lit up. "It would definitely take a lot of pressure off us."

He was trying to keep a straight face. "Let me have a word with him and see. Thing is, you wouldn't have to go through bank loans and whatnot."

Mentioning this to Kenny was not nearly so uncomfortable.

"Sure." was his reply. "When does she need it?"

"I don't know. In the Spring I guess sometime. How much do you wanna give her? I suggested three grand. What about five – would that be too much?"

Kenny smiled and took the cigarette from his lips "And do I look like I really care? . . . Yeah whatever ya think. Only - try to hold off for a little while if we can. For reasons which you know about."

Of course it did cross Kenny's mind to wonder why Bernie did not offer his sister the money from his part in the loot. Presumably the answer would be that Kenny had twice as much of the money as Bernie. That was true and he would be happy to get rid of some of those twenty dollar bills when the time came. But he was also aware that it was in his comrade's nature to grab all at every opportunity. Being the bird of prey that he was.

But to be fair to Bernie he was a man of considerably more tricks. Some days later he called Kenny on the phone.

"Say, do you know the Grimes here in Washington? Remember Joe – did you Meet him? I was his best man at his wedding."

Kenny was not really sure "I don't know. Did I meet him?"

Bernie went on "Well see – he's got this area of land up at Bonny Lake. A kinda forest area mostly. There is actually an old house on it but it was in a bad state as I recall – unless they have fixed it up. I wonder if he would sell it. If you were interested? What do ya think?"

He continued "I mean, depending on what he wants, you could pay partly with a mortgage and partly with your own. That sorta thing."

Kenny was naturally interested – especially if the house was not dazzling and super-desirable. A run-of-the-mill place not to raise too many eyebrows. And so, arrangements were made to take a look at the real estate and see what might be on offer. When speaking to Joe Grimes Bernie explained that he had a friend who might be interested in the particular real estate but that he might be a – well, a part-cash customer, that there was likely to be a mortgage involved but the official price of the house might show less than what was actually going to be paid for it. To many Americans an off-the-books deal sounds good. Bernie did not want to say too much on the phone so it was agreed to talk it through with Kenny in person.

Meet the Grimes – Ann and Joe. An average couple in their late forties. Bernie brought Kenny along to see the land and was politely introduced to them.

The house was an old dilapidated thing that would not have looked out of place in the 1920s. A poor looking shack for sure. A typical wooden construction bungalow that was common throughout the USA. Kenny did not say too much yet he wondered if it was even worth salvaging, though it did have a nice front terrace so it had potential to be homely. But the condition of the building was not his main concern.

It overlooked a sweeping green area out front while up the back there was a fairly dense forest on a steep hill. Down to the front corner of the site there was a small crossroads with a couple of commercial buildings including a Seafirst bank branch. A place that just about qualified as a village, maybe. The rest of the area was rural and quiet. What more could anyone want? Especially in Kenny's predicament.

After they had walked the area enough and inspected everything the four of them sat down to talk it out.

Kenny spoke first "So look, how much do you want for this place?"

Joe glanced at his wife "Well it depends on how much of it interests you. Do you wanna just buy the house and the main plot here or the hilly area up back as well?"

Kenny took a deeper breath "I think in the end I would be interested in it all but as I am trying to swing a mortgage of some kind for this, it might be easier at first – to just get a price for the house and the main area here in front."

Ann spoke up "We think $16,000 for the house."

Kenny and Bernie exchanged glances. That was a fair price for what it was. They knew that they might be able to get better value by buying the whole lot in one go but any such haggling was not really on the agenda here. The goal in this instance was not to save money but rather quite the opposite, to get rid of it.

Kenny agreed "OK. So I suggest I put in for a mortgage for it and depending on how much they approve of, I can pay you the rest directly. In cash."

The grimes looked somewhat confused. Kenny continued "Basically, as soon as it gets approved from the bank, I will sign you a promissory note saying that I will pay you the balance in cash by a certain date, if you're agreed. We can get it notarized. Then, only when you get my payment in cash should you sign to officially close the sale. So you have the cash payment in hand before the cheque arrives from the mortgage loan."

The idea of the notarized payment was to protect Kenny and offer him some proof in case the sellers were to suddenly withdraw. He was not going to insist on actually going to the notary office as written receipt of a cash payment would be enough. But to the Grimes, it made it look like he was kind of organized . . . Which he kind of was.

Also, he was not worried about law enforcement cross-checking such legalized registered notes. This was in the early 70s and the computerized alarm triggers that were to be commonplace decades later were simply not a thing.

They seemed to like Kenny's plan. Joe asked "What percentage of the 16,000 dollars will be cash payment?"

Kenny did not know for sure "We have to see what the bank approves of for the mortgage. It could be half maybe."

Ann butted in "So . . . like, that would be a lot of cash."

Kenny began to grin "It will help you with your retirement plan I'm sure. Better you have it than Uncle Sam."

This brought laughter all-round and seemed to dis-spell whatever stillness was in the air. Kenny added "And if that works out all right we can do something the same with the area out the back of the house assuming you're happy to sell. Maybe farther down the road. In a few more months. I am juggling with funds as I am waiting for payments for things. But it won't be too long I think."

As the boys said their goodbyes the Grimes seemed uplifted and buoyant. And why wouldn't they be? They were getting a good price for an average site with a poor building.

Selling it privately and with a very good prospect of repeating the deal later on. A deal in which they were getting a lump sum under the table – off the books and out of sight. Cash was king!

Chapter 29 Kenny loves Bonny

When the dust settled after the hijacking, with the Christmas holiday that followed a few weeks later, the public had come to terms with what had happened and there seemed to be the distinct possibility that D.B. Cooper might have gotten away with his crime. This held an increasing fascination for people, especially for those living in the North West. It was to be an interest that would grow and grow. For a long time to come.

While the evidence and callers were steadily flooding into the police investigations, articles and letters from the supposed hijacker were also being sent to various newspapers in the district. One noticeable item landed on the desk of the Portland Oregonian that was sent in just a few days after the event, postmarked December 1st.
It was a paper montage of lettering, later found to be taken from Playboy magazine. It read -

"Am alive and doing well in my hometown P.O. - The system that beats the system." - D.B. Cooper

The letters P.O. meant of course Portland, Oregon.

Kenny and Bernie both chuckled at this so much. The crime had obviously struck a chord with people who felt inspired at their actions. No doubt it was speaking to the mostly mundane lives that many lived. And it also added to the already complicated pool of things that law enforcement had to consider.

As time would march on the amount of callers to the FBI claiming they were DB Cooper was to be staggering. The logic of why people would do such a thing is questionable. Firstly, they are running interference in police investigations. In addition, there might be some chance the person gets wrongly framed and incarcerated for a crime they did not commit. The bureau merrily shrugged this off as being part of everyday life at the office.

Then there were T-shirts, posters and even songs.

"With your pleasant smile and your dropout style, D.B. Cooper, where did you go?"

A folk hero. A legend. But he got away. And why *did* he do it on Thanksgiving?

One person not enjoying the Cooper celebrations was J. Edgar Hoover. The FBI head passed away at his home in Washington on May 2nd 1972. But his style of surveillance would continue for decades and be a factor in the erosion of society.

* * * * *

Following the agreement on the sale of the house and land to Kenny, things were moving along nicely. By March the banks were processing the loan in the normal way and the

Grimes, being delighted with the fairly sweet deal, with no real-estate marketing or fees and a nice ball of cash off the tax books, were happy to let him move some stuff into the house and make various arrangements. He was, as such, a good customer. And there was the prospect of him returning again for more trade. One good turn deserving of another.

At any rate, both Kenny and Bernie were reasonably confident that, based on the measure of the Grimes, just from the point of view of tax accountability, as a couple they were not likely to simply dump a quantity of very precious cash straight into their bank account. They were well able to play the game.

On a Saturday Kenny rolled up to his new home, the building still looking like a dismal shack. That did not worry him. His car was loaded up with stuff from his apartment in Sumners.

Bernie was already there with his wife as well as his sister Dawn and kids. They were all poking and inspecting and enthusing over the property, the soon-to-be renovated new house of Kenny Christiansen. The feeling overall was of great cheer.

He got out of the car and waved to all with a welcome, making small talk. He saw Bernie moving toward him with a slightly frozen look on his face. He was staring at something. It soon became clear what was troubling him. Kenny had attached his famous little pipework to the roof rack of the car. The special pipes he had prepared to hold currency.

When they were out of earshot from the rest he spoke in a low voice "Is that what I think it is?"

Kenny kept the manner of speech seamless "Oh yeah. Good ole Gun Barrel. Can't beat it! There's a couple of those with

your name on them I believe."
Bernie had to double-check. He looked like he was gasping for air. "I take it that all is intact with them?"
"Why of course!" was the reply.
He was scrambling to look calm, not something he ever did as well as Kenny. "And you came flying down the highway with that arrangement tied up on your roof – just like that?"
His companion shrugged.
He continued with a mortified look. "Well I am not going to take anything today. Where will you keep them? I mean-"
"Later!" was Kenny's whispered interruption, seeing that Dawn was approaching the car.

'Later' did indeed come. But not before everybody spent the day unpacking, cooking food and snacks and lounging around talking. Night was falling and both groups said their goodbyes before politely leaving. A nice time was had by all.
Exactly what to do with the pipes had been on Kenny's mind all afternoon. Two of them would soon be given to Bernie now that his mind had been refreshed about his share of the money – not that the latter would ever forget.
Kenny was looking around the house for a good place to put them. Due to the current state of repair of the place, he did not see anywhere safe. With plumbers coming in to do the heating system he wouldn't relish any potential mix-up. What a comedic howl that would be . . .
There was not a chance to check for manholes or shores around the house as yet. He wondered about the attic. Next morning, he decided to check it out and soon noticed that while there was no immediate door or stairs into the attic, it was actually a forty five degree roof angle. So there was some space up there. After inspecting the outside of the

house, he noticed a small hatch where a window might be in the apex at one of the gable ends. It was in a poor state. So he fetched a ladder and found he was able to open it. The little door came away and there was enough daylight to allow him to see inside. There was the usual attic insulation and wooden beams spread out to support the roof structure.
He thought for a minute. This would be a good place to hide the pipes for the moment. Meantime he would prioritize installing a new round window to give him better access. Then he could take forever and a day about fitting a stairs directly into the attic area – maybe never. That way, you would always need to get a ladder to the outside to gain access. He would tell people he was hoping to convert the attic. Sometime.
After placing the pipes easily under the attic insulation, off to one side, he came up with an additional plan. There was an off-cut of Formica from the kitchen that was being reworked. He found it to fit neatly over a square area in the floor of the attic to make a little false hatch – a perfect compartment for storing money! It was directly over where his bed would be.
This was altogether a better idea. Later, when he acquired more land from the Grimes up the back, he could look at possibilities of finding some places to bury dollars, here and there.

Chapter 30 The real McCoy

For every well-produced, refined and secure product that makes it through to market and has a celebrated success, there would surely be quite a flood of wannabe, loose-bracket, casual imitators. Especially in America. The land of trial and error.

By mid-spring of 1972, there had already been a few attempts at copycat hijackings prompted by the spectacle of D.B. Cooper, including one across the border in Canada. Kenny read about these in the newspapers with some bemusement. In his case his actions had been an outcrop of what was deep within him, his desire and his background with carefully hatched ideas and planning. But the notion of someone hastily arranging such a crime based on what one person had recently pulled off seemed to him to be giant idiocy, inviting jail time and even worse. How people would flippantly risk so much based on a news item, however sensational, was beyond him. Had they no value put on life and limb? That would never be him. Nor indeed would it even be Bernie – that super-reliable overseer of all things dollar-related.

In the early days of April that year, Richard Floyd McCoy Jr, a resident of Utah, sat in a bar, talking freely to a friend about the Cooper Hijacking and how he would have done it better.

"He should have asked for more money – much more. Are you kidding? Those companies and banks have plenty of it! If it had been me I'd have demanded more – would have got it too."
He went on at length about it.

Hubris aside, such an activity was indeed on his mind as his plans were nearing completion. His wife Karen was already typing up the instructions for the air crew to follow during the forthcoming ordeal.
To be fair to McCoy, he did actually have some proven credentials in Aviation.

Originally from North Carolina, he moved to Provo, Utah in 1962. Being an energetic and dedicated Mormon his career as a young man started brightly when he was assigned to Vietnam where he served as a helicopter pilot. While there, he was awarded with a Purple Heart medal and was sent home after being wounded in 1964. While recuperating he met Karen at Brigham Young University. They got married the following year.
As soon as he recovered from his injuries he decided to do a second tour of duty in Vietnam. This time he won the Distinguished Flying Cross Award for bravery. On a day in November 1967, he took it upon himself to fly his aircraft to defend a compound of friendly forces which was suddenly being over-run from an attack. He was said to have, in a single-handed fashion, wiped out a squad of about twenty enemy combatants thereby saving the lives of many of his comrades – firing down on the area from the helicopter gunship and using all his ammunition.
On returning home things were difficult financially for Richard and his wife. With two young children and a

limited income, just $240 per month from the GI Veterans bill that was passed through congress, things were a bit bleak. Although he expressed his desire to return to Vietnam for another term of duty his wife blankly refused. He managed to take up Sky-diving as a hobby and he also returned to university to study Law Enforcement. He had often mentioned to friends how he fancied a career in either the FBI or the CIA.

By the early 70s he turned 30 years of age and as the kids were getting bigger and more demanding, things were not good between Karen and himself. Theirs' had become a strained relationship for the most part. Being out of pocket meant he relied on his wife for much of the time.

Getting his inspiration from D.B. Cooper's action, he argued with her that he was well qualified to replicate such a lucrative stunt. She had been skeptical that he would go through with it but on the off-chance that he might, she gave him $500 to plan it. He had after all earned good medals in Vietnam. And there had always been a certain fun-seeking aspect about him.

At last his day came, the 7th of April and Karen was on hand to drive him to Salt Lake City International Airport where he would begin this daring adventure in the air. The fifty mile drive was to bear some heated conversation between husband and wife. She maintained he was crazy – maybe just crazy enough to try it. Still she had made sure he was organized for everything – short of a packed lunch. When they arrived she just wanted him out of her hair. "C'mon, c'mon get out of here for Christsakes! I must be mad . . . ” She tried to stay composed till he was at least out of sight.

They parted company and he made his way across the country to Denver, Colorado where he would go through the normal motions of awaiting his target plane United Airlines flight 855 to Los Angeles, California.

From careful study, he had known well that this plane was a stop over coming from New-ark, New Jersey. As Colorado is a bordering state to Utah that made it a good point for interception.

When he bought the airplane ticket he gave his name as James Johnson.

At the terminal building Richard made sure the aircraft was a Boeing 727 which was all important for his exit through the back stairs. As it had already been done he felt quite confident about the jump but needless to say as boarding time approached he displayed some nerves.

The passenger count was about 80 for this particular flight so the plane was not too over-crowded. He had his designated seat down the back of the plane, seat 20D just where he wanted to be.

While the crew and passengers were settling in he decided it was time to go into the bathroom down the rear and put on his disguise. When he emerged sporting a mustache and wavy hair piece he heard a voice behind him as he was climbing back into his seat.

"Sir, is this yours?"

He turned round to see an air steward holding a large envelope.

"Oh yes" was his awkward reply "Thank you very much".

It had a label on the front which read "Hijack instructions". He had left it in the restroom. Inside the envelope were the two pages of typed instructions, a bullet and a grenade clip.

A few minutes after the plane took off for L.A., McCoy made a deliberate point of exposing a grenade that he held in his hand. He made sure the stewardess noticed it and watched her retreat up front, no doubt to seek help.

After speaking to the crew an off-duty pilot casually took a walk down back to get visual confirmation of this well dressed passenger. As he came closer McCoy was in full anticipation and quietly drew a gun and handed him his large envelope, saying "Give this to the girl. She needs to bring it to the captain". He shot him a stern look.
The man complied and moments later the "Hijack Instructions" were in the hands of the captain and crew up front. There was no going back now.

The typed-up instructions told the captain to divert to San Francisco International Airport and park specifically at Runway 19. Strict orders were detailed about all people and vehicles to be near the plane while refueling. Meantime, $500,000 plus four parachutes were to be delivered onto the plane.
Instructions were also given to empty out all cargo from the 727 during this time.

The Captain's voice duly came over the intercom and announced that the aircraft was having some technical difficulty and needed to make an emergency landing in San Francisco. As had happened on other occasions like this the Captain gave direction to the crew to adhere to all instructions given by the hijacker.
Passengers toward the rear of the plane were offered first class seating up front which they gladly accepted. McCoy was now alone down the back. Waiting for his ransom.
By the time the demands were met in San Francisco, the sun was setting. As with Cooper, he knew that darkness would be an important ally.
After landing, all instructions were executed pretty smoothly.

The passengers were cleared and while the plane was being refueled, the money and parachutes were brought on.

McCoy took some moments to do a visual check for the money and saw that it was stashed into a duffle bag that met his satisfaction.

While the ground crew were finishing off the refueling he picked up the intercom phone at rear, asking the crew to send someone back for more instructions. When the stewardess came down he gave her a hand written note for the crew. Its detail was to head east and fly at a height of 16,000 feet.

Later he followed this up with more notes specifying a speed of 180 Knots and to keep in a meandering pattern over Utah. This would give him more time over his home state when he was preparing to jump. He also made a point to retrieve the notes back from the crew to remove evidence.

After being airborne, with the cabin lights switched down, the crew were able to quietly peer through gaps in the doors and curtains. They observed McCoy putting on a jumpsuit and helmet in addition to preparing some parachutes.

He then turned off the lighting and asked for a report on airspeed and weather conditions.

As the minutes passed the crew realized they had moved out of the winding fly zone prescribed for the Utah region. One of the crew members cautiously went back for a look only to see that the cabin was empty. The hijacker had fled out of the plane. Into the night . . .

Having been five hours since this ordeal was triggered by the lone passenger at rear, the flight crew now diverted to Salt Lake City International to make their landing.

As with previous hijackings, the security forces stormed the plane with the FBI combing all evidence. All areas were searched for fingerprints, including an on-flight magazine which the fugitive had handled. In addition, the crew submitted one of his notes which McCoy neglected to take back. This provided a sample of his handwriting.

With daybreak, police began a wide search of the area around Provo but with no signs of immediate success from the manhunt.

Still, after some 48 hours had passed things were happening back at the desks of the FBI. Some meaningful calls began to come in.

One report was from a driver who gave a ride to a hitchhiker who was carrying a ruck-sack and jumpsuit on the night of the hijacking. He had dropped the person off near a roadside bar.

When officers went along to interview a girl who worked at the eatery she claimed to have served a milkshake to a person fitting the hijacker's description. So they had some verification of this lead.

Then there was another call. It was from McCoy's friend to relay the detailed plan for such a hijacking he had heard in their conversation at the bar. He was saying how he did not take such talk too seriously – until he actually heard on the news about the hijacking. So now they had a name.

Law Enforcement duly made contact with McCoy who was very calm and they requested he supply a sample of fingerprints and handwriting. He courteously complied while at the same time denying involvement in any such criminal activity.

With McCoy back in his home and continuing with his normal life, the police beavered away to get confirmation from lab tests and analysis. His fingerprints and handwriting were a clear match with those taken from the

727. They would wait no longer.
On the 10th of April police made a move on his home. His young daughter Chanti answered the door of their small street corner brick built house whereby police stormed in, searching every room.
McCoy was handcuffed, evidence was seized, including typewriters which would later show the ribbon print of the hijacker's note that his wife had typed up. And of course, nearly all of the ransom money was found, tucked away in a back room closet.
Television news carried the images of him handcuffed and being led away by police.
Despite a mix-up in paperwork and warrants relating to the raid of his home, federal court proceedings were enacted swiftly as it was a plain-sailing case and a good opportunity for the FBI to be seen to get their man.
The trial took two months to pass and in June Richard Floyd McCoy Jr. was duly tried and convicted receiving a lengthy forty five year jail sentence. In just a short time the situation for he and his family had changed from difficult to devastating.

Chapter 31 The spirit of Richard

Some days after the much publicized McCoy trial came to a verdict, Kenny was sitting in his new fixer-upper home at Bonny Lake when Bernie dropped by for a visit.
They sat out front on the porch sipping cool beers.
"Have you done much on the house yet?" asked Bernie as he adjusted his deck chair.

His friend looked a bit off-color. "A little. Here and there. The kitchen is nearly finished at this point."
"I saw that, yeah. Oh it's lookin better already."
Kenny switched the subject to what was on his mind "Did you see the news about this McCoy guy?"
Bernie's eyes looked down as his expression changed. "Mmm. Wow . . . " He did not like to dwell on the grim forty five year sentence that was handed out. "The TV showed him being hauled up in handcuffs."
Kenny pursed his lips "Looks like he was all over the place. I mean he did not even hide the money or anything. What was he thinking of?"
McCoy's situation bothered both of them a little but they knew they had to keep calm. Over the last seven months they had been doing just fine. Still they had some degree of interest in the details of any imitator hijackers. Naturally.
Kenny continued "It bugs me that people are so simple and impulsive. It's not like we should have any monopoly on it but it seems guys are reckless when they try this on. Not to mention stupid. It looks like a matter of time before someone gets killed in one of those operations. Like innocent people."
Bernie drew a smirk on his face "You're hardly gonna preach to people about aviation safety, are ya? Like waggin the finger."

Kenny was not in the mood for it "That's not what I mean. It bugs me that people could get killed as a result of trying something we did originally."
Bernie tried to appeal for a change in conversation. "Well look you don't know this guy's situation so don't judge." He could sense what was making his companion so uncomfortable - his conscience. "Jesus you crack me up, ya

know that! You do what you did, months ago, without losing a wink of sleep. Cool as you like. And now you're worried about what someone else does. Something that's got nothin to do with you at all. Man, just when I was beginning to feel more relaxed about things."

* * * * *

In truth, Kenny would become more relaxed for the rest of his life, built on his dramatic, high-impact accomplishment. Bernie for his part would be less so, always being to some extent locked in a kind of restless loop.

While life appeared to continue smoothly for the two over the next couple of years, at least from the outside, from the inside of his gray prison cell Richard Floyd McCoy Jr. was in a very different world.

The shock and stigma of the long term prison sentence did not seem to affect him too much. Nor indeed did the new physical reality of the prison complex. He seemed immune to that and would always look to his tomorrows. The natural built-in spark of enthusiasm, that thing so valuable in humans having served him so well in the war zone in Asia would also serve him here. At least until he got out – by means of escape.

The getaway would be actually Richard's second since receiving his heavy sentence. He had previously escaped from Denver but was quickly captured before getting transferred to Pennsylvania.

It is said that we can tell what a country is really like if we look inside its prisons. In that respect, despite his heavy sentence, McCoy's new home in Pennsylvania's Lewisburg Penitentiary was, on a certain level, an outlier as national prisons go. It was not a place that seemed to bother him and he busied himself with energetically taking on chores. He had not lost his buoyant ways. He hit it off quite well with some of the inmates. In his section there were some guys who got decades for doing armed robberies. So he wondered if there might be a way to tap into them as a source of collaboration in his endeavors going forward.

There seemed to be a fairly relaxed atmosphere in the prison for the most part. An observer would say this was a well run outfit. Inmates were engaged in activities and experienced variety from day to day. Richard McCoy did not fancy spending his life there but as the months passed he was far from bored or depressed.

He would be bright and cheerful in all things and participated in whatever he could, using whatever services the prison had to offer. This would help him know and explore the layout of the place and expand the possibilities in his mind.

One of those services happened to be the dental service. On a visit there for a scheduled checkup he could not help noticing dental cement that was used to implant dentures for patients. It came in different packages, tins and containers but however it was shipped, mixable powder or paste, it looked immaculate when prepared. A brilliant white shiny plastic. "So impressive" he thought. What if it could be molded into the shape of a handgun? If you had enough of it.

A prominent inmate was Melvin Walker, a guy who was in for armed robbery. Richard had a good rapport with him and bumped into him at meals and elsewhere. He made a point of expressing his interest in the dental cement, if any of it could find its way to him with the help of some sticky fingers. While out taking exercise Richard explained to him

"It's in various cartons and tins. Different brand names I guess. There may be powder versions or paste. Whatever could be got. Not too much cause we don't want to raise any alarms. Just enough to be able to play around with. Ya know."

Melvin said he would do what he could to get some of the guys to sneak a little out. He had a liking for this lively go-getter. And besides he was curious to see what could become of dental paste.

After a few days the request bore some fruit. Richard received some dental paste powder. It was not in any tin but in a bag for the convenience of smuggling. He waited to get a moment in the bathroom and took the opportunity to wet it and mix it up. After it solidified it had morphed into a nice rectangular shaped solid. Better still, he was able to cut grooves and channels in it with the tip of a kitchen fork. This really engaged him so he got creative after a couple of days and worked on it when he could, beavering away in his cell. He wanted to create a diamond crisscross pattern for the handle in a typical pistol. A fine blade would have been better but he made do with what he had. Before long he was rewarded with a very impressive pattern. It was still white so he would need to address how to color it but the pattern was very realistic. The lump of dental cement was not big enough to pose as a gun handle but it showed what could be done. He would need to get some more of this magic paste.

The following day at the dinner table he kept it under the edge of his plate while sitting next to Melvin. Mid conversation he tapped it with his spoon to discreetly bring it to Melvin's attention. When he saw it his companion froze, then slouched back on his chair before continuing to chew, finishing down his food. He stretched casually, looking round the food hall before bringing his eyes back to the little prototype effort. Before leaving the table he shot Richard a look of acknowledgement.

Later, out walking, they got to talk about it.
"You've been busy. That was impressive."
Richard responded "Not bad. Pretty pleased. I need more of it."
"Was that what I thought it was?"
"It could be made to look like a fire arm, yeah."
Melvin had a half grin "Well now we need to put a campaign out for more of that sauce, don't we."
Richard was pleased to have someone row along with him. "Well, maybe don't exactly tell the guys what I am at. Not just yet. If they all took a notion the supplies might suddenly run very low at the surgeon. That could turn into a mess."
Melvin ventured to ask "You had me fooled with your craft work. Any idea what you might want to do with such an item?"
Richard was not so sure. He had broad plans about escaping but they were not really finalized.
As they turned around to go back indoors he gave his reply. "Don't know. Any ideas for an exit strategy?"
Melvin let him in on it there and then "There is a certain garbage truck service. Comes in all the time. The guys have been studying it real well. Those things are pretty big. A few fit, strong men might do well with one. We think it can be used to crash the gates."
This startled Richard. He was not yet ready for such drama but he knew he would be up for it. If his chance came he would take it. He was not going to say no.

As they were entering the main building with the usual large contingent of inmates Melvin was the last one to speak. "Well don't spread it. Don't mention it till you hear about it. And that piece you are working on could be very useful indeed."

Knowledge is power. Richard Floyd McCoy Jr. had figured out how to make a convincing gun while inside prison. As a result that unexpectedly got him into a tight group that had plans underway for an upcoming escape. He was as much an asset to the group as they were to him.

Before too long, more of the dental cement was delivered to him. He thought there should be plenty for his needs but he did not want to waste it. He had been grappling with the problem of color. All this casting came out in white. He was not exactly offering a dental service at this time but something darker. He needed it to be black.

He did a trial mix with some black ink he managed to extract from some pen refills he broke up. Messy but enough to give him a result. This helped to darken the dental cement a little so he would run with it in the hope that he could find some other way to stain the gun more when it was ready.

In order to have a casting for the barrel of a pistol, he needed some kind of elongated container. He decided to make do with a candy tin he got hold of from one of the other prisoners. This was five to six inches long and came with a lid. He filled it with paste and allowed it to set but before doing so he inserted half a plastic pen body that he had cut. This was to create a convincing hole at the inner sleeve of the barrel which some poor soul would eventually be looking down. After he retrieved it he had a nice blank section from which he could scrape and chisel away to create a convincing gun externally. He was well familiar with hand guns as were many Americans. He created the thumb grips and side slots and little dents here and there. He also rounded the edges to make it take the shape of a square barreled pistol. A bit on the short side but convincing.

Giving Melvin an update, he discussed the issue of effective dark staining for the pistol. It was decided to raid whatever resources were provided for art classes within the prison. Not much as it turned out but one or two of the guys who were artistic had been given ink bottle supplies by visiting relatives. For an inflated price they parted company with some of these.
Richard decided to roughen up some surfaces of the gun barrel, like the sides and top, in order to create a mat finish while the edges were left shiny. This would hopefully give a more machined look when the ink dried out.
There was one last problem, how to shape the trigger and trigger guard. If that did not look right it would be a give-away. So Richard decided to do a separate molding for that. A small slab of dental casting from which he would cut sections out of to create the trigger and guard. The trigger in the end looked like a shutter type – more like one on a kiddie's water pistol in shape as opposed to appearing hook shaped. He felt it would be fine as long as he got his finger in front of it.
So with the trigger section, handle and barrel all glued together and with the staining of a few coats of black ink it looked immaculate. Like something at a gun show.
Larry, a guy in his thirties and Joe, aged sixty were the two others who were in on the proposed jail break. They and

Melvin were working in the laundry section when Richard quietly showed them his very appealing gun which he was keeping in the rear inside of his belt line. Their surprised reaction was visible though they quickly managed to keep calm. It seemed to serve as a shot in the arm to everyone's confidence.

Richard had already made the point to Melvin that nobody was to be hurt at any moment in the escape. The threat at gunpoint would either work or it wouldn't. He was after all a Mormon and was not happy with the idea of physical assault. He hoped that his wish would be adhered to but he could not be sure.

With all the arrangements and preparations, the guys were hungry to make a move. The time for action came on the morning of the 10th of August, 1974.

The prison was perhaps too well organized and too regular for its own good. The Saturday morning routine was a good example. Dozens of inmates at a time would be released to get out in the morning air in half-hour sessions. With good weather there would be a lively feeling around the grounds. Plenty going on, including routine garbage collection service.

The four guys had it well prepared. At one of the collection points in a lane way between prison blocks they waited until the driver was out of the truck and at the back, busy with the operation of the large bin loader.

With the engine running Richard and Joe quickly climbed into the cockpit with Joe at the wheel. As soon as the driver heard the truck going into gear with the hydraulic trash ram stopping he came up front to see the problem. Opening the door, he was met with a gun which Richard was now pointing at him from the passenger's seat. This caused him to step back in shock and surprise while at the very same second the truck pulled away. Instantly, both Larry and Melvin jumped on the rear running board of the truck as it zipped down the lane way.

A second later it had turned a corner and the two had climbed in the back with the garbage.

Though it only took seconds to get the back gate of the compound it seemed like ages in the heat of the moment. With no visible or audible signs of any alarm being raised, they could see prisoners out walking in the area off to their right in the distance where the open field was. Finally, they reached the rear perimeter gate amid an arch way with still no guards visible anywhere.

Richard spoke up amid the tension "Go go go, NOW!"

Joe at the wheel fed it as much gas as he could. With considerable speed built up for a large heavy vehicle it was sure to do some damage but nobody really knew if it would actually succeed in breaking the large gate with its deadlocks and bolts but they were bracing for impact. The impact was felt by all four men but the sheer momentum burst the gates with a deafening crack causing the windshield to smash. The crash also resulted in the truck losing most of its speed even though it had won out against the gate.

Richard yelled at the driver "Were through – we're through. Keep going!!" And so they sped out the country lane.

They had arranged to head directly for the hills which were not far from Lewisburg. The whole area on the way looked decidedly sleepy with no police sirens evident anywhere. They did not know how long it would take for the prison authorities to wake up and respond but every second here was vital.

Very quickly they reached a wooded area with lots of trees and knew it was time to abandon the truck. Joe stopped up under a tree so as not to be seen from the air and everyone climbed out. The boys in the back were now looking and smelling like garbage. They would need to put some distance between themselves and the abandoned truck – and quickly.

After crossing fields, hiding and gathering their thoughts they knew they had to get out of the zone fast and so they hijacked a passing car at gunpoint, throwing out the two occupants. The exit from the county was made by the four in a green sedan before the police search could get properly underway. They had won the day.

* * * * *

Successful escape from Lewisburg prison was thanks to the element of surprise and the sharp focus of the group of four, not to mention the ingenuity of Richard McCoy with his mock gun. But now that they were out, nobody had a plan. They managed to go to some safe houses in other states, change cars, get clothes and money to help them on their way.

Before long they had split up and went their various ways. McCoy accompanied Melvin and soon the two made their way to Virginia beach where they were staying in a house together.

On the evening of November 9th when the two were returning home three plain-clothes police officers approached the house. Realizing this, McCoy opened fire – this time with a real gun. He was killed by the returning fire. As he lay in a pool of blood Melvin Walker fled the scene in his car but was quickly caught by the FBI agents in

pursuit.
What can we say of Richard Floyd McCoy Jr. and about his powers of estimation of those around him? He was able to conceive and craft clever ideas that fooled authorities yet would not take care enough to cover his tracks. Might it be the signature of someone who was half passionate and half dying?

William Shakespeare once noted how sharp and bitter it is to have a thankless child. But how much sharper than a serpent's tooth it must be to have a thankless country.
The lack of acknowledgment returned from the unfeeling machine that had become his nation had left him mortally wounded. His heart was broken long before the bullet killed him.
America, yet again, had created, then destroyed.

Chapter 32 The crime of all seasons

Gravity is a bitch! No doubt about it. She'd kill you in an instant.
Make one wrong move on a fold-up step ladder while changing a light bulb and you run the risk of having a bad day. Take the wrong step from twice that elevation and you could easily be in a wheelchair from a broken spinal cord - paralyzed and devastated. Make that ledge over fifty feet in height and it would increasingly be a case of dear oh dear oh dear . . . Gravity would exact her toll not just sometimes but always, regardless of what day it is or where our

sentiment is at. So exact that you could even engineer machines to harness an entire precision mechanism to her. And some people did.

Karma on the other hand is an altogether more nebulous creature. Supposedly operating along some social justice narrative whereby the will of the people over time gets served as a response to acts of wrong-doing or infamy. She had recorded some serious screw-ups in history where she did not deliver and the terrible injustice went unpunished forever – Stalin in Russia and Chairman Mao in China each being recorded as a notorious fiasco. Not among her finest moments.

But once in a while her mechanisms would come into line and function properly. The public conscience of the day would perform correctly and out would come a result that would be endlessly pleasing to all irrespective of any legal approval. The people's sense of justice would get served for a change. Perfectly.

Our case in point, one Andrew Jackson. He is the guy whose face is on every twenty dollar bill. That guy.

Jackson in his day, did not want equality or currency. He distrusted paper money, as slave owner and later corrupt president in the White House. Bloodthirsty to the last, his treatment of the native Red Indians of America was an historic disgrace.

Yet, whose face did Kenny get to look at every day? None other than Jackson himself. He now had thousands of copies of Jackson reprinted on all his bank notes and would have to look at it for the rest of his days as he paid his way. A lofty elitist in the back pocket of an unlikely laid-back rake like Kenny – literally. Strange bedfellows, a chap with huge entitlement in contrast to a guy who had to fake and forge a better life, not so he could have palatial luxury and privilege but just in order to simply exist.

Talk about coming full circle.

But there's more to tell. It seems that Karma might have slipped up on this occasion too.

The very people who put this scoundrel on the twenty dollar bills were not really like Kenny, they were more like Andrew Jackson.

Laid back or not, you don't pull off a thoughtful and colorful stunt as Kenny did in the winter of 1971 without knowing a thing or two.

More than most, he was aware that the dark side of the USA was the background radiation of American life. People lived with it without properly digesting what it all meant or what was actually going on. That is exactly how the country achieved self-preservation: by people not properly understanding it. Still, folks invariably had some sense of it now and then. At some time or other they saw the real America and probably denied it because it did not fit the official narrative. Or even their own.

Of course most people were involved in the system one way or another through their careers, a mortgage, a family and all the rest. When you already had a stake in the game you did not complain about it. But when you were at the bottom and felt totally victimized as Kenny had been, you were delighted to rebel. And, if for whatever reason, you came to know about things beyond your domain, you might at least object.

State lies were going unchecked due in part to the brevity of the human lifespan. People were busy with their lives and seldom had any in-depth knowledge of state affairs. To ensure this, popular media such as Radio, TV and Newspapers were all too often rigged and pitched in order to reflect the government narrative. Even after what happened to JFK the establishment would conveniently pick a date far into the future to release vital reports to the public detailing central information critical to the event. That release date would not be for decades to come, long after people can likely remember well enough to enact a valid public inquiry. People at an individual level were not stupid but you don't have to be dumb to do dumb things. Being busy with your well-intended humble life would do the trick just fine from the viewpoint of those at the top. Not to mention the deliberate practice of focusing on distraction stories in order to avert public attention.

Kenny had seen this with the Vietnam war where he himself had been happy to avoid the draft. The government had drummed up reasons and 'the need' to attack a race on the other side of the world, savagely killing men, women and children and employing Agent Orange chemicals to enforce misery for god knows how long on those who survived. President Eisenhower had warned America in 1960 about becoming the Military Industrial Complex. War was big business and it looked to Kenny like it was here to stay.

In 1910, the biggest bankers in the USA which included J.P. Morgan made their way by train to a secret meeting in Jekyll Island, Georgia. They knew that, given time, the federal government would come under pressure to properly address the taxation of financial institutions. On top of that, there had been the 1907 bank panic or 'run on the banks' so they could feed into the public agenda of creating more order in the banking system. In this way, when it reached the public arena it could be paraded as a progressive entity for the good of all while in reality it would be serving another purpose. Known as the Federal Reserve Act it essentially allowed the big banks to become the master of the mint for America. The emerging proposal was passed onto the US congress and it was rubber-stamped into Federal law in 1914. These financial corporations had in effect landed a permanent seat in government. The whole idea of a republic as outlined by the American Constitution was that the government would not allow such a thing yet they had completely broken that rule and nobody seemed to notice. Because, of course, they were too busy in their everyday lives.

A few months previous in August of 1971, while Kenny and Bernie were planning their little stunt, the nation suffered what would later be called 'the Nixon Shock'. This meant that now the United States Dollar was not tied to anything and apparently came about as a solution to mounting problems for the American economy and offering an opportunity for the authorities to reset the situation. The fact that countries like France were also asking the US to return their Gold bullion was no doubt causing stirrings in the world economy. So the FEDs had behaved just about anyway they wanted with no international consequence.

By going off the gold standard he suspected the government would still be stashing gold while they generated as much US Dollars as they liked. One currency for the rich, another for the poor. This enabled the Feds to commit two forms of plunder unchecked by the American people. On the one hand they could still trick around with Gold reserves while on the other hand they could print dollars as they liked. The Federal Reserve was never audited by the public. Nobody knew what went on in there behind those stately walls with time honored plaques, much less be asked to vote and give public approval for the next half billion dollars to be generated. Back in Roosevelt's time the federal government banned citizens from owning gold supposedly to combat the 'fundamental dis-equilibrium' issues it faced. Yes . . . something like that. Whatever story the authorities put out would be propagated by the media and gradually be accepted as fact with no proper rigorous public examination. "In God We Trust" was on every banknote. That is what America was becoming – no verification needed, just trust.

Worse still, there was a correlation between runaway creation of money by governments and horrible wars resulting in deadly conflict. Every state-level war criminal in history had access to huge finance. Mass money results in mass murder.

No doubt, all that minting of currency would mean the dollar (including Kenny's tricky twenty dollar bills) would decrease in value over time. He did not understand fully what the Nixon Shock would mean for the long-term fate of the dollar but he was absolutely certain that he did not trust anyone in Washington. In his view, almost everything they said or did at government level entailed lies and deceit. In fact, they had such a long history of deceit that it seemed they hardly remembered how to do things honestly. Compounded layers of lies become increasingly harder to cover up.

Whatever had happened to all that Spanish Gold? The plunder of South America. It made its way to the elites of Europe – give or take the occasional ship-wreck, one of which had a recovered mother-lode that was used to start the Bank Of England. But the Spanish people never did feel the benefit. By the 1930s they were impoverished and plunged into civil war. Kenny was not so sure if America would go in a much different direction in the end.

It was not that Kenny Christiansen was being complacent now that he had all this money. But it seemed to shift his perspective since he was more relaxed due to the new situation. Those dollars were vital in basic provision for himself but not much else. He wondered if he had not been successful with the hijacking, would he feel the same. He knew that even if the police were to suddenly come knocking on his door to have him nailed and jailed, he would forever enjoy bragging rights for doing something imaginative. Even in prison. In a sense this was the jewel in his crown – his proof of something that no one would ever take away. His creation, his accomplishment. His art.
Staying free and undiscovered would, of course, be the icing on the cake. He had to continue working on that. And part of the effort was to maintain secrecy thereby not having immediate recognition by sharing his past with someone, however tempting that might be over time. To many that restriction might be a source of agony but to Kenny it was the lynch-pin of his success. The very vehicle which had got him to where he was and transformed his life.
But the precious Yankee Dollar which he and Bernie had helped themselves to was only precious to the normal hardworking people of the world. To the super-rich and elites, those who were in power and quite above the law, it was merely a construct to enslave the public. A kind of joke to those at the top while they toyed with society.
When the public had allowed itself to become conformist to everything, its expectation levels became trampled by endless inaction. The battle was already over – or rather, would never begin. And he felt there was nothing he could

ever do with that nugget of wisdom.
While Kenny had done something exceptional in the way of getting ahead, the same ability to do so helped him understand that the self-seeking short-sighted greed that drove the masses would also rail-road them away from questioning government and that in turn would lead to dark places. Not everything in Nature makes good.

Chapter 33 Enter Tena Barr

What do you give a man who has everything? An early morning call maybe?
Kenny stepped out of bed and across the room to open a window overlooking the steep hill at the back of the house. The sunlight poured magnificently over the land and the air filled his lungs. Combined with the scent of the wooden house it was so sweet. He raised his two arms to yawn and stretched and smiled broadly, thinking how heavenly all of this was. However long it lasted.
He had never found himself wanting the usual trappings of money. The yacht or the Manhattan apartment or the lifestyle of those on Wall Street. Or all the hi-strung posturing that goes with those types of people. That stuff would only bore him. That was fine by their standards but it was crap by his.
No no. To impress our boy you had to be much better than that. It would take the expansive blue sky, the fresh air, the song of the birds, the changing of the seasons. And the

simple ability just to witness it all, often referred to as life. He was a creature of Mother Earth and he had fallen back into her open arms . . . at 9.81 meters per second squared.

Today was a bit special. This was the calendar date of Thanksgiving 1976, November 24th – 5 years to the day since he had taken that glorious fall. It was an extra broad smile he wore this morning. Today was the day that the statute of limitations was due to expire. This meant that he was free from prosecution for that particular crime-related skydive. He could even go into the FBI headquarters or throw a press conference and tell all if he wanted, without consequence. At least on paper it would hold up in legal terms. Not that himself or Bernie would ever be so stupid to do such a thing. They did not trust faculties of power at all. At any level. Not as much as a regional office, federal outpost or police dog.
In reality, the main significance of this five year mark was that police investigations were essentially set to die off.

He wandered into the kitchen and was thinking about breakfast when he decided he would first check the mail as a matter of routine. Opening his mailbox he found a letter from Northwest Orient Airlines addressed to himself, K.P. Christiansen. He did not see too much of them these days, just enough to keep the job on paper and certainly not for the money. Enough to be seen to make it pay his miserable bitty mortgage that he took out with Sea First Bank.
When he opened it, he found a letter of congratulations. He was now twenty five years with the airline. He grinned to himself "You don't say . . . " The letter went on to give details of an upcoming large get-together party that was being organized for staff from all departments, company-

wide. It was to be held in Minnesota. He would be sure to stay well clear of such gatherings. It might be safer for him to be absent or even fired than to show up at the wrong end of the airline.

The danger of him being recognized was not entirely receded. He and Bernie had discussed this often. For his comrade who no longer worked on an airline and had not actually done the hijacking it wasn't such a problem but for Kenny it was not to be taken lightly. He had made a point of not looking anything like he had in his disguise on that night five years ago. He never wore the toupee since then, usually sporting a cap instead. But he was also aware that airlines often changed and shared staff from one company to the next. From airports to airplanes he had to be really careful. So despite his fondness for aviation, every day he spent away from that environment was a good day.

As he was preparing some breakfast he leaned over to switch a TV channel when he came upon a mid-sentence end to a report -

"- because of this 11th hour John Dow ruling by the court for the state of Oregon."

There was an image shown of the D.B. Cooper fugitive. The commentary continued in the report.

"The hijacking happened almost five years ago to the day. So this last minute application by Law Enforcement in the courts means that a five year extension is to be added to the statute of limitations for this notorious case."

Kenny was startled. He stopped what he was doing and froze for half a minute. He soon got the scoop from the other channels. This news was unexpected and bad. The Champagne would have to be put on ice . . . or poured down the drain.

Aside from the disappointment he felt a little alarmed. His mind was restless as he paced the house in silence trying to analyze what this meant. Did it mean the FBI were beaten and made this move because they were out of ideas? Or did they think they were near a breakthrough and just needed a little more time? It could mean either though he suspected it was desperation on their part.

He was not super confident either way. But he had scanned all articles about the case whenever he could and he got a feeling they were really grappling with Cooper. There had been confusion from the early days of the investigation. Mix ups in communication with the air crew. He read about them searching in the wrong place, some forty miles to the east of where he jumped. Then there seemed to be confusion between FBI labs over the handling of physical evidence taken from the 727 that night. Apparently it passed through four different labs and there was some suggestion that some of it had been lost, in particular the eight cigarette butts he had left behind on the plane. That kind of half-ass goofing around by police departments did not surprise him. He could well believe it. At the same time they were capable of ploys or setting some kind of bait in the public. Some kind of trap. He always felt that for he and Bernie to do absolutely nothing in reaction to D.B. Cooper news would likely be best practice. This should surely be the case now too. Still, it was unsettling.

At the same time, the proof of the pudding was in the eating. They had not come breaking down his door as yet. Not like with all the other cases, including McCoy who ended up dead. And as far as he could see there was nothing out of place in his system. Nothing to attract attention. Both he and Bernie had been hard-working for decades. No lavish lifestyle and in his case a mortgage which he could,

if anyone asked, just about manage from his lousy job in NWO. His life had after all been a hard graft – twenty five years with that crumby crew. It all added up to a very strong alibi.
After a while he lightened up. He could not help but laugh a little at this game of cat and mouse with the FBI. For sure they would be sore losers. That might explain a lot of it.

Being Thanksgiving he made his way over to Bernie and Margie for dinner. Throughout the evening he was processing the news in his head but could not tell whether Bernie had heard it. Since Kenny was staying over, the next morning he got a chance to quietly bring it up with his buddy. The latter had caught the item on TV but was not previously aware of the statutory issue.
While they were both calm outwardly Kenny did not want to stir panic. He knew Bernie was not exactly like him when it came to such things but he was certainly more relaxed than he had been five years ago. Time had been a good healer.

As the days wore on he thought about things more and a germ of an idea formed. At first it seemed flimsy but there seemed to be something about it that appealed to him. It gradually took some shape in his mind.
While out walking up the back of his house, the land which he had purchased from the gleeful Grimes, he decided to go and check the place where he had buried some money near the foot of one of the many trees in that forested hilly area. It had been hidden for a couple of years now. He had abandoned his beloved pipework storage trick being concerned about metal detectors used casually by hikers or anyone else. So he had opted for plastic bags to keep a few

thousand dollars. To his surprise and dismay, he found that some water had leaked into the bag and some dollars had deteriorated. Not too many but a few dozen of those twenty dollar bills. Stolen money burns a hole in your pocket . . . so to speak. In this case it had rotted and looked fairly eaten round the edges. Easy come easy go.

Kenny wondered how long it would take money to rot like that. From what he saw it was clear that two or three years could do a lot.

What if he could plant some of the loot in order to have it found in public? In the event it was turned in this would mean Law Enforcement might conclude that Cooper did not make good with the money. Maybe he did not make it out of the woods alive. They were forever putting out statements in the news media that the fugitive was probably dead. But of course there had been no body found. Too often the public were so stupid as to not realize that finding a body was kind of important to support such a narrative. Especially as they had combed the area so much immediately after the event. It was not that any one person was inherently stupid but by not studying in depth a particular topic they allowed themselves to be hoodwinked by the authorities.

But this was America and the FBI were at times equally lacking in critical thinking so they would be happy to use it as an explanation. At least on occasions. Over time it might get accepted as fact. The FBI would have more than one log to kindle in the public relations fire.

Kenny could not provide a body or dead corpse but he could provide cash. Maybe a substantial sum like a few thousand dollars that would be verified as being part of the ransom. This would be touted as a failure or at least partial failure of the hijacking. That might soften things at the FBI or even serve to divert attention away from more accurate lines of pursuit.

But planting money in a public area needed to have some more tangible benefit for him. The very act of doing so would put him at risk of being caught and at any rate would increase the body of evidence for police. So where was the advantage if it did not result in the law being sent off in the wrong direction? To the wrong end of the woods as it were. He felt it was possibly a good idea but how could he round it out and make it work?

The answer for Kenny was to come from water.

While he was idly gazing at the maps showing the stretch from Seattle down to Portland he realized he had forgotten all about the Columbia river. This caused him to sit upright and he started thinking hard.

He remembered this was a busy place with shipping moving up and down the river and choppy waves slapping onto the water's edges quite briskly. A large river, deep and wide. If some money was found there along the banks it would provide very strong evidence that the hijacker had landed in the river. With parachute entanglement, dark of night and the sheer cold, it would surely be a problem to get out alive, let alone bring the ransom with him. After drowning, the body would decompose and perhaps be dragged out to sea by a passing vessel. The tragedy of the parachutist who hit the drink. A very compelling story!

Water indeed, the giver and taker of life . . .

To decide where exactly on the map to insert such a plant of cash was another matter. The Columbia river was wide and long.

If the money – even a small amount of it - was found anywhere along its banks washed up it would have the same effect of convincing the police that Cooper landed in the river. No matter which bank, really. The supposition would prevail that it was washed up or down the river gradually. It would be enough to allow the FBI to conclude that they pretty much knew what happened to Cooper. At least in the public arena.

At the same time it would be a substantial distraction for them. Surely some officers would be convinced that it provided the root explanation. It should catch on.

Looking at the original Victor 23 route that the 727 took for the jump, the main part of the Columbia ran alongside it but to the west. But not too far to the west. The parachute could conceivably have drifted over easily, especially in a storm or in difficulty.

This way, law enforcement would likely get its thinking colored and crossed, something that was not lost on Kenny.

In the new year and throughout early Spring he took to his car to explore the main strand of the river along where the 501 ran south. With some checking he came to the conclusion that the most attractive beach was on the east bank. The map showed a curve on it. It was an attractive place where people wandered for a stroll in summertime. Known as Tena Barr, this spot had a better chance of the cash being found. It would be the best option.

Kenny explored the ins and outs of setting up this ruse. He did not simply want to toss the money into the river near the beach. Instead he would bury it so that it would be some time before it was found. That way the cash would decompose a bit, giving the impression it was there for a long time. He could use some of the already decomposed bills he found out back.

Taking a closer look at the bills he wondered if he might give them a little help on the path toward looking aged and corroded. Somehow. What if he cut some edges away from the perimeter of some of the bills then rough up the edges a bit? This should make them appear shrunken and hopefully withered by the time they came into the hands of a passer-by.

Kenny experimented by cutting a few bills round the edges with scissors along a random perimeter. He decided they were not jagged enough looking. So he took a hacksaw blade to the edge. This achieved the desired effect but took too long to do. So he then tried it on a bundle of bills. He was mindful of leaving a clear saw-tooth print that might give the game away if examined by law enforcement. It seemed to work fairly well. So to speed things up he decided to separate each bill out of the bundle, trimming the edge off first in a pattern that duplicated the edge of the first bill he had cut. With that done he could reassemble the bundle and take the hacksaw to the edges of the pack, gently introducing a frayed appearance to the bundle before reinstating the elastic band. This was a protracted business but after a while he felt enough was enough. Nature, he hoped, would do the rest.

Now was a good time of the year to activate this little scheme. Before the long stretch came into the days of summer. Things would be quiet and he would go visit the sanded river banks on the cusp of darkness. He would wait up in his car near the beach for a while until everything seemed still.

He decided to take three bundles of the twenty dollar bills

which included the damaged ones. That was a total of six thousand. Just to make it more realistic he took a few of the fresher dollars out of one of the bundles, just at the end, to make it look like they might have slipped away in the river before drifting into the sandy banks. The elastic bands were all intact on the bundles.

He placed all three into the inner lining of his overcoat as well as a small, single-handed shovel trowel that he used for digging weeds in his garden. That fitted perfectly into the inner pocket.

As it was an evening in mid-week, at a couple of hours before darkness it was time for a drive. He got to the entrance area to Tena Barr off the 501 in nice time. There was an unofficial car park loosely arranged with gravel here and there. He saw two other cars parked up. Nobody in sight. It was time to take a walk and get some air. He pulled a small folding deck chair out of the trunk of his car. A bit undersized but he didn't mind. It had a canvas carrying strap so he slung it over his shoulder. And off he strolled down toward the strand. With his deck chair, dollars in his pocket, cigarettes and a can of soda, he was all set to see off the remaining daylight!

He saw a small family playing around at the other end so he headed the opposite direction from them, due north. He set a completely casual pace as you would when you were out for a stroll. The evening was not really one for sitting around, hence the scarcity of people. In terms of temperature it felt a bit raw. It was perfect – not so much the criminal returning to the scene of the crime as with some of the loot instead. Being Kenny, he felt proud of his alternative approach.

As he strolled along his eyes were peeled for suitable possible sheltered dunes where it was easy to bury money and maybe obscure his presence as it got darker. After a bit, near the end of the strand he saw something that he fancied. As the water line curved out before coming to an end there was a slight cavern in the sand as it rose on the beach, being a little hilly. Lovely – less digging. He decided that looked good for later. But now it was time to move back down a bit and pick a nice place to sit and observe across the Columbia river.

After a couple of minutes there he was seated, relaxed with his cigarette and can of soda. The boats were moving up-river in the distance. There was still an hour to go till darkness fell. Nice.

A little while later, with the place to himself and the light levels going down it really looked like time to make a move. He grabbed the fold-up chair and stretched his legs, moving close to his chosen spot. As it was in full view now he studied it better throwing away what remained of his cigarette.

It looked like a steep part of the river bank, like a miniature waterfall with a pool of water which had washed from the river and got lodged.

He figured he could quickly make it more cavernous with his little garden scoop. Then it would be easy to scrape down some sand from the dune around it to cover it over.

Moving his chair slightly closer he sat there another while till it was almost dark. Just enough for him to see what he was doing. Time to act. Out came the shovel as he started scooping. He had been wary of someone seeing him from a ship in the distance but that possibility was now eliminated. Once again, the darkness was a friend.

In no time he had dug a narrow channel just the width of

the little shovel that went back two feet into the dune. Enough space for the bundles. Dropping them in he heard a little splash. They had hit a tiny puddle of water. Great. The channel was well covered over in what seemed like less than a minute. As he worked with the tiny garden tool he made sure not to pat anything down. With some rain and wind it should soon look quite normal. Bye bye Dollars!

Making his way back to the car it was now all silhouettes. Not a soul nor a sound around.

As he drove home it felt so strange throwing away six grand. Easy come easy go. Except in this case it was not easily obtained despite the means used to get it. Still he looked at it as a chance to, perhaps, secure his future, not to mention occupy the police for a while. It might even add to the Cooper folklore.

He would not tell Bernie about it. Hell no. Bernie would be out looking to dig up the cash himself if he knew about this. The man who could never have enough money . . .

Kenny did not know if he would ever hear about it again. Maybe it would be found next summer though he had his doubts as it was well buried. But he did not really know. Maybe next year. Who knew? Only time would tell.

Chapter 34 The sands of time

After the events of 1976 the dust settled once again on the Cooper case, at least in the eyes of the public. As time marched on there were no news items on TV or Newspaper about the crime and certainly not along the lines of any breakthrough developments by the FBI. This led to Kenny feeling increasingly that law enforcement were cold on the trail in terms of getting to him. That of course was his hope and Bernie's. But they had been surprised before. If they had needed a wake-up call they got it. Once was quite enough. As such, it was just about as close to actually being found out as they would ever want to be.

Meantime, life had been comfortable for the two. Bernie continued to work away at his job in the boat company while his comrade would be more laid back attending his official job at NWO only on the odd day when he was called up, which was exactly the way he wanted it. He was enjoying life and celebrating it much more now. As far as anyone was concerned he was getting by and scraping his mortgage repayments. In conversation with anyone he would always comment on how the airlines paid very well.
Kenny was still great friends with Bernie's wife Margie and they saw plenty of each other. As time went on they seemed to adore each other's company ever more. As for her husband, he seemed to be always away with his work and whatever else kept him occupied. Certainly it was not his marriage that was in focus as far as Kenny could make out. He had sensed the increasing drift between the couple ever since the time of the hijacking, really. He did not see too much of his old acquaintance these days except on occasions such as Thanksgiving or the odd holiday meet-up.
The nineteen seventies turned into the eighties and it waved perhaps a vague flag in Kenny's mind. It was just a reminder that he was moving continuously away from that memorable dot on the timeline that changed his life. Like something in his rear-view mirror that he hoped would fade

to dust. It did not trouble him so much as being a shadow that followed him. It was part and parcel of his success. It came with the territory.

On the tenth of February Kenny was idly turning the dial on his radio when he caught the tail end of a conversation that gave him a stir.

"- whatever that money found near the river turns out to be."

The radio bulletin moved onto a different news item and reporter and he found himself scrambling through the channels to get the full story. After searching extensively through television channels there was not a trace of this on the airwaves. He tried newspapers also, heading to town in his car to catch any headline he could. Nothing.

The following day there was nothing either. This left him wondering if he was going crazy. Yet what he heard was unmistakable. He was sure.

One day later, on February twelfth it became clear with the news swamping the airways.

An eight year old boy had discovered the money in the sandbanks of Tena Barr while on vacation with his family. Brian Ingram had been searching the strand for some wood to make a campfire. He came across three bundles of withered cash and after some debate it was decided to turn it over to the police.

Kenny soaked up all the television coverage like a sponge, taking in the piecemeal images that were being broadcast of a few banknote samples. Some of them were totally blackened with the others in bad shape, while the details were slow to come through for the first time as he went around the channels. All were similar. But they did reveal that the FBI had confirmed that the money seemed to be part of recovered loot from the Cooper Hijacking. This explained the delay in the details for the last two days. They no doubt had to check the serial numbers on the bills.

Of course with this realization by law enforcement the need quickly arose to move an investigation team into the site along the river banks. In everybody's mind there was a chance of finding more loot so police were anxious to secure the area. Trenches were dug and even geologists were brought in specially to study the sandbar in order to advise the people in forensics.

A newspaper article was saying that the top specialist employed was a geologist from Portland State University by the name Dr. Leonard Palmer. He was going to study layers on the sandbanks to determine how long the money had been lying buried there before it was found. This gave Kenny a chill and a bout of nerves. Like he was being hunted. He had great respect for people in such scientific disciplines. He knew how they could deliver and had a feeling that he might be found out. But after a time logic prevailed as did tranquility. They would have a long way to go to connect it to him. It was not like the money was planted last night. These little worrying scares were often the cost of progress. Scary but fun.

One person who did not wear the scare thing too well was Bernie. Within a couple of days of the news breaking, he appeared at Kenny's door – looking scared. He had not called round in quite a long time. Now, he looked rattled and uneasy. Worse than he had ever appeared at any time in the past. For the first time there was an unfriendly aspect to his countenance. He did not look happy.

Kenny could read his old chum like a book. Well, maybe.

"Do ya know why I'm here?" He looked edgy as he stepped

toward Kenny who was now sitting on the sofa.
Kenny gave him a half zombie look as he opened his mouth to insert an unlit cigarette.
"Ah yeah."
"What the hell is the story with the money the police found?"
He sensed that Bernie was hunting for answers. On the one hand he did not like feeling vulnerable to law enforcement. On the other he no doubt thought he was missing out on money that Kenny might have stashed away.
Kenny saw the funny side and blew out his cigarette smoke with his huge smile showing laughter in his eyes.
"An investment in our future!"
His comrade looked puzzled. His facial expression froze.
Kenny continued "Sit down, buddy. Relax. I planted it."
Bernie plonked onto the chair with his jaw fully dropped. He looked like he was gasping for air. He tried to speak but the words did not come out. The second attempt got some traction.
"You what?"
Kenny explained "About six grand as I recall." He relayed the full account of how and when along with his reasoning behind it. After speaking at length he wrapped it up by saying "It was worth a shot to see if they will take the bait. The FBI are so corrupt and narrated and propagandized when it suits them. They are likely to conclude that the hijacker died in the river and his body washed out to sea or enthralled by a passing vessel. This will save them face with the public. Even if half the officers involved feel that way it will put wind in our sails. So let's see."
At this point Bernie was climbing down from his high-tension position.
Kenny continued "And anyway, It came out of my pocket,

not yours. I am happy to foot the bill. It's on me."
Bernie lit a cigarette and with a half stern expression made his point "Look if there is something you should tell me – like this - something I need to know . . . then now would be a real good time."
Kenny looked at him squarely "Well Bernie, you above all people are entitled to say that. And to question this as much as you want. I said after this event nearly a decade ago, that I was grateful for your participation and that I would stay loyal to our cause in this thing. And I meant it. Other than this revelation today there is nothing else to report to you. You now know everything that's relevant about the entire case and nothing has changed about our strategy. Nor should it."
He went on "Given that you might not be the type of guy who would take this tactic, I don't blame ya for coming round to query it."
The inquisition pressed on for a bit. "Why didn't you tell me about it anyway?"
"Well, I didn't want to bother you with it – especially if it was not going to be found. I figured it would not be your thing, really. It was my little experiment. And I still think it will pay us dividends."
His friend seemed to be taking it on-board. It did after all cost Kenny to try this out with the police. A financial venture that Bernie himself would never have entertained. He knew it was not his style. Six grand for an experiment? Not in a million years.

After some days had passed and with more media regurgitation of the Tena Barr money matter, the FBI put out another picture of some of the better surviving ransom notes. This caused Kenny to cringe quite a bit. The embattled bank notes had been neatly stacked and to him they were all too familiar as he could see evidence of obvious human intervention. It was clear where he had cut the borders off the bills and it was a bit too orderly looking for nature's random erosion. He had to bite his lip at the way he had not been meticulous enough. To his eyes, being on the inside of the hoax, the problem was gaping. It suggested a contrived interfering hand. He felt sure that at least some investigating officers were likely to share the same view.

He thought about it some more and remembered that many would prefer to push the other narrative that the hijacker failed in his attempt when he hit the water. In the fog of public opinion this planted seed would do just fine. It just needed time.

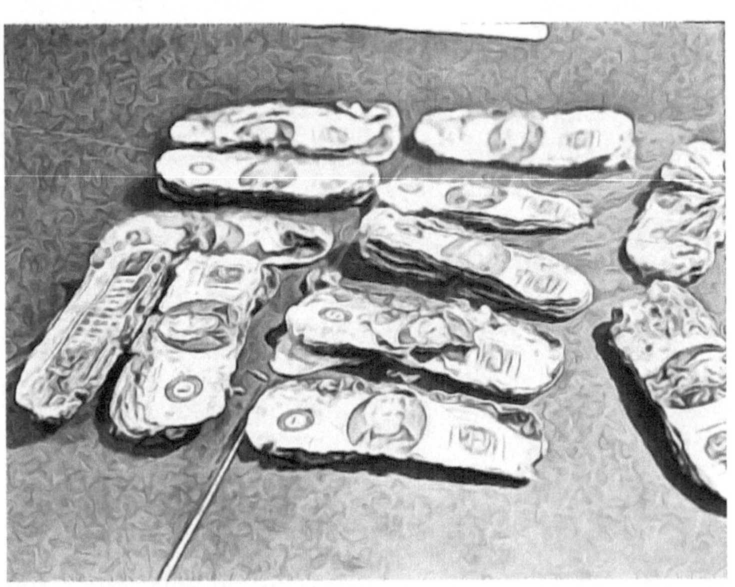

And time it got.

Dr. Palmer's scientific report was duly published and detailed his findings on the sand layers that his team had studied at Tena Barr. His conclusion was that the money was found in a layer on top of that produced during a 1974 dredging of the area that had taken place. The money would have been washed up by wave action of the waters probably a year or two after the river clean-up. This he claimed would account for the relatively good condition of some of the bank notes.

Following that, some commentators offered the opinion that the money survived so well because it had spent a long time being protected in the hijacker's bag before eventually drifting loose and making its way to the sandbank. Well exactly. Just what Kenny was thinking too.

Days later, on February 24th, Kenny stood at the newspaper stand in a large magazine store doing one of his favorite activities – browsing through the various publications. He came across a familiar face mid-page in the Chicago Times. Agent Ralph Himmelsbach was photographed in his office smiling, with hands raised pointing to his shelves full of D.B. Cooper files. Kenny had remembered him being interviewed years earlier when he was put at the head of the investigation for the bureau. He was interested in what he had to say so he bought the newspaper.

The article was titled -

Retiring FBI Man may not get his man – hijacker D.B Cooper.

The first half was mainly a recap of the case outlining what happened. Over a thousand people had been investigated and all ruled out as viable suspects. Then came the juicy stuff.

Asked whether the hijacker was dead or alive, Himmelsbach replied: "I have not reached a conclusion. Investigators do not have the luxury of reaching a conclusion . . . "

But barely pausing, the agent then described what facts were known about the case as if attempting to establish a case that it was highly improbable that the hijacker survived.

He noted that Cooper jumped from the jetliner on a "freezing, windy, snowy night" in a light business suit, and that his actions and comments aboard the plane suggested that he was not an experienced parachutist and "makes me think he didn't know what he was doing."

"I felt on the night that it happened he had only a 50-50 chance of getting away with it," the agent added, "and as time went on I began to feel his chances were significantly less than that."

The discovery of the ransom money last week "leads me to assume more and more to the possibility that he didn't make it."

The agent said that, based on the tattered condition of the money, he felt "morally certain" that the money had been exposed ever since the hijacking rather than having been buried by the hijacker, and added "This lends support to the conclusion – it doesn't prove it - that it is likely he didn't make it and he is lying somewhere near where he fell."

Still, Himmelsbach acknowledged that only the discovery of a body that can be identified positively as that of Cooper, or conclusive evidence that he survived, will end the mystery.

"Its ironic isn't it?" he asked "I spent thousands of hours on this case; it's taken a significant part of my life for eight

years, and here it is – the first and only concrete bit of information comes only 17 days before I retire."

All this gave Kenny cause to chuckle as he thought to himself "Thank you Ralph. I knew you'd see it my way."
It was not that others in the FBI could not hold a different opinion but he felt that the first tangible evidence to, literally, come ashore in eight years would help to blow a favorable wind in his back. With Himmelsbach retiring the sands of time were serving him nicely. And the sand at Tena Barr had certainly done its job.

Chapter 35 Kenny dead

Throughout the nineteen eighties Kenny lived his sweet life almost entirely as he wanted. A man of leisure for the most part. Living in comfort in his humble ordinary house at Bonny Lake he loved every second of what nature had in store with her simple surroundings, going for walks in the woods and above all, spending his time for his own use. Many would have asked for more but not him. With time being so precious, unlike the majority of folk in this enslaved world he had managed to steal it back.
Civilization, despite its wonders, came with a set of imposed laws and protocols, often for the good of society but included constraints that enforced conformity of the masses. A sort of spell that was cast. If you recognized this you had a chance of breaking that spell and at some point

break free. Yet that notion was the raw definition and core of criminality.

The question quickly arises as to what breach of law is acceptable. To some, the killing of a fellow man or imposing his suffering was acceptable. Whatever held your position and preservation could be justified. Certainly this would apply to people like Andrew Jackson.

But not for Kenny. He was much more like the American Red Indian for whom all life was one.

Ever since the hijacking and even before it, his mind was very clear on the morality of it. He had also been lucky that it all came off so well and he never carried a tinge of guilt over it. But there was one thing that had occasionally given him pause for thought.

Reading the news that Tina Mucklow had left her job after the hijacking and joined a convent gave Kenny a bit of trouble that he would never quite put to bed.

He had no idea about her goals in life or if she had some long term religious calling. But he was always pretty confident in his reckoning that the incident he had imposed on the airline of November 24th 1971 had caused her to leave her job and become a nun. Maybe the incident served as some final push of her conviction or perhaps it wholly triggered her decision making. A delayed trauma? This troubled him from time to time. He never wanted his actions to impact the career of anybody in this way, especially giving up a job in the airlines and replacing it with a nunnery. If she was genuinely happy with this outcome and that was really what she had always wanted then that was great. But he did not know what she would ever have to say on this.

What was more, he never had a way of knowing given that

she never made a public appearance or gave an interview anywhere other than the immediate statement right after the event. And he had always watched out for it but it never happened. He had to assume she wanted it that way. Certainly the media would have been happy to talk to her had she come forward.

With his security and secrecy in mind he really saw no way of contacting her, giving her money or helping her in some way. Yet part of him had always wanted very much to sit and chat with her for half an hour. To give her the proverbial hug to help her on her way in life. She was someone who he regarded as a friend, at least somewhat and would love to know her better but he did not see how. Even a letter to her posted anonymously might be a risk. He was not going to venture there. He would have to make do with thinking she made her own call in life and that she had not suffered too much as a result of his actions.

He had sensed that ability and integrity in her nature during the airline incident so it seemed like the best explanation overall. She had after all acknowledged in the media how nice he was to her and they certainly got on well together on flight 305. He had intended it to be a victimless crime. By and large he had succeeded but Tina joining a convent was unsettling.

By the early nineties Kenny started to have a turn of bad health. With his system occasionally faltering, medical checks were run and cancer was duly detected. He knew it would spread and that his days were numbered, unless of course he survived it. Stranger things had happened. The news was not completely surprising to him as it came with age and no doubt it was brought on by his life-long fondness for smoking. But there was something else in the

back of his mind. He had always remembered his time working in Bikini island where lots of Atomic bomb testing was taking place. He had no doubt the radiation level there was now having its say after all those years.
Some days were bad but others were good in terms of his energy levels. After calling Marge he arranged for a drive up to pay her a visit as he had not seen her in a while. And a great cheerful meeting it was for both. With his slightly bloated appearance thanks to his prescribed medication and the sporting of a baseball cap, he was more than happy to live the moment. Any day he was alive was a good day.

Bernie Geestman would never change. Always on edge, hungry for more and working the angles. The never-ending grab-all mentality. Age or ill-health might one day bring a different conversation to his door but as time passed there was no other signature to him except that of the all-American restlessness.

By Spring of 1994 his union with Marge was well at an end and divorce proceedings in the court were under way. Marge, having deep mistrust in her husband, had already moved out to a ranch she had in Twisp, Washington State, about one hundred miles to the north east of Seattle. She would battle at every station with her ex-husband over what was hers and what she was entitled to as she felt she had better do so. She understood their relationship had become a cauldron of lies and deceit having long past the stage of coming to terms with a failed marriage.

In late July of that year Kenny spent the days being cared for by day care staff who were medics. They were terrific people who looked after him really well. One evening he

was woken from a slumber by the nurse who handed him the phone. There was an in-coming call for him. It was a lively-sounding Bernie.
"Hi, Kenny. What's the story with ya? How you doin."
Kenny eased himself into the conversation by making some small talk but was cut off by his old pal.
"Listen are you alone there? I need a word in private."
Kenny took a moment to beckon to the nurse that he needed privacy and she politely exited the room and closed the door.
He got back to the phone call "Yeah, go ahead."
Bernie continued "Look man you need to be very careful there about who you talk to. I mean about events of the past. Right?"
Kenny reassured him as he had a long time ago that his lips were sealed. That he would never mention it to anyone.
But Bernie's campaign call was not over yet. "Obviously it would leave me in a lot of difficulty. And not to mention Marge. She might not be able to handle things too good."
As if Marge could not handle her own corner when it came to anything. That would be the day. But they both knew that Kenny and Margaret were very close. Bernie's stab at showing concern for others seemed a bit hollow. As usual.
Kenny felt that Bernie was calling to check his mental state in order to try to make an intelligent guess as to whether Kenny had perhaps spilled the beans to anyone. He was inclined to hunt for information. As soon as he got that clarified and felt that the matter was squared away he made some excuses saying he was busy and had to go.

After hanging up the phone Kenny began to feel great sadness as the evening light levels dimmed with the sunset. Sadness like he had not felt in years – perhaps never. It seemed to hang in the beautiful summer air which his body was no longer capable of handling. He realized that he just had his last conversation with Bernie. They would never meet again.

He was, to this minute, ever-grateful to his old friend for his collaboration all those years ago, for the vital assistance in an operation that transformed Kenny's life, making it worth living. But Bernie had participated only because there was something in it for himself, not to salvage Kenny's well-being. Forever keeping tabs. It was even the same just now with the phone call. He was anxious about himself and his own position. It was not about Kenny's departure. Kenny could not help noticing that there were no tears in his voice over the phone. No sentiment or reflection. After all this time. He hadn't even bothered to come to visit him. This thing would not change. That was the nature of the beast regardless of occasion. Deep down he always understood this difference in character between himself and Bernie. He had always worked around it. But no more. Now it got to him. Here at end-of-life, he was feeling its sting. He could only guess that this was part and parcel of dying.

Thankfully, he was cheered up by the accompanying medical care staff around him. He would drift in and out of sleep and be ever-mindful that the next time he closed his eyes might be his last. He sensed by the concerned look on faces around him that the end might be near.

He perked up in form and liveliness with visits from his family in Minnesota.

He could not help thinking how this was turning into a celebration of his life. He had always been frustrated that he could not openly share his hijacking success with people. That was the way of it, for Bernie's sake and his. As if to underscore the point, in came his brother Lyle for a last meeting. He felt such joy to see him. He sat by the bedside talking for a good while. Kenny, seeing that others were out of earshot, spoke softly as he could not manage much more. "Listen!" He started taking deep breaths. Deep but not effective in the normal way.

"There's something you should know. I did a bad thing-" He paused in speech, thinking of Bernie. He would keep his word. " . . . but I can't tell you."

His brother moved forward. "Never mind. We love you anyway." Taking his hand he added "None of that matters now."

At that moment, at least for Kenneth Christiansen, it was true.

Kenny died on July 30th 1994 at the age of sixty eight. In his will he left the house and land at Bonny Lake to Lyle as well as some $180,000 in two bank accounts. In addition, there was a coin collection he had guarded which would later fetch close to $40,000 for the family.

* * * * *

Around the time of his divorce with Margaret, Bernie had been granted legal permission to enter her real estate to retrieve any and all of his personal property. This came with a limit of ninety days from June of 1994. That limited time lapsed without his required appropriate action. He reapplied for such permission twice more, in 1997 and in 1998. This time the application was rejected in accordance with standard legal reading and protocol. Having failed in the courts he took it upon himself to get satisfaction on the

matter.
After being away from her ranch, Margaret discovered a broken entry to her garage where the door had been kicked in. At first, she did not know what, if anything had been taken though clearly some things had been disturbed. Finally, after weeding through the details, she noticed some pictures missing - old photos of Kenny and Bernie together as well as one or two other documentary items connecting the two. She decided to check through a stack of work logs belonging to Bernie that had always been there. There had been many that were stored long-term showing work attendance for each year. This was in relation to his job at the tug boat company. Suspiciously, the volume for 1971 was now gone. It had clearly been removed.
His tracks, it seemed, had been covered. For now.

Chapter 36 Life After death

For Kenny Christiansen life had given him nothing but lemons yet he had managed to make spectacular lemonade. And the taste of that unprecedented concoction would linger for a long time to come.
In the years after his passing, his brother Lyle gradually began to piece things together. The house in Bonny Lake was duly sold on. While not actually looking for clues of anything, a theory of Kenny's life story and behavior gradually crystallized in his mind.
Most unexpected was the mock-up hijacker photo of Kenny coming through the door. Going through a scrapbook photo

album in Bonny Lake, this was found hidden behind another photo tucked away inside the album.

Lyle was able to weigh up the change in fortune for his brother after the time of the hijacking, Things were apparently stable in his work and he bought the house having never had financial worries after this time. Kyle had known all about Kenny's previous situation through the letters that were sent back home during his many years of hardship.

After rounding out a dossier that outlined this evidence Lyle handed it into the FBI in Minnesota where he lived. While this never resulted in anything, the 'Kenny' narrative of the DB Cooper case made its way to an article which was published in New York magazine in 2007. At that time he spoke to a writer by the name of Skip Portus who noted what a good movie it would make. This put Lyle thinking and he actually employed private investigators to put the dossier into the hands of a female movie director – the director responsible for the movie *Sleepless in Seattle*. He never received any contact from her.

Still the story outlining Kenny as the real DB Cooper persisted with author Geoffrey Gray who published an acclaimed book about it titled *Hijacked*. The 'Kenny camp' was beginning to gather cult status. This set the scene for the History TV channel to make an hour-long documentary on the topic. Brad Metzler's Decoded series examined mysterious stories like this and when his on-screen journalist-styled investigators turned their attention to the case it would come to a head.

As part of their time in Cooper-land, the crew brought their cameras to Kenny's house which was now a spruced up print shop for its new owner with the shop all painted in terracotta red. They explored all round the building. After befriending the owner he gladly allowed them to use special scanning equipment on all the walls and surface areas, in case they would find anything stashed away – like money.

Within minutes of scanning before the camera crew, a curious compartment was identified over the ceiling of what used to be Kenny's bedroom. A step-ladder was quickly organized for the external circular attic air vent at the gable end. One of the TV hosts removed the dummy window and climbed into the attic being followed by the film cameras. The compartment cover that Kenny had devised was discovered. Naturally, they assumed he was using this to keep money.

But there was more to follow for the making of the documentary. The broadcast company managed to contact Bernie Geestman as they had done their homework on both himself and Kenny. Amazingly, he agreed to meet up for an on-camera interview. Perhaps he hoped to do his denial case good or maybe he was just too old to care and threw caution to the wind.

The three TV hosts along with the rest of the crew met up with Bernie in a motel that had been pre-booked. After the interview was edited, what the public saw was a nervous Bernie on camera. There were some fringe questions asked. He denied any involvement with the hijacking. The panel did not press him too much but reassured him that whatever he admitted, the statute of limitations had run out and he could not be arrested for anything. He continued to waffle. His memory seemed to be sketchy at best. In the end, when asked, he agreed that Kenny could have been responsible for the hijacking, saying he certainly looked like him. People would later say that he had thrown his old friend under the bus.

The TV show concluded that Kenny probably committed the hijacking but it stopped short of concluding that Bernie was his accomplice on the ground.

After it went out on air, Bernie's family was shocked and surprised. They did not even know he had any plans to participate in a TV interview. And they certainly never suspected either he or Kenny to be involved in such high criminality.

But after a few months some members of the Geestman family reached out to Robert Blevins of Adventure Books of Seattle and so he met up with some of them in the Washington area for interviews.

He spoke with them for two hours in a restaurant. During this encounter, the daughter of Dawn Andresco (then in her fifties) claimed that after seeing the Encoded documentary her memory was jogged and she recalled the incident where she walked into the shed to find Kenny at work on his fake bomb. She distinctly remembered Kenny taping wires to coin rolls with red tape. She did not know what it was but after seeing the TV show put two and two together.

Blevins later brought forward a witness who was a neighbor of Kenny's in Bonny Lake. As a young boy, he found $800 in the wooded area out back of where Kenny lived. This had been buried in heavy plastic bags. Before they handed it in to police they photographed the bills. There were bills issued in the mid 1980s so they would have been laundered by Kenny and were not the original $20 bills from the hijacking. The particular spot where they found it has since been converted into a busy public road.

Tina Mucklow, the long lost air hostess, moved out of her convent and back into normal life in Washington State. When she was approached by a reporter about the hijacking she abruptly turned him away from her door.

Her colleague Florence Schaffner, who Kenny first approached onboard the 727, when shown Kenny's photo, claimed that he looked most like the hijacker that anyone else she had seen.

After the Decoded program went out, Margaret Geestman sold her ranch at Twisp for just under half a million dollars. She left word with her lawyer and her bank official that she did not want her future whereabouts disclosed. She died in 2016. She was in her eighties.

Until the intervention of Lyle, the FBI never knew anything about Kenny Christiansen as a possible suspect in this crime. Had they decided to include airline staff on their radar they would surely have found Kenny with ease. Public embarrassment by admission of this bad mistake is avoided with the bureau's frequent dismissal of Kenny as a possible suspect.

Earl Cossey, one of the people responsible for the supply of parachutes during the hijacking, was murdered in his home at Woodinville, Washington in 2013. He had been clubbed to death. Cossey was known to be an advisor to the FBI on parachute rigging. His opinions on the Cooper case were at times at odds with those of law enforcement over whether Cooper could have survived such a jump from an aircraft. But the actual motivation for his killing is not established. Was it connected to the case or is it an entirely unrelated and separate incident? Doubts will remain but we may never know.

* * * * *

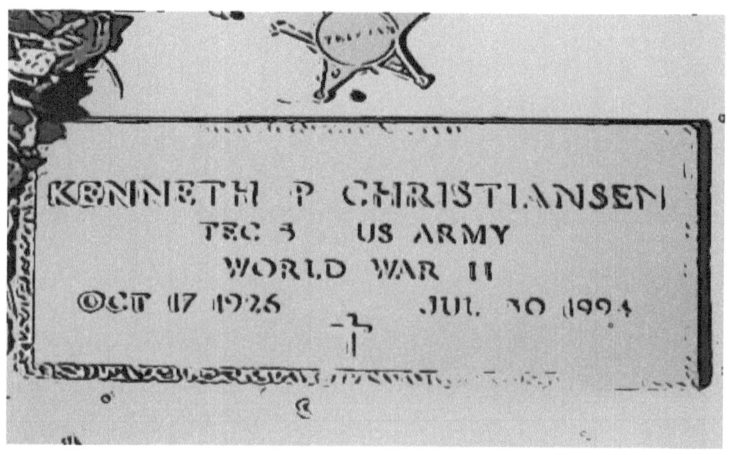

Here we stand by Kenny's grave in Minnesota. The wind breaks the silence through the trees. Just another day in the Earth's record keeping.

Society creates laws for accepted behavioral guidelines. The individual must decide whether to conform to those laws or not. What is at stake? And for who? Where do we paint the moral red line?

That was answered long ago by Lennon and McCartney

And in the end the love you take
is equal to the love you make

THE END

Acknowledgement

Special thanks should be given to Robert Blevins of Adventure Books of Seattle. Robert has been a leading advocate for the Kenny Christiansen narrative of the DB Cooper story. In my view he has been the person more than anyone who has done due diligence with his on-the-ground investigations. He is a credit to good journalism.

We should also note the critical role of Lyle Christiansen, the brother of Kenny. Without his intervention, there would have been no Kenny in Cooper Land and this book would never have been written. May he rest in peace.

ACFAS

About the Author

With a background in IT and a wide range of interests including Science Radio, Electric Cars, Audio and more. The first installment in publishing is *A Crime for All Seasons – A True Story.*

Read more at www.acfas.blog

www.ingramcontent.com/pod-product-compliance
Lightning Source LLC
Chambersburg PA
CBHW030621310726
48979CB00003B/829
9781739600655